# The Looking Glass Water

## The Water That Woos

An Allegorical Novel
by
Terry E. Lursen

TEL Publishing

# Acknowledgements

The Looking Glass Water is an allegory, a story that was given to me early one morning that took me a couple of hours to write out in long-hand and after telling it to a few folk, decided that it was ready to put it down in book form. All of the characters are fictitious and only from coincidence would they resemble any actual person… with the exception of the characters of Alfred and Pete and Floyd and Ruth whom I knew in the wonderful town of Folsom, Louisiana over thirty years ago while attending seminary. I honor their memory by including their personalities as keepers of the water for they certainly kept me while I was a young minister in training so many years ago… I'm grateful to the Alfred Pittman family and the Floyd Rogers family for granting me permission to use their names honorably in this story.

There are certain dialects used throughout the story, the southern rural, the western rural and a few types of preachers. No apologies are made to anyone for actual people speak like this or very similar to this in these current days, as well as in the past, with these very certain dialects.

I also want to thank our review team of Ben and Emily Goins, Jerel Law, Sherri Daull, Bill Liebler and Jane Lursen for reading portions of the manuscript and keeping me on point throughout the journey. For Ben Goins in particular…thanks for contributing the story line on the honey in the portal and for your continued personal support as a friend. Thank you to "Lewis and Diane" for your friendship!

Thank you, Jane, my loving wife, who has permitted me to stay home and write what I believe needs to be written. I love you, Jane!

# Dedication

*I want to dedicate this story to Jane, my faithful and loving wife, and my three adult children, Jessica, Stephen and Christian. Throughout the years, you have endured with much grace my whims and desires, my faults and changes, my leadings and misgivings. Through it all, we've all seen the Lord's grace in us all to move us into Him in a most fantastic and Godly way. I pray that this story helps others to see that there is a treasure beyond our comprehension that is not found in four walls, but is found in the constant denying of ourselves in the ever-abiding life in Him.  I love you all and I love Him all the more!*

# Contents

## Chapter 1

## The Confrontation

**1929**

The sanctuary was dark as only a few candles remained lit from the long, exhausting day of being the only light in a very dark world. The candles seemed tired as they flickered, breathing their last breath. The room was cold and lifeless. Stone and wood and tile and brass bore the fabric of the tapestries strewn above as even they seemed lifeless with absolutely no movement in the air. The air was thick and rich with the spirit of something sinister lurking within, hiding in plain sight, but not within the purview of the bishop.

"I don't know what to do with you. How could you do this again?" Pondering his next thought, "How can I fix this?" the bishop clenched his staff, not knowing his next words.

The priest knelt by his employer and looked up into his eyes with trembling fear.

"You have to leave!" the bishop told him as he looked down at him kneeling at the altar as he gritted his teeth in seething anger.

"You need to get out of here, now." he said with resolve.

Rejected, the priest begged on his knees with clasped hands, sobbing as he spoke, "Why? I can fix this. No one knows. I am sorry..."

"*I* know! How is it that you believe that no one else does?" screamed the bishop in haste. He was becoming rather unbecoming at this juncture as he paced in the conversation.

The priest knelt quietly interposed in himself, palms sweating, his undershirt now soaked with perspiration, thinking, thinking, yet nothing came to mind to get himself out of this one this time.

Bishop Cache', or Bishop C, as the brothers knew him, was trembling, not with fear, but with anger, no…no, no, no he was way beyond angry for he was not only angry with the priest, he was angry with himself for allowing this to go on for so many years. And here he was again.

Father Miller, the priest, was shaking his head back and forth as in times past and Bishop C knew the words that were about to erupt.

Bishop C interjected first, "Another, another, another, no, not another! Enough is never enough with you, is it? Is that what you were about to say? No, it won't happen again? Do you understand how sick you are? And now, I've let you do this to me again!"

He stammered from his anger, about to fall from the blood rushing through his brain as though it was to burst from his temple. He caught himself at the edge of the table and caustically chuckled at the thought of the communion that had been shared earlier that morning in mass and the vain hypocrisy that had darkened the room.

"It's always one apology after another with you, isn't it? One regret following a remorse. One, 'it will never happen again' after another. Your kind of an apology is nowhere in the scriptures, but sorrow leading to repentance is." Bishop C spit as he spoke erecting himself and screamed, "You have to leave and you have to leave NOW!"

Father Miller sobbingly responded, "But, where will I go? Where will I go *this time*? Leave and go where? When should I return? This is all I know, this is my life!"

"I don't care, you can go to hell for all I care!" Bishop C wiggled his finger in his face, "Because that's where your pathetic soul is going to end up! But first, it's laicization for you."

Bishop Cache' was exasperated and exhausted from the afternoon of disgrace, for this time, more than a few people knew what the priest had been accused of and even the smoke from the candles and incense in the darkened sanctuary seemed to know and refuse to no longer obnubilate the secrets of the priest. The vapor of the holy water was void of any life. The bishop had not prayed, he didn't feel like it; he knew His Maker was waiting on him for an account. He could not pray and the priest knew it. The bishop was now in his past and his present had caught up with his future. Time stood still as one, past, present and future all rolled up into a moment that had become a nightmare. Hauntings were on his face and the gulp of his swallow to catch a breath was evident to the priest whose sin seemed to fade quickly away.

"But what about *you*?" The priest taunted him as he rose from the floor and gathered himself to the back of the bishop.

"What about me?" the bishop glared.

"You know that the spirit knows the spirit…" Father Miller disgustingly portraying the accusation of satan while wrangling his neck as a snake around the back of the bishop.

"You're sick, everything about you is sick. You will leave and you will leave by sunrise!" stammered the bishop.

"Get out of here, get out of my sight!"

"But where will I go?" Father Miller said frantically clasping his hands in humility, "I have no, no means."

His disposition had changed dramatically in an instant. He stood before the bishop at the altar lifeless, accepting the demand this time, twinkling his brows back and forth seemingly not understanding the words coming from his own mouth. He was vacant of mind and spirit. His demise had finally arrived within him, the demise of his vocation, his calling, his life as he knew it. For what he had done, he thought as his brow twitched, what he had done again and again and again had been done and he could not undo it…ever. It finally dawned on him that the things he had done were irreversible. Neither he, nor anyone else, could undo them. He had been found out and there was no going back. Repression no longer worked, he was becoming undone.

In his mind he could hear the crying of the mother of the boy he had been with. She was not there, no, but her spirit was the only life abounding in the room. The sanctuary had gone colder, "Is there any heat on in here?" he thought to himself.

The bishop had slumped on the steps of the altar exhausted and frightened of his own future. And just as the priest had changed in an instant from worming his way around the conversation, he suddenly had an epiphany. He turned away from the bishop towards the front door and with a hideous gaze, he whispered to himself in a voice that only some other spirit could comprehend.

## Chapter 2

## The Decision

Father Miller immediately took the vacation he thought he deserved and found himself standing over a precipice almost a thousand miles away from his past. He had not climbed far, but the way down on the other side of the rock was endless. There was a deep crevice and he stood there wondering how it had been made. The sun was beating so hot, beating down relentlessly for at this point there was no shade in sight. He had gone as far as he could go up that side of the mount.

He stood there transfixed by the edge of the cliff and the burning rays of the sun peeping down into the crevice…dark and darker still it went.

He thought to himself of something he had read long ago, "The murky waters of unforgiveness are thick with history and resplendent with all it holds. In the land of sowing and reaping, one never quite imagines that if you sow unforgiveness, you would also reap it."

In all of it, he thought that heaven would surely wait for him, yet the murky hold of what he had held onto for so long now had its hold on him. He was held by what he had sown because it had been sown into him in his childhood and he had never let it go. Yet, here at the precipice, time seemed to be running out and a decision was waiting, curiously waiting.

He had become what he had hated, the history, his past so long ago and hate filled his heart once again for what they had done to him. Could it be that he had been doing for these many years was some sort of wicked revenge? No, it wasn't *revenge*, it was something deeper than the superficial art of an eye for an eye for his pain had compounded the interest due on the one he believed was truly responsible. He did to others what others had done to him, yet even more sickening things did he do for his mind never rested and his flesh was at his beckon call.

The sun was beating down on his back and as he looked up, it seemed to ask him, "Well…what are you going to do?" The sun seemed to be forcing the issue and he still refused to get it as a result of his repression. He was strong there, even stronger than the sun, he perceived.

Sunbeams striating, like waves in the breeze, burned down upon his back. And then the chill set in, the breeze from below on his face. To his back there was extreme heat; to his face there was the chill of darkness rising and then sucking its breath downward. He moved closer to the edge of the precipice and moved back again to gather more heat. He carefully moved to his left to find the hottest ray of light to stand in. The sun going down began to filter through the trees seemingly showing him the perfect place to stand as well as the perfect place to…well.

"It's time, I know it's time, there's no going back." He whispered to the chill. Nothing could save him now, no one, no God, no thing to call him back. The sun's rays pointed to the edge of the ledge, the perfect launching point to the darkness that beckoned him from below.

"He said I had to go and I know I can't go back," he was talking aloud to himself. "They'll come for me and I do not want to face those boys again."

"A tear, why a tear?" he wiped his face indignantly. His eyes watered again. But was it really tears? "Why am I welling up now?" He thought. There was no feeling of…of anything within.

He could feel the sweat in his boots, his socks soaked from walking and climbing; he seemed to have been climbing all of his life to get out of the hold where he had hidden the touches. He did not want to be touched again as his mouth quivered and twitched. He would not be touched again and yet the touching, the faith, the lies, the cruel breath and the stench of old coffee smelled like it was on him forever to never wash away.

As the chilling air whisked up from the darkness, he could smell his own breath and the coffee he had had that morning. He had become the stench that he had hated for his hate bore the fruit of the seed of hate and blossomed into a tree ripe with anguish, bitterness and revenge.

"*You have to leave*," wrangling his neck as a snake, mocking the bishop's words.

"That bastard of a bishop…You have to *leave?*" he hissed aloud as the hissing echoed throughout the crevice.

"You HAVE TO LEAVE!" he squeamishly screamed, convulsing, losing his balance and almost fell forward, scaring himself with fright.

"History…history, *my history*?  What about *your history Bishop Cache*?" as he stepped backed a bit, biting back at the bishop who was only in his mind. His anger was focused now on the bishop.

He tasted blood in his mouth and spit, wiping his mouth with his sleeve and hand. He had bitten the inside right of his cheek in the moment of imbalance. He spit out a tiny chunk of flesh remaining in his mouth and the blood seemed to be filling his mouth quickly. Spit after spit, spitting out into the dark crevice his blood spat forward. Crying now a bit in pain, he started laughing at himself. There were always two emotions at work in his flesh with him and this time was no different.

Striations of heat mixed with cold caused his inner emotions to shift. His inward energy had pushed him as far as he could go with his fear, his hatred of all things past; it pushed him until there was no breath. He had not washed his hands. He always had to wash his hands, but where could he do that? He remembered beneath the stairs, where he used to hide, he could feel the safety there, but hear the creaking of him coming. The sound was imbedded in his memory and would not go away.

"I need water!"

He cried out and shook himself from his mind.

"I need water!" again, he exclaimed.

He had just stepped to the edge, a pebble trickled down, bouncing, like you see in the movies, but it was real this time, it was here.

What was he doing *here*? The pebble trickled and bounced until it didn't and then he heard it no more. A grimacing smile came over his worn chin as though he was still considering the fall.

In his mind he thought, "The rock has taken my place," "Glory!"

He shouted in relief. "Yes, no need to fall, to jump, no need, not now. The Lord placed that rock there and it fell as I would have. It's done. I need water!"

People miss their present preparing for their future and yet, all he had done was re-live his past. He could never enjoy the present for his past was all he thought about. He turned towards the sun and the heat on his face closed his eyes. He thought back to the shades in the sunlight in his study. The warm afternoon glow on the papers drew him back to a time in his boyhood bedroom when the afternoon sun gleamed through the shears and you could see the dust in the air. His bedroom was thick with dust and the glow of the afternoon sun revealed the air in the room so much it seemed that you could count the flecks of dust as they wandered aimlessly throughout the room.

Now that was a time, a memory worth holding, lost in his childhood in the afternoon and no one there to touch him. His past had become his present as his mind stood at the bedroom door piercing through the dust-filled air at the drapes so colorfully displayed with shears allowing the afternoon sun's warmth to fill his mind with comfort. His arms reached for the window to open the shears and there he was in his room full of peace. A tear rose to his eyes as his mind continued to dwell in the past from the sun's rays by the shades in his study to the sun's beams through the shears of time…a time when time had not yet been and he was still safe. In that moment, he was in a dream within a dream taken back in time, but only in his mind.

"I need water," he said aloud as he stammered down the angled rock, sliding recklessly down the steep. Had he climbed so high not realizing the climb? All he could think about now was water, "I need water!" he kept whispering to himself.

He fell again; his buttocks sliding down the rocks, re-gaining his footing, tripping and falling forward quickly down the mount. He looked to be rather athletic in the jaunt, but was anything but, haphazardly falling forward, disgracefully falling and laughing he couldn't stop falling forward from his weight and the steep decline.

Once at the bottom of the mount he didn't stop running, he ran into the forest, the same forest that he so dreadfully feared. The forest thick with green and trees higher than sight settled his fast-paced mind. He slowed from running to tripping over brush and realizing the extent of the vastness of the green, he slowed, stopped and sighed.

"I need water…" was the extent of his thoughts as he proceeded determined towards the goal of finding a brook he just believed was there, but had never seen. It was occurring to him that the thoughts of his past were driving him to a place, an unknown place with an unknown completion. This forest was his end, he thought. All of this had to end somehow, possibly here.

His clothes were drenched from the earlier baking sun and the ensuing gamble down the ridge. He had survived the ledge and the thoughts, but his clothes, as wet as they were, were beginning to attract the chill of the deep of the forest. Here again, his heat was turning to chill, this constant changing wind and temperature was not only in the heights, now it was in the depths. He proceeded with care through the thick where it seemed that no man had been for some time, or ever.

He wandered a bit, turning round and round, stumbling, falling forward once again as though some magnet were wooing him invisibly towards a very specific destination. This was that kind of forest that you couldn't tell where you'd been or where you were going, so he just kept one foot in front of the other moving, almost gliding along the top of the brush.

He hadn't been born with an internal navigation, so he didn't know what from where, but could smell something fresh in the distance. The closer to the freshness he got, the wetter the forest became. He was drenched from the wetness and stopped to remove his backpack, sitting on a fallen tree log that was just at the right height for relaxing.

The breeze felt wonderful.

He remembered riding his bike as a youngster and feeling the same cool breeze on his face. He felt relaxed enough now to think back to that time and asked,

"God? Do you see me? Did you see me then? Are You there?" Only the breeze responded with a chill.

As the chilly breeze surrounded him, his mind went back to a far lesser time when he was that age on the bike, the time when he was hiding from Father Spruzzare'.

"No!" he said aloud, with only the cottonwoods, willows and red squirrel to hear the faint shout. He was in his past again; he was not there where he was, he was where he'd wished he'd never been. Then the thoughts came to his being alone so much in the evenings after choir practice, sitting in the bathtub, washing and washing and washing and washing 'til he bled from the scrubbing. He could never get the stench of Father Spruzzare' off of his skin.

"Why couldn't I ever get clean?" he grimaced as he remembered the reason why.

He noticed his own breath, the vapor, the air was chilled, and he was panting about ready to run again, but he had nowhere to run and no one to run from. Hyperventilating, he was in himself and he knew he had to get away from that one thing that was destroying him, his own wicked self.

This place was a place he had not visited in over 30 years. In his mind, he was in the tub, spitting, washing, crying, sore, sick, untouchable.

"Why God, why?" he ached in jeers among the spirits present. The tub water was murky in his mind, but it was always murky.

"Why, God, why?" He would always sit in the tub alone until his mama came home.

As he continued to think within himself, he'd gotten up from the log and continued to walk with no attention to where he might be going. Time had passed and yet it hadn't. The breeze was a bit too breezy now and provided a chill that went from his balding head down the back of his spine.

"Where am I?" he pondered and questioned aloud. He was different now, angry and disparagingly different for everything was different. The trees had grown taller; the foliage had parted a path in the way. The wooing of the way was drawing him forward and he thought to himself, "I smell water."

He wrestled through the open cattails and willows as they bowed beneath the breeze in the direction of the lake that lay before him. The breeze was guiding him to the one thing that he needed…water…the kind that all men need.

## Chapter 3

## The Wooing of the Water

It was a sense of *meros*, destiny, his lot to bear, that called him and wooed him forward towards what he did not know. He felt what he thought were the eyes of the forest watching him and as he stumbled through a tiny pathway in the brush, he could sense someone was breathing in and drawing him by their breath.

As he approached the opening beyond the tall trees, there it was… the most beautiful lake he'd ever seen. He ran to the water and fell to his knees splashing the water on his face, not noticing the stirring he had created. He brought the water up to his mouth with his hands and drank with exuberance unaware of the movement of the water and the spiritual current that was flowing from the water to his body.

He rested back for a moment to catch his breath and the sensation of being watched was as strong as it had ever been.

"Where are you?" He thought to himself, springing up from his knees, looking around and slipping on the substance he had created beneath him as the water had touched the ground. Falling backward to his buttocks, he fainted another demand to the invisible observer,

"Who are you? Show yourself!"

Crawling back to his knees in amazement and fear, he realized that it was the water pulsating and calling to him in his spirit, breathing as the breath of a man.

He leaned over the water and saw its crystal clear perfection. He could see to the bottom of the lake, like looking through glass, but no, like a mirror. Not only could he see to the bottom of the lake, he could see himself. And there in that moment, when he no longer saw the bottom of the lake, but seeing himself as though looking into a mirror, the water began to speak to his spirit as a spirit speaks in the inner being with a still, small voice.

"Dru..."

It whispered his name, it knew who he was. The clarity of the water was clearer than a bell. At first, it spoke in warm tones of his past… with scenes and events, then all of a sudden, faster than lightning...zip, zip, zip, he quickly saw his past.

He saw his mom, the loss of his dad in the war, his aloneness, his fear, the terror, the running, the priest, the priests, sitting, touching, running, he was running so fast to school, to church, the water spoke and spoke quickly in his spirit, but he had never had that happen before.

It spoke of the priests, the boys,  the children, to fear, to the terror, to fright, to touching…the water spoke and spoke of him and told him all that he was and where he had been.

It told him who he really was and what he had done and all that had been done to him. All the things he had done heartlessly, but willingly, it told him and left nothing to chance and it was all true of who he was and all that he had done, it was all true, all that he had done and all that he was…it was true!

"NO!!!" he screamed, clasping his hair, pulling out what little hair he had on the sides.

"NO!!" he screamed again, shaking his head back and forth.

"It was their fault, they made me do it, they made me do it, they made me like it…I hate them! I hate them! I hate You!"

He screamed in terror and the water was not finished for it was saying all that it needed to say and he could not move. The wooing water had wooed him into it and he was spitting out profanities and doubts, fears and terrors, screaming curses to the hate, curses to the priests, curses to the men who had had their way with him. Falling forward in his hate, the water wooed him with passion, but he would have none of it.

"You're just like them, you made them, you made them do it and so I did it to them just to get you back…I'm not sick like they said, oh, no, I'm not the predator, they are! I'm the victim! I did it just to show you and I showed you good, didn't I?"

The water spoke in passion, in tears and wooed him forward, but again, he would have none of it. He broke back to the rear, away from its spell, its trance, "You're wicked, you unjust one, you caused all of this to happen just to kill me. You have no control over me, You never did! You are not my god!"

The water became silent and still.

As the stillness had come over the lake it all seemed bizarre, yet he knew it was real. He was dazed from the tantrum. His head was spinning and the clearing was slowly stopping around him as a merry go round at the end of its turn. No sound. There was no sound, not even the sound of his breathing. All sound had disappeared. He was there, but seemingly in a hollow vacuum.

With gritted teeth and clinched fists, he screamed at God, "So this is what it's like to defy You! You take my life and You make me miserable, I hate You, I hate everything about You!"

And then with all the hate that was welling up within him, he glanced over the water and saw what he had never seen before; the terror of a creature that only nightmares are made of. His erupted hate spewed at the creature in the mirror…in the water, for the water had turned to glass, no, a mirror, the creature was above him, or behind him, no, it was him! Him? It was him, and he screeched out a torturous screech, "NO!!!"

Turning to run from the mirrored lake, he ran for all he could, maddening, running, frothing, running, screeching, frothing, bleeding, he tore his face and forearms running past the trees.

The rocks he knew; this time it was to the rocks as he ran at a maddeningly desperate pace. He was running faster than he'd ever ran before.

"To the rocks, to the rocks," he breathed aloud. "To the rocks, I'll show you what I can do, to the rocks this time for you!"

He was leaping as he ran like a cheetah in a race for its life, he ran beyond his might with fright and fear and terror as his mate. He enjoined his hate for all that was, for man, for life, for God and right he ran with all his might through the brush ripping his clothing from his body by the broken limbs of brush and tree.

Reaching the rocks, he climbed like a bear in a frantic pace, he was chasing death and it was death he would beat.

"You have no power over me!" he exclaimed as he reached the top of the rocky ridge where he'd been just hours ago. He didn't stop to see, he didn't stop to feel anything anymore. He leaped and flew forward downward, screaming his last scream,

"You have no power over me…"

Down into the dark crevice he fell to his death. In his final falling thought, no power would ever have any power over him again.

## Chapter 4

## The Water Never Changes

**1931**

Gertrude Whitegold stood with her brothers mourning the death of their father whose life had been lived way too short on love's highway to family and togetherness. Her brother, Samuel, had made a silent commitment that his life would not be taken so shortly as his Dad's, but at the very least he would make a go of it as he always did, solving the world's depressive state in his neck of the woods. Gertrude looked at Samuel and said encouragingly, "You know you can't fix this one, Samuel, I know you want to, but Daddy's gone and that's just that."

Samuel trusted his sister's words, for the most part, but he had this feeling that of all the things that needed fixing, death wasn't one of them. He had accepted his father's fate of passing as he did and he had already moved on in his mind to working on other people's problems that he could fix. He was a realist when everyone around him saw him as the perfect idealist, always after the worst problem in the world and spending time, energy and money on companies and people that others had left to die.

His brothers would shake their heads in despair every time they asked Samuel's wife Elizabeth what he was up to and she would respond with another dose of frightening news of the next best deal gone bad, but invariably Samuel would pull the company through unscathed with him coming out with a pretty penny to boot.

Time was passing way too slowly now in these hard times of

oppression, loss and the death to tomorrow as many had learned to survive only on today's bread and that not enough.

Not so with Samuel, he had a knack for prospering where others were mired in their failures. His was a mind that never gave up, never gave in and never let go. He was the consummate warrior of the stalwart man, the every-man that many had learned to turn to in their times of loss, remorse and failure. If depression was the doom of the day, Samuel was the boom of the way. He could take a failing company and in no time, like lickety split, have the operations operational because he knew how to see a problem and not be intimidated by it. Not only could he see the problem at hand, he would have a variety of solutions to the problem that actually worked, when other so-called consultants didn't have the faintest clue of what to do other than to cut their losses and run.

Over the brief years that lasted way too long for most people, not even the day was long enough for Samuel. He was prospering where others were losing and he never made mincemeat of the loser, he was always there to lend a hand and help where others couldn't see beyond their noses. In his time, he was the consultant to the generals, the owners and the presidents of firms who needed that extra push and nudge to turn a company in the right direction before they fell off the cliff of bankruptcy.

In all of this, he had privately built a stash of cash that became the envy of everyone he met. He was driving high in the car of choice, his favorite, the Auburn 851 Speedster that he and his cohorts would travel quickly through the mansions pleasantly plucking their collectibles at auction just so the former owners could pay their taxes or buy their groceries. No one seemed to have any money but a few folk and one of the few was Samuel Whitegold. He had money to buy what he wanted because he had worked hard for it and it was all safely in the security of, well, not even he would say.

He loved to collect things; that was his hobby. His was a life lived in love, purpose and service. It just so happened that he made a substantial return on helping others with their businesses and everyone he ran across was rewarded somehow just by meeting him.

During the 1930's, there was so much poverty and loss, that people speak of the time as the only known time in America that life was lived in darkness and despair. Whatever people owned, it had to be given up for a smidgen of the price…pennies on the dollar and whoever owned the dollar was able to buy up the pennies.

Samuel was collecting the wealth of the land and soon he was on to collecting land itself. He had sent his land-fare representative out west to spy out land that was in foreclosure. He only wanted the choicest of properties because eventually each of these land purchases would grow in their investment value, but oddly enough that wasn't Samuel's main objective.

His objective was first to help in the greatest of needs and secondly to obtain the choicest of collectibles. He thought differently than most business men, most different indeed. While most savvy business men who had the bucks to buy for their rate of return on investment, Samuel was out buying for the collectible value. He had a mind of his own and what he valued most was the aesthetic, not the monetary gain. He valued what the collectible held in intrinsic value that could not be determined by a dollar amount. He was of a classic golden gilded age type of mind where true beauty was in the eyes of the creator and he had the 'eye', so to speak, to see what the creator of the object, the collectible, the artwork, or even the land held in the beauty of its Creator.

This train of thought led his land-fare representative, Stephen Bentley, not to the major cities where prime real estate could be bought for a song, no, the land-fare agent was searching for properties that held a particular value to their owners, but they would have to let it go at a substantial bargain. Even though the money was abundant, it was not unlimited, so the art of negotiating became an evident gift in the Whitegold name.

The ideas of Samuel were fixed in Stephen's mind and in his business acumen. It was as though any inspiration that Samuel had received from the sun…Stephen was imbued with it as well. He was not in the major cities; he was where the other scavengers of promising land refused to look and that was out in the countryside in states where land was plenty and the landowners extremely needy.

This led him through Idaho and Wyoming where the ranchers were trying to co-op deals with Mr. Vanderbilt and the government to create this new national park by the Tetons, but not everybody wanted in on the money grab from the government or from the Vanderbilt's. Offenses and fences had abounded in the land for years during the debates and fightings among the locals.

One man had still not resolved to sell out to the government for the park reserve. He wanted to keep his land for very personal reasons, but not for a family inheritance. There was something on his land that was not for sale, not for nobody, especially the government.

This left the most pristine land vacant; a lot of about 1,000 acres, mostly square, with dense forests, wildlife and a setting just below a ridge of mountains that not too many people cared to venture into because of the time it took to get into the area and an even longer time to get out of. Still, it was evident that this very large partial of land was not a part of the government reserve open to the public and the public stayed away from it for some reason or another. It could have been the broken down fences of days gone by or it could have been the ridge of mounts and yutes that gave a glance to the public that you could just keep on going…just not through here.

Pristine, lush, rich and dark with green…all shades of green, indescribably dense in places, this forest land waited to greet the right person at the right time.

The landowner, Jefferson B. Case, was a smiling sort, even though the snake agents abounded like slithering beasts on the prowl for their next feast. He lived in a shack on the lowest ridge where his daddy and his daddy had lived for years. Their's was an extremely grueling life of hunting, fishing and plowing for their daily meals much like all of their forefathers who had long gone before them. Jefferson had no heirs and only lived for the day that he could offer his land to the right person who would keep it and its treasure safe from the land agent snakes, the government and the ilk that would usually make their way out to his shack with all kinds of made-up stories in desperate need of his land.

Stephen had a personality that could calm a rabid raccoon and a smile that could turn a cold heart to a summer's warmth. Jefferson was of the same mind, so when they met, they hit it off like two old friends who had not seen each other in forty blue moons. They talked and talked and caught up with each other's families like they used to know each other, but didn't…but they really did somehow…in the spirit.

Jefferson was hesitant about selling the land to just anybody, yet the similarities of he and Stephen were strong and the stories that Stephen told of Samuel Whitegold, his employer, were quite telling of his mindset. Jefferson needed to know Samuel's heart in the matter because there was a part of this land that required it to stay put and not be sold off to the public or to put it on public display.

This intrigued Stephen to take a complete hike to view this special piece of property, but he was wise enough to keep his mouth shut about his own personal desires. It just made too much sense to Stephen that this Jefferson fellow sounded like Samuel in such a way that the land was actually a collectible. This land was to be secured and kept safe and protected. Stephen didn't know exactly why, but the uncanny nature of Jefferson seemed to be extraordinarily similar to Samuel's. According to Jefferson, the land needed to be purchased by only one person and that person had to keep the land and do absolutely nothing with it except keep it as a collectible. That was a promise that had to be made and kept forever. Jefferson continued to speak about a secret treasure that was in the middle of the property that no one could ever know about. He spoke in code and Stephen could only be assured that Jefferson's heart was telling the truth and that he wasn't some senile old man protecting a treasure that had never existed.

A moment came when they walked outside and the fragrance of fresh water was in the air. Jefferson called out to Stephen,

"You smell that?"

"Smell what?" Stephen pondered.

Throwing his nose up into the air, the fragrance of evergreen and lavender, pungent wet air mixed with camus lily and pine was ripe and real. The air was so fresh and clean and there it was, the smell of water and he didn't even realize you could smell water.

"So, that's what water smells like, Jeff?"

"Yep, I didn't knowed if youse gonna smell it or not, but I'm shore glad you did," Jefferson smiled his smile full of spirit and warmth.

By this time, Stephen was full of fresh air and full of whatever there was in the air.

"You knowed that you don't exactly know where the wind's gonna blow, but it's gonna blow out chere and it checks you out when it does," Jefferson smiled a little Mona Lisa smile at Stephen.

Stephen replied, "I think I know what you mean, Jeff, but I know that smell, it's already in me and I love it! I love this place and I guarantee no one's gonna harm the beauty of this place ever, Jeff, no, not ever, I declare!"

With that mutual declaration declared in the midst of the air, the mist of the air wet their hands in a bit of rain as they shook on it and they walked off together over the ridge with Jefferson explaining to Stephen where he wanted to be buried when he died.

## Chapter 5

## The Transfer is Complete

With all of the confidence of a hunter who's bagged a prize buck, Stephen made his way back to Florida to deliver the papers of what he believed to be the greatest collectible ever. Samuel was overwhelmed to see his land agent and to hear the news of all of his exploits, especially his journey to Wyoming.

Stephen had gone to the water, the treasure that Jefferson spoke of before he left the land and saw for himself the power of its self-sustaining flow. It was filled to the perfect brim by an underground spring of the purest of fresh water. He got to know the water as the water had already expected his arrival. His understanding of the promise he had made to Jefferson was growing deeper all the more with time spent by the water that spoke. Stephen had touched the water and the water had touched his spirit and told him all that he was. His experience with the water was one of reception and positive change unlike anything a man could do for himself. It was in him and there was no going back to any business as usual.

Samuel could see this on his face and in his disposition when he arrived back at Samuel's estate. Stephen had been changed for all eternity and Samuel was so taken by Stephen's demeanor that the overwhelming sense of a father son relationship began to flourish in their last remaining days together.

Samuel's daughter Sarah also delighted in the relationship that Samuel had with Stephen as a son for she had already seen him as a man made in heaven just for her for she loved him more than life itself. She knew it the first time she laid eyes on him and could only speak of very good things when Stephen's name was mentioned.

Being in his presence was breathtaking to her heart for she fluttered as a child overwhelmed with joy anytime she was around him. Everyone seemed to notice her infatuation with Stephen, but to her it was the real thing. She had to work at her self-control when it came time for dinners or parties when the two of them had a chance to be in the same room.

She was not overly confident of herself or of her reception of Stephen. He was so very kind to her, but she didn't honestly know if he was just being kind because of his position or if he really liked her even a smidgen of how much she loved him. She was reserved and sophisticated, extremely non-assuming, always dressing with the flair of sensibility and presented herself as a lady in waiting, but waiting with much patience. She was mature and maturing the older she became. She had never known anyone quite like Stephen and now that he had returned from his travels across the states, she was desperately hoping that her father would see  to have him work closer to home.

Over time, her father Samuel completed his travels abroad and across the nation collecting what later would become the riches of the rich. There were so many people in dire need of cash to make it through these truly desperate times that they were willing to give up their most prized possessions. One thing about Samuel that was not in most men was the sense of priority. This was his greatest asset to any company that he helped succeed and it was to his own personal success in these explicit expressed priorities. This is the main reason he was able to succeed where so many others had failed. He was never deterred from his focused priorities. He was strong in keeping the main thing the main thing in business and in life.

Because of this, he did not see collecting things as a sense of achievement or pride, as a selfish hoarder might perceive himself to be. No, he saw things for their aesthetic value, their beauty, again, as the thing's creator would see it. He valued these collections of his as a hobby, but it was not his life.

His life was his family, his wife Elizabeth, his daughter Sarah, his health and his faith and not necessarily in that order. He knew how to have fun, but all within the confines of strict, yet not overbearing priorities.

Samuel knew he would not live forever and so he had built up a trust fund that would keep all that he had collected through the years in mint condition, well-kept and secure for the rest of the future to see the creations of what others had admired in the past. He could afford all of this somehow for his fortune had been gathered in serving and the giving of his gift of success transferred to the businesses he had saved during the depression.

Sarah had his heart for what mattered and Stephen did as well. In a few short years, their love became a match made in the halls of heaven. If there ever was the perfect marriage, it was found here in the giving of two lives that came to adore one another. Stephen shared the treasure of the water with Sarah and they lived in their part of the world in a gilded age of romantic enlightenment, seeing past the dreariness of the depression and using the gifts that had been transferred to them by the most generous of men.

Throughout the years, they lived among the tapestries, the silver, the brilliant cut glass and the ornate crystal. Their everyday was the dreams of what most folk who only saw what they saw in the magazine publications put forth as a part of the business ventures Stephen had invested in.

Sarah lived in lavish luxury with a fur for every occasion and a crystal goblet for every known beverage of choice. Opulence became them and they enjoyed every moment of their lives as they saw their surroundings continue to grow into the more and the more.

The affordability of marble floors and granite seating, precious stones inlayed into statutes of the heroes of the past, glaring stained glass, and layers upon layers of the finest of linens and cloths created by man were at their beckon call. They enjoyed the fruits of their father's labor and they built upon it with each vibrant day. Like Samuel, they did not cherish the things of the world as their world for they shared his priorities of love, faith, family and togetherness, especially the day that their only child was born, a son named Victor.

Victor was born in 1947 and never knew what it was like to lift his hand to work a day in his life. He lived his wonderful life with this mother and father in the most aristocratic wealth known in the states.

By this time, Samuel was aging quickly and stayed sick most of the time and, as most people discover eventually, even the richest of the rich cannot buy health to live in the flesh forever and so it was with Samuel. No matter his priorities or his goodness, no matter his generosity or his expressions of the greatest of works, he came to his end as all men must and died, albeit he died as one of the wealthiest men in America. He died with his dignity and his valued character intact, his wife and family by his side and not once imagined that any of the stuffing of the collections that he and his family had accumulated through the years would go with him into eternity.

Samuel had kept the promise of the water that speaks with Jefferson B. Case as he had been laid to rest and now it was up to Stephen and his heir to maintain the promise of secrecy and care for the land that was so rare. Stephen knew Samuel's priorities and kept them all his life as he and Sarah lived in agreement as one and the same.

Victor, on the other hand, had only seen what he had seen and all that he saw had been given to him. He didn't like to travel and he didn't like to socialize, therefore he simply didn't go out much, not much at all. He was educated by the finest tutors and trained in French by linquists in the home surrounded by the very history that he studied without much care. If he didn't want to do it, Sarah didn't push him.

In their agreement, they tended to agree on everything and Victor grew up thinking that all of life was about marble, crystal, lush silk tapestries, the richest of French foods and most of all…pleasing himself.

Victor grew up, literally, with the silver spoon in his mouth, but oddly enough, unlike most spoiled brats that inherit wealth without work, he never portrayed himself out of line with any of Stephen and Sarah's love and priorities. He learned Stephen's business practices and his management skills, but didn't venture out much to put anything into practice. His was a life of maintenance and he learned from his mother that when something big had to be paid for, you sold something of equal or greater value.

With that type of mentality and business savvy, his negotiating skills were put to use in finding buyers of all that had been accumulated throughout the years of his grandfather and father. The land was the greatest of assets, along with the houses that had been built by some of the most creative architects. What Victor discovered was that much of the land holdings that dwelled within the family portfolio had become ultra-prime real estate in the most growing cities in the nations. The fastest growing cities were sprawling out to these mansions that sat on tremendous amounts of acreage. He learned to obtain the best realtors money could buy as the years past and his need to sell the properties became his way of life and his way of making a living.

Over his lifetime, he had sold just about everything that could be sold that his granddad had loved to appreciate. The bottom of the portfolio was reaching the top of the stack by the time he had reached his sixties…a time when there was no one around to remind him of the promise to keep the water that spoke secure and safe from the public.

The water knew that the time for a transfer was in order and the water waited for the right person and the right circumstances to come along.

## Chapter 6

## The Water Still Speaks

## 1985

Leaving Los Angeles, Miguel decided he would make a trek through an unbeaten path. Too many failures in this short life had left him cold and alone. He had completed his undergrad degree to move on to higher heights, but the one thing that alluded him, which alludes many young men his age, was the perfect girl. Was it the girls on his pathway or was it all the mess he'd gotten involved in as a child in a home without a real father?

The substitute dad he'd ended up with was a freak, of sorts, so he basically had to go out on this thing alone. He tried every drug there was to alleviate the sense of darkness from his childhood and all of the philosophies he had heard along the way.

He had to say no more to the cocaine, but he would never give up his weed; this he carried with him always. All kinds of girls, yes, anything to make him feel like a man that he ought to feel like, instead of that queer he grew up with that was supposed to be taking care of him. As a boy, his step-father's friend had had his way with him, and no one, not anyone knew or would ever know.

So, he figured he would be with just about any girl to get those scenes out of his mind, but he just couldn't shake it. Marijuana was his weapon of choice and, oh, the traveling, just keeping busy to keep his mind off of his past and improbable future. It was in his mind that he could go both ways and so to avoid what he perceived might be his inevitability, he traveled with his buddies to keep his mind at ease.

Life and love was way too messed up in his world and he felt the need to try and fix it for everybody else but had never accomplished that feat for himself.

He would laugh to himself, as was often the case, that one day he would be a superstar that could fix everybody's problems. He'd be the modern day Robin Hood, taking money from the rich and giving it to the poor. Better yet, he'd just get rich, yes, that's what he'd do… but how? He'd never done anything and the only thing his mother had taught him was that nobody takes care of anybody, especially the wealthy…they just take care of themselves.

He wanted to help people, but didn't really have a plan or a place to start. So, here he was traveling again thinking about it. He felt as though someone was watching over him and he would one day be that star, but getting to the top of the mountain, he'd need some help.

He was not too far into the hike that he had come upon the forest that was as deep and thick, rich and green as any picture he had ever seen. Everything was overgrown, but it was all so beautiful, unimaginably gorgeous.

Curiously though, he felt strangely safe. He had not felt this safe since his real father had come to visit him. It was only for a while, but the feelings of those moments had logged into his memory and here they were again…safe and secure, even if he was smack dab in the middle of a forest where absolutely no one knew where he was. He had left his friends behind and he nor they knew where he was and what made this time so fantastic…he didn't care!

Here, he could continue his journey with his smokes and dream his dreams of tomorrow. He was tomorrow's man, the man of the future, who, as he laughed to himself was so high now from his weed that he didn't know if he was walking into the forest or out of it.

Hunger and thirst were calling and he had nothing to settle the urges that were welling up deep within him. Stillness was in the forest and the sense of someone watching him was there again.

"Hello? Anybody out there?" he let out an inquisitive yelp. "Hello, I know you're out there, or here…hello?"

The break in the foliage led to a clearing where breathing became easier and the relegation of his thoughts fell back to his friends that he had left behind hours ago.

"Where are they?" he thought to himself, as he threw a pebble through the brush.

"I feel so alive here," he wondered to himself, breathing easier and the rays of sunlight beaming through the sway of the trees woke him up even further. He seemed to gain new strength with each breath.

He dwelt on the possibility of his purpose in these moments alone, yet what he really desired was significance. He wanted to be known… he wanted to change the world…he wanted to be truly significant in such a way that it didn't really matter to him how he attained notoriety, he just wanted to be known by somebody…by everybody. He was quite ambitious in heart. He'd been told he was an over-achiever, but what did that mean? He felt like he could rule the world, at least his part of it, anyway, and he could feel the unction brewing inside of him to achieve, achieve, achieve and just like he was walking over the brush, so he would walk over anybody that got in his way.

At this point, he began to run and run at a pace that he ran when he was a boy on the island. The faster he ran, the more swift he could run through the brush sweeping over his pants legs like people grabbing at him trying to hold him back, but no thing and no one was going to hold this man back anymore…so, he galloped through the brush dancing and bouncing off of the trees, darting back and forth like a point guard on the basketball court. He was empowered here and he felt like the wind was at his beckon call. The forest was his in these moments and he owned all that he saw.

Running faster now, he was running through the forest at a pace that was good for him. No one was going to catch him and no one was going where he was going. He was his own man and all of a sudden he jumped over a downed log, rolled and tumbled with his body falling forward and rolling all the more. He rolled until he rested on his back and looking up into the rays of sunlight piercing through the trees, he thought to himself, "I'll even own you, I'll even own you."

"No one is going to tell me what to do ever again!" he said aloud all the while looking around sensing the lurking someone still listening, still watching him in his aloneness and his pride.

His self-assurance was confirmed now, yet what he was going to do at this very moment, he had not the slightest clue.

Looking up through the striations of the branches of the trees with the sunlight waving at him in the movement of the wind, he asked,

"How do people…no, how do I," as he was probing deep within his own thoughts now. "How can I…" still thinking, forming the phrases in his mind carefully with even more prodding from some spirit that seemed to be calling it out of him,

"How can I change the world to my liking...the way I want it to be?"

Still lying on his back, he started to look around to his right and his left, and he sat up to the sounds of rustling water. It sounded like someone had just come up from out of a pool, the sound that water makes when something is going through it and rising up out of it. He could swear that he could hear a dripping noise coming from just over the ridge.

"Is someone swimming over there?" he thought to himself.

He rose quickly to his feet and threw himself over another log and up over the mound to look below and there it was; the most beautiful, pristine lake he'd ever seen. No one was there and yet the sounds he'd just heard sounded like they were much closer to his ears.

He thought to himself, "There must be some type of echo chamber down there." He stood for a few more moments eyeing the spectacular view of the water that was not moving and then he trotted down to the water to see this close up.

The water was as clear as tap water so he could see the bottom of the lake. Interesting though, there were no fish and as he stood above the water he noticed that the water was moving, kind of like when he would watch an aquarium with a pump in it filtering the water.

"Fascinating," he thought to himself.

"This is almost magical, this beautiful clear lake out here in the middle of nowhere and it's, it's…" he couldn't think up words to describe what he was seeing. The lake was truly indescribable.

"I wonder what it tastes like," again thinking aloud this time. "Well, let's see if you taste as good as you look," for surely by now the glistening water had grabbed his attention and his thirst.

As he bent down at an angle to approach the water, his vision became quite enamored with some type of metamorphosis of the water. While he was standing a bit off of the water, he could see straight through to the bottom and the water was a little deep, but how deep he could not tell. But, as he bent down to his knees, the refraction of the water's surface changed to that of a mirror, very much like any pool of water when at the right angle, you can actually see yourself on the surface reflection.

This was different, though. It was as though he were looking straight into a mirror. He looked up and there was hardly enough sun to create the mirrored image he was seeing on the surface of the water. He saw his lightened dark complexion and slender face, his big elephant ears and flattened nose. The intricacy of his own image as he looked at himself in the mirrored image in the surface of the water was extraordinary. He could see himself.

He snickered to himself and thought, "Man, if Joanna and Robert could see this, they'd flip!"

Yet as he thought this, he was thinking the thought and not talking, but he saw his mouth move while he was thinking the thought.

"Woah!" he exclaimed in his mind with his mouth moving and then he really did say, "Woah!" out loud.

He fell back away from the water a little frightened, but not fearful, no, it was more magical than creepy.

He lunged forward back to his knees and looked over the water thinking thoughts to himself and yet his mouth was moving.

"Extraordinary!" he thought to himself and this time in the mirrored water, his entire face moved with his mouth in elation.

"You can read my mind," he said to the water.

In that moment, his hand moved forward into the water and the most exciting shock came over him from the water, through his hands, through his arms and shocked his entire body into his spirit. Flashes of light and images began to pour through his spirit of yesterday, his past, his mom, his meeting with his dad, the guys, at home, the travels, the travels, the travels, Ri'card dressing up in front of him, and the thoughts, the memories shockingly pierced through his mind faster than lightning. Zip, zip, zip, the thoughts zipped through his spirit of his yesterday's…his life flashed before him and he was shocked, agitated, and frightened at the same time.

"Stop, stop, stop this, you fool!" he was talking to the water in response to his past that he'd just lived through again.

"You don't know me, what are you?" he shouted to the water.

"That's just all in my mind, you don't know me!" as he gritted his teeth in anger. This wasn't funny or fun anymore and he started to investigate in his mind what had just happened.

"This must be the weed talkin'," he thought to himself, shaking his head back and forth and there his mouth was moving again in the mirrored water as he thought his anxious thoughts.

"No!" he screamed at the water, breaking the surface with his fist as though breaking a piece of mirror. The water cracked like broken ice.

Yet in his frightened anger and pent up rage, the water was on his hands and he sunk his hands deeper into the water past the water's edge and a warmth came over him unlike anything he'd ever felt.

"Come," said the water, as he released his clinched fists and flattened his hands to relax. A peace came over him, again unlike anything he'd ever felt. It was as though the water had something to offer him…a freedom from his pain and his past…all his yesterday's could be washed away, it seemed as this wonderful water was calling his name and powerfully freeing him at the same time.

"NO! You're not real, you've never been real," he said again with gritted teeth. "It can't be that easy to simply let go and let you have me, you're not getting me!" he retorted to the water for his conscience was not receiving anything the water had to say.

"I'm my own man and nothing has power over me! I am my own power! "

By this time, his defiance had propelled him from his knees to standing over the water cursing it. He could see straight through to the bottom and he began spitting into the water with what little spittle he had left after his long hike into the woods.

"You're not real," he said to the water as he was shaking his head back and forth in the fashion of "no, no, no". The conversation was brief here and a resounding rejection was in order. He had stood his ground now and nothing was going to tell him what to do, take his life or have any power over him.

"I'm my own man!" he yelled back to the water. "and there is no god, I tell you, that will ever tell me what to do! In fact, you know what I'm going to do, don't you," laughing at the water, mocking it, as the water remained silent and still.

Just then, Joanna and Robert had come over the same ridge at the top of the hill, calling for him, "Miguel, where have you been? We've been looking all over for you, we need to get back, it will be getting dark soon."

Miguel had turned away from the water and looked up towards his friends and said, "I'm coming!"

Miguel looked back towards the water one last time and whispered with gritted teeth, "I'm my own power, I just proved it to you. You'll never have me bending my knee to you ever again!"

And with that, he ran up the slope to Joanna and Robert and said, "Let's get outta here, this place gives me the creeps. You gotta smoke?"

Robert laughed and said, "Of course!" handing him a newly rolled masterpiece of nirvana. "You gotta let me take care of ya, don't chu?" patting him on his back like a brother.

He smiled his big smile to Robert while Joanna just looked at him strangely. "You two are two strange dudes!"

"Yea, we may be strange, but we're gonna change the world to our kind of strangeness," he jokingly said to Joanna as they walked through the forest.

"Rob, what do you think about politics?"

Robert looked back at Miguel with a sense of overwhelming agreement in a very dark sinister kind of way and said,

"Politics?! Now you're talkin'. The world hasn't seen change like our kind of change 'cause our kind of strange is our kind of change."

They laughed at each other knowing a good hit off the weed would get them through today and the rest of their lives…with no one or no thing to tell them what to do.

## Chapter 7

## The Looking Glass

## Present Day…

The door chime chirped as the door creaked open to the complaints of the woman walking through the door.

"Hello! Welcome to the Looking Glass!" he cheered.

"Hi, Ms. Dee," he smiled at her sneer.

"I hate the sound of that door chime! Have you gotten it in yet?" she inquired about her order that she'd placed weeks ago. She had not been listening when he said that he would call her when the mirror had arrived.

"No, not yet, it was actually due in yesterday," as the delivery truck's wheels squealed in the distance. "I think it's coming in just a few minutes, do you hear the roar of the truck?" he said as the truck passed by the mirror store not stopping.

"Yes, I hear it and heard it, and I think I've heard this before…I want my money back. You told me it would be in last week," as she glanced in the mirror behind the counter, noticing the redness of her face and neck. Now she was embarrassed at how she was acting, but it was his fault, so she stammered all the more, "I want my money back and I'll pay you when it comes in, if it ever does."

"Ms. Dee, you know I have no control over it," he retorted, but she interrupted,

"Yes, you do; now you've gone to lying. Give me my money back," she demanded fiercely this time.

He had to do it this time. There were no more promises to make or keep for this small time shop owner. Looking down at the open register, all of the money in the till was exactly what she had paid for the mirror.

Breathing a sigh of resignation, he looked at Ms. Dee, looked back down at the open cash register drawer, looked back at her with her mean grimace on her face, and started pulling bills out of the drawer.

"I think I owe you $301.50, right?" he asked.

She winced as her right eye twitched in angry stress as though she wanted to hit him and then proclaimed,

"That should about do it!"

As he was counting out the dollars the door chime chimed its chirp and in walked the delivery driver,

"This thing is heavy, can you hold the door open?" he sighed, breathing an exasperated breath. "I almost forgot you. I actually didn't want to have to pick this thing back up, but I also didn't want it in my truck another night either."

"What do you mean, 'another night'?" Gigot inquired, sensing some kind of rationale for excusing himself from not making the delivery on time yesterday.

"What? 'nother night, naw, I didn't mean to say that," he brooded, knowing that he'd just given himself away.

Ms. Dee looked at Gigot realizing that he'd been telling her the truth. But, as was her way, she merely gumpft and yelled at the truck driver,

"Just hold up right there, I'm sure that's mine and you can place it in the back of my car."

After the delivery guy and Ms. Dee left in their peaceful agitation, Gigot was alone again with his menagerie of mirrors. Chuckling to himself he thought, "What have I done? What have I done with my family's money? Who is going to buy all of these mirrors?"

Then the chuckling was no longer a chuckle, but a reserved gratitude that he had dodged another bullet of possibly having to give money back to a customer. If this place had been a shark tank, he would have been eaten alive.

Gigot stood behind the counter and pulled out his Bible. He found comfort in the Psalms. He would read about how God provides and how he personally did not want to be left abandoned and ashamed; he would read and read some more. Then, he would go to praying. He would walk around the store praying and hoping that God would send in a customer to help supply his need. Sometimes they would come and other times they would not. The incredible sense of aloneness would set in and he would find himself breathing so deep that if he could breathe up the earth, it would fill his lungs. He was alone, but oddly enough, with all of those mirrors, he seemed to be alone multiplied.

## Chapter 8

## The Heretic's Hallelujah

Gigot had a heard a local southern preacher say, "There's nothin' you have to do to be saved except believe." To him, that message sounded good, but deep down he knew it simply wasn't true because it wasn't complete. Later in the message, the preacher drawled, "All you have to do to be saved is to repent and believe…" and then he went on to preach about what Jesus did on the cross.

He thought to himself, "Now, which is it? He knew that was half right, but what exactly does this preacher believe?"

He knew something about it all just wasn't right, the message, that is, but he just couldn't put his finger on it. He had sat listening to this preacher for some time. His message, after all, was almost identical to what he'd been hearing from other men of the cloth. And he knew that this guy was very forgiving for it was there in his church that he was allowed to rest after what he had done.

It was what he had done that was at the forefront of his mind, almost all of the time, and he'd always sensed the judgment. The judgment was always lurking around, but did it come from others or was it coming from his internal guilt? What he had done was what he had vowed he would never do and yet there it was now and it would not let him go. The self-inflicted stigma was with him…this scarlet letter seemed to be imbedded on his forehead and in his meandering thoughts.

He had seen in a dream once, this female quip with an English accent, "He talks 'bout others sins but never confesses his own," and the words haunted him. It was as though some spirit was constantly accusing him and haranguing him incessantly of his past.

How could he have done what he did? He knew all that he had done but he did not know all that he had done. He had been living the guilt and the consequences for so many years, yet no matter how many times he had heard and really believed he had been forgiven…he had not forgiven himself.

It was far more than stealing a loaf of bread. He had stolen innocence from his children. He had stolen privacy from his wife and the privacy of another. He had stripped himself of any virtue, if he had ever had any to begin with.

"How could I do what I did?" He constantly harangued himself with that question.

It was even printed on a page of his personality profile that he was incapable of ever doing such a thing and was abominable in his thinking. He had stripped himself of proper demeanor and of any and all pride, for in that there certainly was a bit too much of. Judgment is not always swift, but it always is. It will come sooner or later in that he feared. He had not understood the depth of his sin…the adulterer never does.

There was something to this committing of adultery. He discovered that you have to break just about every commandment there is in order to accomplish it with zeal and the lie had been his greatest weapon of defense.

She was the best liar he had ever known and strangely enough, when the lie benefitted him, he didn't seem to care.

"How could that be?" he perpetually pondered. He continued in his ignorance of all that he had done and work was his only escape from the impending reality of what was to come in his not so distant future.

Still, here it was again, another preacher preaching something that just wasn't quite right. He knew there was more to this thing than just believing, he remembered that 'even the devils believe'. Certainly, that wasn't what he was, was he, a devil? Is that all he had done…simply believe? No, that could not be for he knew he had been changed as a teenager, a great metamorphosis even. But the years had been curiously revealing of his inner self, his selfish desires and his personal world of religion. Nothing had turned out to be what he had always dreamed it would be. His marriage wasn't, love wasn't, religion wasn't, work and money wasn't…nothing was what he had hoped it would be in his life except one thing…his love for his children, for they were his constant.

The ever-present love for his children guided him when everything in this earth would vaporize. The gravitational force of love that he knew to be real with his children kept him sane and also kept him alive.

One afternoon, a different preacher came in, who in his own mind believed he was one of the most anointed men of God known to man. Nothing could have ever been further from the truth or, at least, from what Gigot learned to believe about him. Gigot was learning to listen and not play the fool that he had been in times past by talking too much.

This preacher seemed to be the greatest thing walking because he was so successful in making converts to his church. But Gigot saw something different that many folk didn't see or hear. What he heard was the voice of an imposter, a poser, displaying excessive ambition and strangely enough, this preacher confessed his past memories as though they had happened last week and he wore them as laurels on his head. There was a difference in confessing a sin in repentance and remorse and the confession of a braggart where jest and laughter went along with the stories.

Gigot felt humiliated by his ranting of his past life, because the stories were embarrassing. As some men brag of their exploits from last night's drunken party, so this guy bragged of his escapades from days gone by, but by the way that he talked, it could have happened the night before.

As despicable and dastardly as his behavior had been, there seemed to be some type of intimated comradery as a result of Gigot's own personal confession to the man months earlier. To be clear, the things he heard in his store amazed him each week.

Was there a man of the cloth without sin? Did any of them preach the truth?

"My God," he thought. "What is the truth and does anyone know it?"

The arrogance and pride of men and women that made their living from the Word of God were making a killing, that is, the killing of souls for the benefit of their pocketbooks. And all of the stones he wanted to throw at them seemed to be too heavy to lift as a result of his own personal sin. There were no stones to throw here for the weight of his sin had weighted the weight of the stones to a ton.

What brought all of this out in his customers anyway? Was it the mirrors? Could the mirrors be the reason why so many people would come in his store patiently waiting to be alone in the store with Gigot? Customer after customer would browse and browse through the faces of the mirrors and then once they were alone, Gigot would invariably say,

"Let me know if I can help in any way," and then the streams would come.

The heart doors would open up with confession, stories from the past, current dilemmas, adultery in the home, separation from spouses, lost children, sickness and health issues, relationship issues and it seemed endless at what the next customer was going to come in with and want to talk about. The gates of catharsis would open up like Niagara Falls and the tissue box became his greatest ally.

Was it being alone with the customers that gave them the opportunity? Was it something inside of him that drew it out of them? Was there something to all those mirrors being in one place that people could not get away from themselves? Did any of them have an inkling of who they really were? For they would talk incessantly about themselves, their problems of the day, their season of life, their work, their employer, their children or grandchildren, their problems, the issues of life and oh, their problems. Then the tears would flow…and every once in a while, he would make a sale that would pay the month's rent.

At this juncture, Gigot had been open for business for a couple of years just scraping by with the mirror sales. A real friend of his, Noah Kacin, dropped in to see how he was doing. Noah had had a few trials of his own through the years and couldn't get Gigot off of his mind.

Gigot was surprised to see Noah and he could only figure he was in for a quasi-lecture or so he thought, for that was something Noah was known for. He was actually good at it, but the inductee usually didn't think so. Noah was Ivy League, born and bred, but something different was in his heart than most Ivy Leaguers. Anyhow, Gigot was glad to see him and was inwardly hoping for a sale, but that was not why Noah had shown up that day.

"Hi Noah, it's great to see you, how are you?" Gigot smiled and smirked at the same time, raising his brow just enough to let Noah know that he knew that this was a business meeting and not just being among friends.

Noah responded, "I was in the area going north to Tallahassee and thought I'd drop in. How's the business?"

"The same, Noah, the same as it was the day it started, just barely enough…maybe. How's your business?" Gigot retorted.

"Not bad, I'm on the road again to go start up a new region just north of here, the company's expanding and my area is expanding right along with it."

Gigot raised a brow, smiled his smile and whimpered a chuckle,

"I'm happy for you, is there something I can do for you today?"

"Well, you know your wife told Beth that you weren't doing so well and so I thought I'd come up here and see you on my way north."

Beth was Noah's wife and Gigot's wife, Pauline, talked a lot, sometimes too much...which always aggravated Gigot to no end. There never was any privacy when it came to Pauline for she was a talker…a detailed talker. She was the kind that would make any husband shutter when relatives or friends walked in the door with a smirk on their face. So, only God knew what Pauline had complained about this time because nothing was ever enough for her. If it wasn't one thing, it was definitely two, or four, or six.

"I'm fine, Noah," Gigot offered begrudgingly, knowing that he and Pauline would be having a "conversation" when he got home.

"What's on your mind, Noah, go ahead and get it off your chest?"

"You need to get away from this place, Gigot, I mean, far away, so that you can clear your head and see things from a different perspective."

Gigot raised an eyebrow in wonder because this time Noah wasn't offering a new "perspective", as he called it, he was offering an idea for Gigot to go out and see something on his own.

"Perhaps you're right, Noah, it is time for a vacation, but the kids are in school now and it's difficult to go someplace with the kids."

"I wasn't talking 'bout a family vacation, I'm talking 'bout you, just you getting away to clear your head of this place, cause this place has you in a fog. I don't think you're thinking straight. Does that make sense?" Noah seemed to be making sense with his reasoning.

"Yes, that makes perfect sense, I guess." Gigot trusted Noah and respected him. He knew that Noah was telling the truth, albeit, he didn't know exactly how he knew all that he knew.

"I could get Vicki to cover here for a week, she's offered twenty times to work here; she loves it here, for some reason. Why, I do not know," Gigot chuckled as most of the people loved his store, but didn't really have the means to support it like he needed them to. People can only handle so many mirrors in their home.

"What exactly are you suggesting?" Gigot was pondering Noah's idea that seemed to be a pretty good one at the moment.

"I think you need to go on a real trip, a cross-country trip, a quest, a pilgrimage, of sorts, to sort things out about this store and what it's doing to you and your family. Go on a hike, a hunting expedition, I don't know…do you hunt?"

Chuckling, Gigot replied, "No, I don't even own a gun, oh, wait, yes I do, I bought it on 9/11 and have never even opened it up out of the packaging."

Now it was Noah who had the raised brow in amazement at that answer. Who in their right mind buys a gun and leaves it in the packaging for five years?

"Why would he do that?" Noah thought to himself. But, then again, this was also the same guy who had put all of his savings into a retail mirror store and borrowed money on top of that. Noah couldn't think of anyone who ever owned a mirror store. On the surface, Gigot seemed impetuous, but was anything but impetuous. He didn't understand Gigot, yet he knew that Gigot's heart was being led by something far greater than himself and the purpose in all of this had yet to be revealed.

## Chapter 9

## Preparing for the Journey

Gigot had no sooner gotten home than Pauline was questioning him about his day. Undoubtedly, the news had gotten out about Gigot going on a 'quest' for a better mind or brain, whichever one might take the leave.

"So, how did it go today? Make any sales…talk to anybody new?" Pauline simply could not hold herself in privacy for all had been revealed in earlier conversations throughout the day.

"No, nothing new, made a few sales like always… sometimes. And, yes, I did talk to Noah, which I'm sure you're aware of," Gigot responded.

"Oh, yes, Beth did happen to mention that Noah had dropped by the store today. What did he have to say?" Pauline queried as she stirred the noodles in the pot. Gigot just looked at her and watched her stir, easily seeing the irony of what she was doing and what she was asking. Unfortunately, Pauline didn't quite get some things as Gigot didn't quite get others.

"How was your day?" Gigot inquired with ambivalence, moving on to see what the kids were up to in the family room ending what never was a conversation. Gigot had the ability to move about with distinction throughout the home as a field marshal might in making preparation for a battlefield. He wanted to see, hear and feel everything that was going on his home. Work put so much stress on him and he wasn't coping with ease through life, particularly at home. He just wanted to sit down and watch anything, or nothing, on the TV with his kids.

They didn't mind because there was no mind that one would have to apply to watching TV. This was a break time and Pauline simply kept working on supper. Any conversation now would have to wait for later or never, whichever came first…or last. Aloofness, as one might believe they call it. They both wore that very well.

Gigot knew he was going somewhere on a trip and he was already missing his children. As they sat there together watching the television, he had one on the left and another on the right. Bessie was sitting in the chair with her legs sprawled as any very young lady should not, but that never seemed to matter to Bessie, especially at home.

As Gigot perused the room, he was breathing in the time and soaking up the energy of just being with his children. No, none of them were talking and they were all glued to the television. None of them were paying him any mind, but they were together and every moment or two, each would glance over to him and smile their smiles, knowing that he was there. Sighing, as a rested pet might sigh, they would all sigh together at times, thankful just to be together. It was in moments like these that a tear would flow from Gigot's face.

He was ever so grateful to be with his children. He loved them like no other father could love and he would defend them at a moment's cause and spank them even quicker. Time could get captured here and he could live forever in these moments for he knew his future would be coming soon and then these times would be no more.

Not so for now. Now, he savored what he held most dear and that was his children. Nothing on this earth could ever be loved as he loved his children and so he leaned on Daniel as James leaned on him. Heaven on earth and peace was in this moment and nothing else mattered. They were his wonder and his world.

It took a couple of weeks to work through the details of the trip to the unknown. Gigot decided he would hike and hunt, although he'd never really gone hunting before. He'd been out with a few friends doing some rabbit hunting years ago and had learned quite a bit there, but going it alone in the wilderness was not something he was entirely comfortable with. The 410 that he had purchased years ago was still in the box.

He was always leery of guns in the house, particularly with children and accidents. Accidents with guns are fatal and cannot be undone and he had seen that tragedy played out too often in his past with the children of a few friends who had accidentally shot themselves while cleaning, playing or simply taking the rifle out to look at it.

Basically, Gigot was not a violent man and deeply respected what a gun could do…so he kept the shotgun in the closet in its original packaging and his children were none the wiser.

He decided he would go alone and travel west by car, a family van by nature, that way he could sleep in it if he needed to. With all of the expenses of traveling, he knew he would have to save where he could. He didn't mind driving because it was in his blood from his father's side of the family. His dad, uncles and grandfather had all driven trucks, short and long-haul, but Gigot's life was different, an educated kind of different. And, the hemorrhoids didn't encourage long spells of driving anyway.

"Well, it looks like you're ready to go," Pauline sighed not really wanting him to go as she had previously planned. She had cherished separation in the thick of things, but was weak going through with it. "Are you sure you know what you're doing?"

Gigot just looked at her with a wavering brow, knowing that he would miss the kids, but would enjoy the break from the tension with Pauline.

"I don't know what I'm doing. I'm just going to find the one thing that might make us all a little better off. You know I've made so many mistakes in the past and somehow that has to stop. Breathing has always helped, you know, being outside."

Pauline smiled and was becoming increasingly jealous now with the idea that he would be out hiking in the wilderness which was something she had always wanted to do.

"Well, when you get back, I would like to go to the north Georgia mountains. Can we make plans to do that?"

"Sure, certainly, we can all do that together." Gigot's mind went directly to the thoughts of his children. He had already said "good-bye" for days and shed a few tears the night before with them in saying, "Good night". Now, they were at school and that made leaving them a little easier.

"I'm gonna go now," which was his usual and customary exit in order not to have another control his ability to leave a situation.

"You know I'll be praying for you and the kids while I'm gone; this is a praying trip, you know."

"I know, and I'll be praying for you."

Pauline began to cry, not being able to contain her emotion, she grabbed Gigot and hugged him for all she was worth and did not want to let go. In that moment, she did not want him to leave, and started to heave a little in tears.

"You know, you don't have to do this, I don't want you to leave." She cried on his shoulder as he held her tightly cherishing the moment that didn't come often enough in their marriage.

"Maybe this is what this whole thing is about," he pondered in his mind as they held each other tightly. This moment could have lasted a day, but was over in a matter of minutes. Both in tears, Gigot got in the van prepared to go to an unknown destination that could, perhaps, explain why his life had taken the turns that it had.

Pauline had prepared enough food for a few days so that the cooler and the bags surrounded him in the van. He smiled, so she smiled and waved her last good-bye welling up in tears once again that turning away from him could only stop this increasing pain of separation.

In that moment, she decided to make their lives better by ceasing to do the things that he so often criticized her for, particularly being obstinate. She just didn't listen to him and she knew it, but she couldn't help herself, she didn't know how to change. She waved her arms like an eagle as if to fly away from herself and the trouble that she constantly badgered him.

"Maybe that's what made his leaving so easy for him," she thought.

"I'm not going to be that person anymore. When he gets back, he'll see." And with that, she sighed and smiled, knowing that she had to get to work herself, it was going to be a big day.

Once Gigot got on the highway, he immediately put in his CCR CD and started to breathe deep breaths. He opened the window and let in the fresh air of speed. He was sensing Pauline in his heart and began to miss her unlike he had done so in a very long time.

"What is going on here, dude?" he questioned himself, beginning to well up in tears all over again. He had not gone ten miles and yet he was choking with the idea of simply turning back home forgetting his plan of renewal.

Reality struck quickly, or something did, spiritually, possibly, that said,

"Grow up!" And with that he was moving up the highway as fast as he could go.

# Chapter 10


## The Dew Drops In


  Gigot had gotten through Dothan, Montgomery and Birmingham and was hoping to get to Memphis by nightfall. Thirteen hours of driving in one day was pretty good for him with all of his stopping to go to the rest rooms. He was planning to spend the night at Lewis and Diane Hartfelt's home near the western outskirts of Memphis along the Mississippi River. He was about an hour and a half south of Memphis traveling through northern Mississippi when he had to stop again.

  This time, he was about to wet his pants he had to go so bad. The coffee and water had done their job to get him this far and so he took the exit leading to Shallowell, Mississippi, near Olive Branch, just before you get into Tennessee.

  Taking the exit, he jutted off to the closest gas station, eyeing with close attention the outside clientele that were sitting on benches just under the gas pump awning. They were smoking and drinking and one of them flicked his cigarette underneath Gigot's car where it was parked at the gas pump. Having to hurry into the rest room, he didn't have time to frown at the guy that could possibly blow up his car. Relieved he had made it inside the men's room, it reeked with urine and basically knocked you back a step just approaching the door. He didn't spend much time in there.

  Walking by the men smoking their cigarettes on the bench, he thought about saying something regarding one of them flicking their cigarette his way, but he decided it imprudent especially since they were also drinking out of their beverage bags they had just purchased inside.

These were a mixture of men. As he was pumping gas into the van, he noticed that some were hobo looking, but a couple others looked like they were dressed to go someplace and happened to be hanging out for a few minutes before they got to their destination. It was futile to try and make out their conversation as they seemed to be having a great time just laughing at themselves and their stories.

Gigot remembered times where he hung out with guys and laughed, but it had been too long ago to remember the circumstances. He was befuddled as he stood there pumping gas and seemingly, they didn't have a care in the world. One of them got up as he was about to finish with the gasoline and the guy was talking about how he had to go across the street to see what was going on tonight.

At that point, Gigot, who was rather intently listening to their conversation, turned and looked across the street and saw the most decorated neon flashing marquee he had ever seen in a church parking lot. It was one of those roll around signs with a trailer hitch, wheels and lights and had huge balloons floating high from its endpoints.

"REVIVAL 2NIGHT" it said, along with the visiting apostle's name in bold letters, "APOSTLE HANANIAH BAPTISTE" "7:OO PM ALL ARE WELCUME" He reckoned that they must have run out of 'o's', so they just made do with what they had. Apparently, this apostle guy must have been pretty popular because there was a line out the door of folk trying to get in and you could hear the music pounding from inside the doors across the street.

Just then, one of the hobo looking guys brushed by the van, mumbling something to Gigot and Gigot said, "What did you say?"

"I sa-id, 'you gonna go ov-er cher to da 'vival?'"

"We's sposed to 'vite folk to cum to da 'vival, you cuming or not?" He said, begrudgingly, waving the length of his arm at Gigot and motioning him towards across the street to the church service.

"Uh, I didn't know about it and I'm from…" Gigot could hardly get the words out of his mouth and one of the nicer dressed guys, a huge black guy that smelled of some kind of lotion, patted him on the back and said,

"It's ok if you don't wanna go, but youse invited, jus' wanted you to know dat." The big black guy smiled a real big smile and kept walking across the street. He yelled back at Gigot,

"You can leave ya car parked dare. Ain't nobody gonna barder it dare. I promise!"

Gigot looked back at the bench of guys and most of them had left except for two that were getting rather snockered by their bottled bags of booze. He looked into their eyes from across the gas pumps and they were already in a daze and looked like they were going to bed down for the night on the gas station bench.

From across the street, the crowd had lessened and gone inside, but every time the door opened, you could hear the music pounding to the song, "Come on everybody, come and meet da Lawd."

A peace came over his soul as he locked the car doors with his key lock and jogged across the street to the beat of the music. By the time he got to the door, he was laughing to himself at what he was doing, but he was also a little undone by the experience of being swept away by a couple of men, who, in their minds, were doing right by the Lord by "'vitin' him to da chuch suvice".

Gigot slipped in to the back row of the church. This place was rockin'. They must have just been about through with the music as this slow pounding drumbeat was pounding away and the majority of the people were simply swooning with fervor. For the most part, they were standing, and almost all had their arms flailing high and waving as they seriously praised the Lord in prayers, mumblings, speaking in tongues, shoutings, cryings, pleadings, a couple of women screaming here and there and it was all going on at the same time. The music would swell and the people would swell. The music would go softly and the people in turn would tone down their musings as if to hear the Lord if He were to walk into the room.

It was quite reverent at times and yet it seemed something was about to explode at any moment. The piano got quieter and the people in the pews began to sit down, one by one, as on que or something. It seemed as though they had all done this before and as each one had had their peace in praise with the Lord, they would just sit down all tuckered out from the experience.

Not so with the guy sitting next to Gigot. Yes, it was the hobo looking guy from the gas station bench as inebriated as he could be. He looked up at Gigot with dreamy eyes and said,

"Da Lawd is in dis place, ain't he?"

Gigot raised his left eyebrow and not wanting to disappoint the man said, "Yes, sir, He shor nuff is."

The man relaxed a bit and slumped back into the pew. He laughed out loud a bit and said, "I knowed it. Youse gonna git saved tonight. Dats why youse here, ain't it?"

Gigot thought to himself as he was looking back at the worn torn man, who not only wreaked of booze, but also needed a shower, "What have I gotten myself into?"

He smiled at the man who started to doze off, slumping to his right away from Gigot and gently laying his head on the hard wooden pew. Just then, the sound of the air conditioning came on and he could feel the cool air breezing around the sweating crowd. Everyone relaxed with the sound of the A/C with a few women waving their fans to cool off quicker than the others.

With all of the fanning, Gigot could smell some fancy aroma that he had recently smelled, but he could not quite make out what it was. The men behind the pulpit were doing some kind of announcements introducing the apostle speaker and the crowd was jeering, 'dats right, come on!' and 'yea, he's here in da house', 'come on, now!' and 'oh, sweet Jesus'.

Gigot's preoccupation, though, was with the aroma and not the introduction, which was really taking too long.

"That's it!" he thought to himself. "It's that big black guy that smells like, like, honey!" He had finally figured out the scent of the man's lotion and, being that the man was sitting in the pew in front of him, all of the waving was sending the scent throughout the back of the auditorium.

The mixed congregation of blacks and whites had their Pentecostal spirit in common, but it was the women especially, who picked up the scent and were obviously distracted by it. The black man who carried the weight of distraction didn't pay it any mind. Little did he know he was the center of attention of the women in the back of the room. But, they didn't know exactly where the scent was coming from. Gigot could see different women, who were familiar with the lotion, picking up the scent with their nose and turning in the right direction of the man. And suddenly, as on que, the air conditioning would turn on sending the fragrance in another direction. Then, the women on the other side started to sniff and wave their fans as to draw the scent closer to their noses.

Gigot, who was usually intuitively aware of his surroundings was watching and being entertained by all of this from the back pew, not paying any attention to the Apostle Hananiah Baptiste, who was about to speak.

With a name like 'Baptiste', Gigot couldn't make out if this black apostle was French Cajun, Hispanic, or by his accent, from an island country or Africa. His accent was not pure but seemed to be blended from a variety of regions. He was still quite southern in a French kind of way. Gigot had never seen a real apostle before anyway, let alone a visiting black revival speaker with a white pastor and a mixed congregation. This was all totally new to him.

Little did anyone know that the Apostle Baptiste had come by his title by way of a small apostolic church in southeast Lousiana. Hananiah wasn't his real name; his real name was Bapsy Boudreaux from down in St. Tammany Parish by way of Mandeville...where the 89's used to be sent. Anyway, it seemed as though Mr. Boudreaux had gotten into the racket of being the highly popular and extremely deceptive local used car salesman who had duped just about everybody in a particular region of the parish. One night, in his soul-searching to get away from the parish Sheriff, he found himself in the Resurrected Apostolic Fellowship. They were so taken by his repentant demeanor and his slick salesmanship, thinking that it was the anointing of the spirit, they baptized him and knighted him with the hallowed title of Apostle. They gave him a new name of a prophet from the book of Jeremiah named Hananiah.

He had become widely known in the Delta region and, as a result, had been invited by many Pastors to come and preach their revival services, being that the great apostle didn't have a church of his own.

The congregation in Shallowell was overwhelmed to have the great apostle come and bring a word from the Lord. Here, there was complete commonality among the people, black, white, a few Hispanics, not too many well-dressed, some in their Sunday best and even the hobo to Gigot's side was seemingly involved when he was awake. The atmosphere was different…it was free and because of that, Gigot was a bit more relaxed as a result.

"Thank ya," Baptiste's voice pitched high at the end of the line, with a bit of a choke for an effort in emphasis, Gigot supposed. But that just got a few of the women started repeating back to Baptiste what he had just said.

"Thank YA!" differing women would shout back to Baptiste or to God, Gigot wasn't really sure who they were thanking.

Baptiste was dressed in a deep red velour type robe type garment… Gigot had never seen a garment like what the apostle had on, so he didn't really know how to figure it out in his mind. It wasn't so much that the red velour made him look royal…it was that dangling gold chain that draped from his neck to his belly button that really stood out. This gold chain cross was huge and long and dangled with every breath and movement that the apostle swayed.

"Thank ya!" he said again with one hand lifted in the air. He was worshipping the Lord with his eyes clinched tight, a huge Bible in his right hand, his left hand raised high and he was swaying right and left, repeating, "Thank ya! Thank ya! Thank ya!"

The apostle seemed to be swaying to the electric piano music in oneness that only musical performers could do. This was his accompanist because the original piano player got up and went to a pew for the guest player to play while the apostle gave his message from the Lord.

"Ya see, I thank the Lawd for all He's done…"

"Dat's right!" a shout came from the audience.

"And I want chu to know…I sa-id…I want chu to know…" the apostle was reving in his spirit.

"Uh-huh, come on, now," someone else chimed in.

"I want chu ta know…dat da Lawd is gud…and his mercy…(the piano accompanist was emphasizing every word) I sa-id…His great mer-cy…oh…oh…His GREAT mercy…is for yor generashun…" the apostle paused as a woman dressed in white stood up and waved her hanky,

"Thank ya!" she said with a great amount of exuberance and tears,

"Thank ya, Thank YA!"

The apostle seemed to be drawn to her and motioned with his hand for her to continue on,

"Now, now, I know…dares mo' dan one person out dare…yes, I know…dat can praise de Lawd wit me!" as he jiggled his hips to the words.

At that moment, the whole congregation jumped to their feet and shouted, cheered, praised and screamed. Right on que the piano accompanist started playing a jig like a thumping something and a man from the left corner ran from one end of the front to the other and ran around the back and ran and kept on running; folk ran down front as the band chimed into the thumping and people near the altar started dancing, cheering, shouting,

"Praise you, Jesus! Praise you, Jesus!"

The apostle just stood in place smiling with his feet firmly planted where he was and swayed to the jig with his fists tightly clinch in his front and his eyes and mouth clinched shut as well. He was enjoying this and he really hadn't said anything yet, not that Gigot could remember anyway.

About that time, someone screamed,

"Dis is da Lawd, I know it, I know it, I know it!"

Someone else shouted, "He's right on time! Yes He is!"

Apostle Baptiste picked up on that phrase and repeated it,

"He's right on time, yes He is, ain't He, He's right on time, yes He is!" this time doing a little jig himself to the beat, "He's right on time, yes He is, He's right on time, I know! He's right on time, yes He is, He's right on time, I know!"

The entire congregation repeated what he had just sung and sung it back to him,

"He's right on time, yes, He is, He's right on time, I know! He's right on time, yes He is, He's right on time, I know!" and everybody cheered, more people were running up and down the aisles and Gigot didn't know whether to join in or run out of the building. He held onto the pew in front of him tightly as though the pew would save him from making a fool of himself. He clinched the pew tighter and was overwhelmed at the sights and sounds that were coming from the moving crowd of people. Everybody was in on it except for a few folk surrounding him in the back. The drunk was waking up from the ruckus and shouted,

"It's da spirit of da Lawd in dis place, da postle dun brought up da spirit of da Lawd!" and then he slumped back down in his drool.

Gigot wiggled his neck a bit not knowing exactly where to look because there was so much going on. The band was in high gear, the apostle was dancing his jig and the pastor had jumped up watching the crowd smiling as a proud parent watching his children do something special. Pastor Eli believed that he was the father of the house and all of the people in the congregation were his children, so it made sense to him to be proud when they all could join in together in the spirit and he could stand on the platform as only a proud father could.

As the commotion stirred to a fevered pitch, the apostle had now gone from swaying to dancing to spinning round and round with his arms stretched out letting his velour robe hang from his arms like angel wings. The long golden cross was dangling from his right hip as he tressled left in a spin.

Apostle Baptiste must have gotten a little dizzy at this point because he abruptly stopped spinning, stumbled a bit and grabbed for Pastor Eli's arm. With a blank and dazed stare on his face he shouted,

"Ain't dat like de hand of de Lawd, catchin' ya when ya fall!" and the place erupted with cheers.

Gigot had never seen all of this going on in a church service before. He had grown up in the south going to the Baptist church and he remembered that they didn't believe in all of this, but that didn't mean it wasn't real because the Baptists believed a few things themselves that weren't real. It had just taken Gigot too long to figure out most religious beliefs were just that…beliefs and not truths. So, this revival was as entertaining as it was an education.

Time had past and Gigot looked at his phone clock and it was already close to 9:00 pm and yet he couldn't exactly remember anything that the apostle had said up to this point. He knew he had sung and danced and spoken a few lines that made the people cheer, but by now he had sat back in the pew to rest, as most folk had, in order to listen to something real. Gigot analysed what was going on and what manner of spirits that had control of the place, so he listened intently to every word spoken.

"Nows I wants to postulates some truths to you all before I have to go tonight, 'dis won't take long…elder…put me on a timer of, say, 21 minutes…is dat ok with you all?" the apostle inquired of the people and they graciously cheered.

"Take all da time ya need postle", "Preach on preacher", "All right, now", and yet another said, "Come on, talk it to us straight!"

"If you believes I'm the man o Gawd, say, 'Amen!'"

Everyone shouted, "Amen!"

"If you beleives dat de Word o da Lawd is pouring fort tanight...say, 'Amen'"

And everbody screamed, "Amen!" again.

"Now dis ain't just for ev-rybody, but ifins you believes dat you gonna get a special word from da Lawd tanight, come an place a twenty on dis here altar and say 'Amen!'"

One by one, a trickle of started folk going down to the altar, placing ten's and twenty's, one's and one hundred's on the altar as the apostle demanded and he blessed their heads as they passed by him. Many gave, but not all...most still wanted to hear what he had to say.

"You see, when da man o Gawd postulates da trut o Gawd, it means he's been on high wid da highest. You heard it, folks, I have been on high and da Lawd dun sent me down here to tell you what's going on on high."

A few folk stood and folded their arms together and swayed and said, "My, my, my, ain't he sometin'," smiling as they sat back down.

"Now don't you dink dat I'm somebody jus cause I's meets wid da Lawd face to face, no, no, no. I ain't nobody…" the apostle said humbly.

Someone else yelled out, "You de apostle, you da man o God!"

Another agreed, "I knowed dats right."

"Da Lawd dun sent me here to say one thang, and one thang only… do you want to know whuh tit ih?" the apostle shook his neck as the crowd began to stir madly by his question.

"I sa-id, do…you…want…to…know…whuh…tit…eih?" and the piano started back on que.

"All right, now" another responded as the crowd was beginning to stand one by one. "Preach, preacher!" another exclaimed.

With a stirring frenzy, he kept repeating, "Do…you…want…to… know…what…tit…eih?" and the more he repeated the phrase, the more crazy the crowd became with exuberance, shaking hankerchiefs, waving their arms, standing with folded arms swaying back and forth and on and on the people responded with shouts of agreement and praise.

"Let me tell ya what da Lawd dun said to tell ye, but ya got to sit down to hear it, cause you gots to gits dis and git it gud." Apostle Baptiste was quieting the crowd from their frenzy because whatever it was he was getting ready to tell them, it must have been important to him; he wanted it quiet.

"You see, when da Lawd speaks to ye, ya can't keep it to yoself, naw…shoose, shoose, da Lawd is speaking now, honey, we'll talk later," the apostle spoke directly to a beautiful mixed Milatto girl who was swooning not far from him.

"Ushers, help dis poor girl outta here and take her to my room so dat we can pray for her later…"

And with that, other ladies seemed to go into swooning, saying,

"My, my, my, dat poor girl gonna get her healin' on tonight!"

When that commotion was over, he knelt down on stage in front of all the people and wiped a tear from his eyes, saying,

"I'm so humbled to be so exonerated in da presence of da holy One. He dun purified my soul and washed me clean in da fountain o life. He reconciled me with da po'er of da reconciliation. He put a hot coal on my mout to wash my mout so Ise could speak his wonders…I touched da robe o his garment and it made my hand white and lebrous, but He healed it right, dun, dare jus ta let me know I wus his own man o Gawd."

Gasps, whimpering and cries were coming over the room as he continued, "Yes, da Lawd himself touched my infuhmuhty and gave me a new name."

"Uh, huh," someone quietly spoke and all could sense the swaying coming over the room.

With great tears, Apostle Baptiste rose and said again, this time, in a little louder voice, "I sa-id, da Lawd told me himself, he gave me, a new name," waving his head back and forth, breathing heavy, exasperated in tears, "He told me dat my new name is…" and you could hear the people gasp and hold their breath. "My new name is… Plenty, and everywhere I's go, dares Plenty to go around." And with that, he collapsed on the platform.

The crowd was frantic, hushes and swoons came over the women and the men got up to stand around the apostle covering him in layers, just standing around his body. The men in front looked militant, almost angry if someone might even get a little close to the unconscious man of God.

Pastor Eli was already by his side as the Apostle was in the motion of collapsing. It seemed they had moved as one. Pastor Eli was praying over him and with both hands held high was kneeling and bowing as one might kneel before a king. He was speaking in tongues, praying and screaming, yelling for God to have mercy on the body of the collapsed apostle.

"Lawd, have mer-cy; Lawd, have mer-cy," Pastor Eli spoke with a cry in his voice. Gigot had heard that voice before, but couldn't remember where he'd heard it. Certainly, he'd never heard Pastor Eli preach before, but his voice was so distinct and yet, now, yes, now it was coming back to him the more Pastor Eli pleaded with God,

"Oh, Gawd, this is yo man o Gawd…" and finally it came to Gigot that this voice was the voice much like that of Mr. Haney, from the Green Acres sitcom back in the 1970's.

His voice cracked as he spoke, "Let's all pray for the 'postle," and with that, just about everybody went to speaking in tongues. As the cries went up to God in their uncertain prayers, there was motion coming from within the circle that the men had created around the apostle.

Pastor Eli reverently said, "Ladies and gentlemen, we have a crisis here. What the Lawd is showing us, I believe, is de Spirit of de Lawd, Himself, ri-ght here, ri-ght now," and the people went silent.

"Yes," he said as his voice crackled, "I see de Lawd right now," he was looking up towards the ceiling. "I see de Lawd, high and lifted up in His chariot on high looking down on us, his little peoples. His gawment's coming down touching da 'postle ri-ght now."

There was more movement now in the midst of the men guarding the body of the apostle and the apostle seemed to be trying to get up on all fours from lying face down in his spittle.

"Give him a-i-r, give h-i-m a-i-r, " cried Pastor Eli and the men parted away from the apostle as the Red Sea must have parted for Moses.

Gigot didn't realize it, but the church auditorium had become so packed with people that there was no room to move. So many people had come in after Gigot had that every pew seat was filled and every aisle space was filled and packed like sardines. The people were very gracious, though, not pushing and shoving, but politely trying to get a view of the apostle as he was rising from his prostrated position.

"Where did all these people come from?" Gigot thought to himself and "When did they get in here? How did they get in here?" he continued to wonder.

Apostle Baptiste fixed his cordless microphone around his face and the people were speechless. He looked as though he had seen a ghost. His dark black complexion seemed a bit ashy and dry, possibly from all of the brow wiping of the sweat earlier, but Gigot didn't quite get what or where the man had been while he was out cold.

Apostle Baptiste spoke, "I…have…" and then he choked. He looked down and then looked back up again, "I…have…been…with…" the people began to gasp at every syllable as it took the apostle every ounce of energy he could muster just to say a word. "I…have…been…

with…JE-S-U-S!" he screamed and yodeled at the top of his lungs.

The women in the front fainted and the militant men that had surrounded him earlier gathered arms together as to form a barrier around the now sacred man of God.

"He looked at me, dear children, He looked at me," and the apostle cried all the more. "His wonderful face looked upon me and anointed my head with His hand!" This caused the place to erupt more so than the other times to the point where women were swooning into the arms of the men around them and movement was trying to be moved, but there was nowhere for people to move, so they just cried, screamed, shouted and cheered.

"He wants me to anoint you with the anointin' He just anointed me with," the apostle described the scene in heaven that he had just had with Jesus. "But you have to clear back," he stated.

Pastor Eli stammered, "Clear back, clear back," motioning with his arms to make room for what was coming next. "Clear all the way back towards the back, I want the front cleard," Pastor Eli demanded.

"Bring the offering basket down chere," he continued. "No, not dat one, bring de big un." Pastor Eli was motioning to the ushers to bring this large basket to the front in front of the pulpit

"Now, folks," Pastor Eli pleaded with his people, "You know I'm your fa-ther."

"Dat's right," many of them replied.

"What's you want, passer?" another one responded.

"Dis man o Gawd has been in de presents of JE-SUS," he screamed triumphantly, "and now he's gonna 'noint you wid da same a-nointin' dat he dun got 'a-nointin' wid. If you wants to gits surius wid Gawd, you gots to gits surius wid Gawd. You bring a love offring down here and fill dis basket up to overflow and dis a-noinded man o Gawd will touch you wid de oil of life, ain't dat right, 'postle?"

"Dats right, pasteh, dat's right!" they continued to say loudly.

The helper men closest to the two sacred men were Pastor Eli's two sons, it seemed. They were the ones who had carried their Bibles, notes, handkerchiefs and now their oil. The tallest of the helper men took out a large silver bottle of oil and the apostle outstretched his arms, pulling back the rich red velour robe so that no oil would get on his garment. The oldest helper man lifted the bottle of oil high as in some kind of ritual and poured oil down onto the moving hands of the apostle. The apostle was mumbling, praying in tongues as he worked the oil into his hands and allowed it to run down his arms. The oil must have been a little cold because by the time it had run down his arms into his armpits, he shuttered and wiggled and gave the helper man a very mean look.

Apostle Baptiste turned to the audience with a very solemn expression on his face and with oil dripping from his hands said in a very deep resounding voice, "Who will come and receive the anointin' of Jesus?"

Again, as if on some que like they had all done this before, the entire congregation parted and passively moved to get into a single file line from one end of the auditorium to the other wrapping and wrapping around the building and throughout the pews because everyone wanted in on this anointing. They believed from their need that every word from their Pastor or their Apostle was from God and so they acted accordingly. Everyone who came walked passively and reverently towards the man of God and placed cash, checks and prayer requests into the basket before they reached the Apostle. This, along with the money already placed on the altar, was the intended love offering for the Apostle that he would receive for being so gracious as to give out the anointing of Jesus that he had been freely given.

## Chapter 11

## The Open Portal

Tears flowed from Gigot's eyes at the heart and sychronization of the people. He could tell in their passion that they desparately wanted the Lord's anointing and this need drove them to submit passively to their leaders.

Gigot was always chasing after God himself because he knew that only God could take him away from who he was and what he had done. He was continuing to learn the difference between faith and foolishness by recognizing his own mistakes along the way. The character of some of his decisions taught him the difference of when he was dwelling in faith or acting a fool. It was uncannily funny and simlutaneously sad at how he could hear the foolishness being preached as faith and hardly none were the wiser. It was though the salesman in the apostle knew that a passive mind was a most perfect kind of mind to receive his offerings so that his offerings would be returned multiplied. Gigot got in line with the rest of the folk as they all followed one another through the pews. The hobo looking guy had awakened and sobered up a bit and they were the last two guys in the line following the huge black guy that smelled of honey lotion.

"My name's BB, whut's yours?" the big black guy asked Gigot.

"Gigot," he responded, smiling as fumbled through his pants pockets for some cash to place in the basket because he could see that just about everybody was giving something to the apostle for his anointing. The basket was getting quite full by the time Gigot and the other two got close to the front. The hobo looking guy was getting more and more antcy with each approaching step and Gigot whispered to him,

"Are you ok, do you have to go to the rest room or something?"

The hobo looking guy replied humiliated, "I ain't got nuttin' to give for my anointin'."

Gigot pulled a couple fives out of his pocket, separating them with his fingers as his hand approached the hobo.

The hobo reached out with his right hand and simultaneously put one five in his right hand and placed the other five in his left hand drawing it down into his left pocket. He calmly said,

"Thank ye, 'dis is for later to git me sometin' to eat."

People were lying everywhere on the carpet down front near the altar where they had been 'slain in the spirit', which was another experience that Gigot had never seen before in real life. Some people were lying there on the carpet out cold and others could be seen with their eyes closed like they were asleep, but they might be scratching their noses or checking their watch or fumbling with their dresses so as not to be indiscreet while planked out on the floor.

A few folk were shaking on the floor yelping like they were possessed by some spirit and still others were just standing there with their eyes clinched shut and waving their arms back and forth like they were doing aerobics. Others stood with blank stares as in a spiritual trance.

One lady was hunched down bending over with clinched fists repeatedly saying, "Thank ya! Thank ya! Thank YA!"

Some folk were crying and others swaying while others were sleeping or weeping. Gigot didn't really know what to expect or if any of this was real. He was hoping that it was real because he had never experienced anything like this before and he felt he could use a strong dose of reality in his life.

"Maybe this church was why he was on his trek," he thought to himself.

Pastor Eli was still up on the platform shouting for everyone to come, and they had, and yet he still kept shouting. He would pray and he would cry, thanking God all the while for His wonderful mercy and for the greatness of the apostle and his great humility in coming to such a lowly place such as his church. With great fanfare, Pastor Eli started gasping for air, pleading with God to let Him see His face as the apostle had seen the Lord and just then, as Pastor Eli was looking up, he screamed to the top of his lungs,

"I see you, Jesus! I see you!"

Then he looked back down at the crowd and said,

"I'm in a portal of holiness, I'm in the portal of holiness, come to the portal of holiness!"

Just about that time, Gigot, the huge black man that smelled of honey and the sobering hobo had reached the front of the auditorium just beneath where Pastor Eli stood. The hobo fell back frightened at what Pastor Eli was screaming about with the spiritual portal because he thought there was a hole in the floor or something and thought he might fall through this portal into Jesus' arms if he took one more step forward. The frightened hobo was reluctant to move any more steps forward, putting the other five into his right pocket. Just then, with the fragrance of the honey lotion strong in the air, the air conditioning kicked on and sent the fragrance right into Pastor Eli's nostrils.

Pastor Eli screamed again, "Jesus is telling me that somebody's gonna get a promotion tomorror and a pay raise...now who is dat? Oh glory to Gawd...come into the portal with me folks, it smells just like honey."

Apostle Baptiste had just put his oily hands on the huge black man that smelled of honey and he could tell where the fragrance was coming from because he had a stash of that kind of lotion back in his room. He looked up at the pastor, who, by now was screaming with elation,

"The portal of honey is right down chere, folks, it's right down chere, I'm in da portal o honey with Je-sus and it's so wunda-ful…"

The apostle quickly prayed over the huge black man that smelled of honey and without a hitch grabbed him and Gigot and whispered,

"You two grabs dat basket and come wit me!"

Gigot was taken aback a bit and the two simply looked at each other as the apostle turned to his right and walked out the choir entrance door.

"He talkin' ta us?" BB inquired of Gigot.

"I reckon so, BB" said Gigot, still thinking that he would get his anointing backstage after he delivered the basket of money. The two got on opposite sides of the offering basket which must have been two feet wide by two feet long and about four foot tall. It was actually heavy with all of the money, checks and prayer letters that had been placed in the basket.

They raced to the back as one of the helpers opened the door to the back and the apostle brushed him back as though he didn't want him around his money. The helper lodged a grunt and wiped his mouth of drool and closed the door back to the room where the apostle had run to.

You could hear the people leaving out from the auditorium as Pastor Eli ran quickly into the back room. They embraced one another while Gigot and the huge black man that smelled of honey stood at attention on either side of the money basket. They weren't even noticed as the apostle and the pastor started jibbing one another about what just went on in the service. They were laughing and mumbling and Gigot couldn't make out a word either one of them said.

You could hear car horns, hollering and shouts of praise outside with all of the people leaving, but Gigot and BB just stood there at attention not knowing what to do next. The service had lasted so long that the people were excited about getting on with their lives leaving as quickly as they could. In no time, the auditorium was empty and the folk closing up the church building were making their rounds. A knock came on the door by one of the helper guys and he asked if there was anything else that needed to be done.

The apostle, overhearing the exchange between Pastor Eli and his men asked,

"Where's dat girl I tolt you to send back here, where is tshe?"

"Let me check," Pastor Eli responded and before he could walk out the door, Apostle Baptiste grabbed a chunk of cash from the basket and stuffed it into Pastor Eli's coat pocket.

"Thank ye, pasteh, thank ye for lettin' me come out chere and help wit da Lawd."

Pastor Eli smiled his expectant smile and returned the thanks, stepping out of the room for a few minutes to locate the pretty milatto girl of eighteen years that had been sent back to the back.

Apostle Baptiste looked Gigot and BB over and without much fanfare said thank you to them for doing the Lord's work tonight and that the Lord would certainly reward them in heaven one day.

"Now, git outta here!" he motioned to them with his right hand in a 'get out of my face' kind of way.

As Gigot opened the door, Pastor Eli was standing there with the pretty milatto girl holding her elbow real tight and ushering her into the room.

"Thank ya, boys!" the pastor wincingly sighed as he entered the room with the girl while Gigot and BB were ushered out of the room with Pastor Eli's eyes and guiding brow.

In a matter of micro-seconds, the apostle had ushered the pastor out of the room, gotten his honey lotion in his hands and was taking his robe off with the other hand, saying to the girl as he closed and locked the door,

"You eva been minstered to by a 'postle be-foe?"

## Chapter 12

## The Applesauce Blend

Gigot ran out of that building as fast as he could. He thought lightning was sure enough gonna come down on that place. He'd never seen so much money in an offering bucket before and he'd sure never heard an apostle of the Lord say something like that to a young lady either. Needless to say, he'd never heard an apostle of the Lord at all…and he still believed he hadn't.

Running across the street, it began to rain and the gas station had long been closed. With no one around, he jumped into his van and got back onto the highway for the short drive to Lewis and Diane's. Lewis and Diane wouldn't mind him driving in so late as their custom was to stay up late and sleep a little late because of Lewis' awkward work schedule.

Gigot knew Lewis and Diane as dear old friends. He had always had a heart yearning for them because he sensed commonality with them like a family member. They were friends and he missed them terribly. When they moved to Mississippi, something left Gigot's heart that he had never been able to replace. It was as though his blood brother and sister had left for good; the kind of blood brother and sister that you're proud of and you want to be around.

As Gigot drove, he drove faster and faster thinking of the times that he and Pauline had had with Lewis and Diane and the huge rib eye steaks that Lewis would grill out. Gigot had a warm rush of embarrassment as he remembered the time Diane invited him and Pauline over and after Lewis had grilled these humongous steaks, Diane said get what you want. Gigot, being the selfish pig that he was at the time got the biggest steak and Lewis just laughed and said,

"You're gonna eat all that?"

It had not dawned on Gigot to cut the thing in two because it was enough steak for at least two or three people. It was the first time Gigot had taken a 'to go' box from a neighbor's house because he couldn't eat the whole steak. Remembering this, though, in his own humiliation, Lewis and Diane never said a word of aingst at anything Gigot or Pauline might do or say for they were the epitome of southern hospitality.

Diane had this heartwarming personality and the southern accent to boot. Lewis was a man of distinction in his own right. He used to work for a government agency, the secretive kind and the government always had their clinches in him because of his creative talent. Lewis was an engineer by trade, but it was his instinctive character to create solutions and solve intensely critical problems that set him above the rest. Gigot could never keep up with Lewis, even though Lewis was ten to twelve years his senior. Lewis never knew exactly when he would be in a covert mind game or the real thing. Nuclear analytics was his specialty.

They had built this tremendously ornate river home that Lewis said would never be under water. Not only was it on stilts off the Mississippi River basin on secluded property that the government allowed him to build on, it could also float if the Mississippi ever decided to take off in a deluge of rain and flood. Lewis designed and built the house, mostly by himself because all the contractors were frightened at the angles and did not understand the newly created components that went into the house structure. Lewis stayed to himself as he worked, kind of like the nutty professor, but with the backing of the "company".

When Gigot finally arrived, as late as he was, Diane ran out of the house to meet him. Lewis was not far behind with his favorite glass of wine that he always cherished after a late dinner. Diane had saved Gigot a plate of food and after a brief spell of conversation, wine and comradery, Gigot was off to bed exhausted from his first day of the journey.

The next morning, Diane was excited about the day, as she always was, particularly fussing at Lewis for running the water so much.

"You'd think we lived on a river, or something!" Diane fussed at Lewis to Gigot as Lewis was preparing the morning coffee.

"Ya'll know I can't stay long today, I'll probably leave right after an early lunch, if that's ok with you, Diane," Gigot said politely to Diane who had just begun to ask when he had to take off.

"We sure do miss you guys," Gigot choked on his words as Diane looked him square in the face. "The neighborhood is not the same, the parties, the good times, being able to watch Lewis take care of that pristine yard and then come out and admire his handiwork with a glass of chardonnay was priceless!"

Diane had a tear in her eye now as she missed the friends of the neighborhood that she had grown to love. Many of them had moved away, yet some good friends were still there. They caught up on old times and as well as caught up on any news that they had not been aware of through various types of communiques. Lewis had had enough of the reminiscing as he never was much that kind of guy.

Lewis had a preoccupation with work for it was his work that kept him and his company going. Gigot excused himself from the breakfast table to step down to Lewis' lower level lair where all of his intricate formulas were envisioned and created.

Not only was Lewis an engineer, he was also a physicist and a chemist all rolled up into one crazy professor type. "What chu working on today Lewis?" Gigot asked as he proceeded down the last few steps to the secluded space. "I can't say…or, I'm not supposed to say," Lewis responded not looking up from the dripping tube he was examining for textual flow.

"All right!" Lewis looked up with a smile on his face. This let Gigot know that whatever he was doing, it had just worked. Lewis slapped his hands together as if to cheer for what he had just created.

"What is it?" Gigot inquired.

"It's a remedy, I hope," Lewis retorted, "from nuclear effects, so to speak."

Gigot raised an eyebrow and winced, "Nuclear effects, what nuclear effects are you referring to?"

"One day, and it hasn't happened yet, but one day, we all might need this. When the right bomb goes off in the right place, there'll be a lot of fall-out everywhere, particularly close to the zero sight. The burns will be excruciating to the point where people will be begging to die. This stuff, if you drink it at the right stage will re-create the molecular structure of the original tissue and cause the radiation to cease and regenerative growth will simultaneously take place."

"That's amazing Lewis! You created that here? You know what it looks like, don't you?"

"What?" said Lewis.

"Applesauce, it looks like drinkable applesauce. What does it taste like?" questioned Gigot.

"At this point, I don't know, I've been testing it on radiated animals and they haven't told me what it tastes like. That's one thing I guess we could add is apple flavoring and see what it does to the chemical structure."

In a matter of moments, time had passed and Diane was upstairs ringing the buzzer for Gigot and Lewis to come up and eat a quick lunch so that Gigot could be on his way. Gigot's time with Lewis and Diane was too little too quick and he was trying to slow down time with his breathing. Lewis and Diane just looked at him, not really understanding the depth of love that Gigot had for the two of them. He could only imagine real friendship in heaven must be like this… wanting to be with someone that you just loved to be with and never wanting to leave their presence.

## Chapter 13

## The Arrival

Most men hardly know themselves, let alone their times. And, as is it with most men, the preoccupation of lesser things is always in the forefront of their minds as the years, the days and the moments pass by into the past without a whimper of acknowledgement until it is often too late. Why is it that most men see the externalities and refuse to look towards the inward parts until the time arises out of grave need, want or sickness?

Gigot was realizing his lost opportunities and his wasted years. Realization can be quite deafening to the fallen as regret seeps in and takes over the mind's ability to reckon with reality. Debilitating opague and false memories have a tendency to stand guard against any truth that might prevail to help push a man upward out of the brink. Instead, his thoughts draw him deeper to a level of depression that no drug can correct. At times, Gigot had walked by his emotion and was oftern led by his feelings perceiving his feelings to be that of the Spirit of God. Even his own desires were justified by his innate trust in his feelings, yet he was completely unaware of the depth of his muddle.

As he traveled north westward, having no clue where his foot pedal would lead him, he would think and think and regret and cry, pout and moan, repent and relieve himself of every past mistake he could possibly bring to light. The longer he stayed on the road, the longer he wanted to stop at whatever local liquor store he might spy on the road and think to drink the drink of blended whiskeys he had used in times before to escape the impending moments of life as he knew it. But, no, not this time, whatever it was for him to discover, he had to do it sober…just so he could be honest with himself about whatever experience awaited him.

State after state, he drove and drove, gas station after rest room, over and over again and again, driving until he was so exhausted he longed for reprieve. Yet, the unction within him was ceaseless; he had to move onward towards the destination that had been appointed for him and only his inward spirit would know when he had reached his final destination. He buffeted his body towards the goal of seeing just how far he could traverse the never ending road of turning wheels and the uneasy smell of exhaust.

He had traveled north out of Memphis through Missouri up to Lincoln, Nebraska and turned west. The Buffalo Bill Wild West Show billboards going on in North Platte got his attention to stop there and rest for the night, but he had entered the town too late to experince the cowboy show. The next morning, he kept to the highway in a north westerly direction. He could see the image of the Tetons in his mind. It was as though the image had been placed there and he could taste the icy snowcapped ridges as one might lick the top of an ice cream cone. It was this marvelous taste of freshness that led him navigationally with a boost of adrenaline that no coffee caffeine could compare.

The excitement of arriving at a final destination reminded him of the eyes of Molly, the golden retriever that his niece had let him borrow to bring a little joy in his life from his failures. His daughter, Bessie, knew Molly best as Molly did anything that Bessie said. She obeyed in every instance, was quiet, comforting and loved to be loved. It was this emotion that was overcoming him now as he was getting further into the forest regions of Wyoming. This was a place he had never been, but had always wanted to go. This was the great outdoors of America, where freedom was free and the air was clean and cold.

Rejuvenated was a mild word for what he was feeling now. Transfixed on the prize of arrival, he pushed his foot harder on the gas pedal to get closer to the mountains that were rising in the distance. He had a few hundred miles to go, but he could see where he was going by the tops of the mountains in the distance. What a view he had from afar and as far as his foot could push in forward on the gas pedal, his perspectives were changing as well.

No more to dwelling on the past, it was behind him and all of the miles he was putting on the van were miles left behind as mistakes past made were fleeting breaths in the wind. The sensation of leaving all behind was only a sensation, of course, for in reality, when he would finally reached his destination, he would then have to turn around and eventually go back home. That thought shot through his mind like the arrow of a warrior on the path and it was that thought that drove him ever onward to see if the wherever he was going was the whatever he would find that would alleviate the wounds of his pitiful existence and the failures of all his yesterdays.

The circle had been brought right back around and he slowed a bit with his speed. He figured now that as he was reaching his arrival, he was also reaching his return, a return he was not prepared to make, and he started to cry.

Gigot was not manic or bi-polar, nor depressed or repressed. He simply needed an adjustment into the reality of what truly was and no one seemed to have an answer for that one. His realization of that kept him on this side of saneness and from the thoughts that haunted him on his roller coaster ride through life. His cries turned from mourning to joy in a brief amount of time as he arrived at the tiny town of Bodie, Wyoming just beneath the awesome stretch of mountain ranges that had risen before him in all their majesty and glory.

It was time to stop and smell the air for he believed he had arrived at the place of his reckoning. This was a tiny town with not much to offer, but the answers to what he needed to get him on his way of finding that which had alluded him all his life...a peace of mind that no money could ever think of buying.

He pulled up to the local general store where two old cowboy looking men were sitting on a bench just outside the front door. The building was worn and torn, like much of the rest of the town. It reminded him of a scene from the old cowboy movies of the west that he had seen so many times growing up on the old black and white television sets. This place looked like an old movie set, rustic and grey with old planks holding the roofs up without much strength.

"Howdy," Gigot smiled towards the men sitting on the bench.

"Howdy," they each responded with a rural flavor and a spit of tobacco in the can.

Gigot laughed inside himself so as not to seem rude because this scene was playing out like a spaghetti western with the exception that there were no saloon doors to break through. It didn't seem quite real, but it was and so he walked on inside the store.

As one might expect, the reason for going inside without much fanfare was that he was looking for the rest room sign and there it was, hanging from the ceiling, a huge white sign with red letters and an arrow to boot, pointing in the right direction to where the men's room door was.

Finishing quickly in the men's room, his excitement was beginning to build again. He wondered through the store a bit so as to look interested in whatever they had there, looking and browsing at the leather boots and hats, hardware and feed, bridles and tools on one side, eggs and refrigerated items on the other.

It was early in the evening, so he thought it would be easier just to go to a diner and then bed down in a motel room for the night. The thoughts of buying a few items seriously crossed his mind, but he left the store without purchasing anything as the store owner didn't look a bit surprised. As he walked out of the store, he could hear the clunks on the floor behind him that the store owner was following him to the door and locking the door behind him. The man turned the open sign to close, pulling down the blinds to close the store down for the night.

As his back was at the closed door, he thought,

"Dang it, I didn't ask him where to go. What am I supposed to do now?"

Just then, he heard a clang in the spittoon, and looking down to his left he saw the two old cowboys looking up at him like a smart-aleck dad looking at his dumbfounded kid.

"You looking for sometin' round here, boy?" one of the men sounded off.

Gigot raised his eyebrow, took a deep breath and choked, gasping for air because a gnat, or something had just flown down his throat. He coughed up the bug and could feel it on his tongue and looked awfully bewildered at what to do next as the two men sitting on the bench raised both their eyebrows to see just what Gigot's next move was.

The other man, laughed a little and said,

"You know you can spit that out, you don't have to swallow it," spitting half his chaw into the can.

Gigot spit immediately off the porch and wiped his mouth, chuckling to himself and then they all laughed together.

"What brings you out 'chere, boy?" the first man asked.

Gigot was honest and didn't have anything to say, but,

"Searching, mister, I'm searching for a pot of gold, a treasure, that's it, a treasure, do you know where I can find it?"

Spitting again, the second cowboy, wiped his mouth and chuckled, knowing they had just met someone who was honest enough to tell the truth about what he was doing in their neck of the woods.

"You don't know what you're doing out 'chere, do ye?" laughingly the man replied.

Just then, the two men parted and sat at each end of the bench, inviting Gigot to sit between them.

"Have a sit," the one said as the other patted the middle of the bench inviting him to sit down and have a brief spell of manly talk as they had waited for years for such a time as this.

"My name's Alfred, his is Floyd, what's yours?" Alfred asked expectantly.

"Gigot," and before he could say another word, Floyd laughed and playfully said,

"Now what the hell kind a name is Gigot?"

Alfred spit, Floyd spit and they both leaned forward and smiled at one another as though they had asked Gigot a trick question.

Gigot responded, "That's what my mother named me, I don't know why she named me that, that's just what she decided to name me. It had a special meaning to the man who leant me some blood when I was born. I was one of those Rh factor babies that my blood…"

"Yea, yea, yea, I know what it means, so your saying this fella who happened to be around to give you a blood transfusion as a baby got to name you your name?" Alfred asked.

"Well, I hadn't really thought about it that way before, but, yes, I guess that's right," Gigot responded inquisitively as he was now preparing himself for their next question, although he couldn't possibly know what that might be.

"You got some place to be?" Alfred asked, looking away towards the mountains.

By now, Gigot felt like he was playing some kind of mind game with Floyd and Alfred, so he said,

"You tell me!"

Spitting again and leaning forward to look at each other, they both smiled a quick Mona Lisa smile at each other and Floyd said,

"'Dis boy catches on quick, don't he?"

With that remark, all three of them sat back on the bench and looked west as the sun was setting over the southwest ridge. It gave a halo to the rim-top of the trees on the southern ridge and the setting sun's rays glistened over the snow-capped peaks as it slowly dropped out of sight.

They sat there…the three of them, just watching the sun disappear over the horizon as though they had had a front row seat to the greatest show on earth. This was the real thing, the sun disappearing in glory over the mountain ridge and all at once, as if on que, they all sighed with deep breaths at the glory of the beauty of God's creation that they had the chance to see together.

"You want some grub?" Alfred leaned his neck out to his right and asked Gigot.

Gigot raised his brow, smiled and asked,

"You asking me?" and he turned and looked at Floyd and Floyd leaned over and spit and looked at Alfred and said,

"'Dis boy ain't too quick, is he, Al?"

And with that, Alfred slapped Gigot on the thigh and said,

"By now, Pete's done cooked up a mess, let's go git some."

With the flick of a thumb, they all jumped into Alfred's pick-up truck, with Gigot in the middle, on to Alfred's house for supper. They had a few stories to tell Gigot before they sent him on his way.

## Chapter 14

## The Night before the Journey

It didn't take long for the three of them to travel to Alfred's ranch house for supper that night. Floyd's wife, Ruth, was there cooking up some home town western grub, as Alfred called it. Braised brisket over a fire and home fries in the oven along with some baked beans made the house a smoky comfort before they walked in the door. Gigot discovered he was salivating to the point of drooling and as was Floyd's custom to observe without comment, he just handed him his handkerchief expecting him to wipe his mouth. Gigot, being a little more germ conscious than that, quickly wiped his mouth with his right shirt sleeve and motioned a 'no thanks' to Floyd and his soiled handkerchief.

There was this quiet snickering between Alfred and Floyd as though they had known each other all their lives. Gigot was enthralled at how hospitable the four of them were with their new-found friend as Pete, short for Patrice, showed him where to wash-up before the meal. Alfred and Floyd didn't bother with that aspect, washing up, that is. They figured they had lived this long with roughing it out in the west; one more meal with dirty hands wasn't going to pay their health any mind. Besides, they hadn't really done anything all day since lunch as they were both retired and only did something useful when somebody in town needed help.

The soap in the bathroom was that hard kind, harder than anything Gigot had ever seen or used as soap. It was as though they had made this stuff themselves out of rocks. He looked at himself in the mirror, looked back down at how hard he had to work to get some kind of suds working in his hands and proceeded to occupy himself with the frame of the mirror. The frame was made of cedar and had aged quite nicely through the years. He could tell it had been hand-made and that, with care. Its rustic dryness gave the room a feel of togetherness and as he rinsed his hands in the sink, shaking them briskly, he looked up and he could swear that the mirror had just moved in front of him. Was it that, the mirror moving within the frame or did the room just move? He was beginning to think that he was becoming imbalanced from waiting too long to eat dinner and sincerely believed he needed some protein in his system in order not to pass out, or something.

"That's weird," he thought to himself as he looked to his right for the hand cloth to dry his hands. He looked back into the mirror intently as he was drying his hands daring the mirror to move again for he had an austere look on his face with his left eyebrow raised. He winced his eyes with the look of "I didn't think so," in his mind and just as he was placing the drying cloth back in place, the mirror moved again.

He stumbled back against the wall behind him knocking the picture frame off of its nail. The picture frame quickly slid down his back and so he pressed himself against the wall as to catch the frame from hitting the floor. He had caused a bit of noise with this and it was taking him so long in the bathroom from the distraction of the mirror, Alfred yelled through the door,

"You still alive in there. Supper's getting' cold."

"Coming," he responded as he hurriedly pushed the picture frame back up the wall and tried to catch the back of the frame on the nail.

Ruth knocked on the bathroom door,

"Do you need some help, young man?"

Totally embarrassed by this point, Gigot began to perspire as it was taking him way too long to place the picture frame on the nail in the wall. He was feeling for the nail with the back of the frame, but looking at the glass of the picture and could see the mirror on the other wall in the reflection. There it was again, in the reflection in the glass, the mirror was moving this time and it didn't stop. So, he stood there and as a calm came over him, he could feel the frame go gently into place over the nail. This calmness was inexplicably tied to the mirror moving behind him, so he relaxed in response, turned to his right towards the door, smiled towards the mirror and opened the bathroom door.

As the door swung open, there was Alfred and Pete, Ruth and Floyd, hunched over in front of the door as though they were spying on him by listening to what was going on in the bathroom. All five of them just looked at each other startled and without another moment of hesitation, Alfred asked,

"Uh, you want bar-b-q sauce on your brisket or you want it dry?"

Bewildered, but pleasantly so, Gigot started to laugh and they all hugged him like a soldier son come home from war.

"Let's eat!" Alfred stated as they all moved around the wooden table to have the smoked feast of the west.

They took their time, the five of them, laughing and eating, passing the food around until it was just about all gone. There was a bit of bread and brisket left and Alfred asked Pete to wrap that up for Gigot's lunch tomorrow.

They all helped clear the table and they all got the dishes washed together. Gigot observed the four of them working together in tandem, moving as though they were on an assembly line…working together in harmony, with Floyd whistling and Ruth singing her gentle words of peace. Gigot was invited to sit over in the large room to the left of the kitchen, a wide expansive room with high vaulted ceilings, all wooden and all sturdy from the years of what a real wooden ranch house looks like with an inviting view to the mountains on the front side and a giant stone fireplace used for warming the house and for braising brisket when the need arose.

It had gotten dark outside and the three men made their way out to the front porch to sit for a spell before they took Gigot back to his van. As they sat on the porch resting from the smoky, comfortable meal they had just enjoyed, they sat there as three men could, quietly reflecting within themselves the remains of the day and what each one had encountered in their day's journey.

With all of the peaceful reflection going on, Alfred seemed to reveal a little bit of intuition as to why Gigot was there.

"You ready for tomorrow?" he inquired of Gigot.

Gigot turned his head left and leaned a bit inquisitively as though Alfred knew something he did not and said,

"Alfred, I think I'm learning rather quickly here that I've come to the right place. It's almost as though you all were expecting me and that you all know why I'm here, but, honestly, I don't."

Alfred and Floyd remained quiet as they gently rocked in the rocking chairs feeling the cool breeze of the evening. There was something in the atmosphere that only inspired intuition could tell and they all sat there not saying a word, just looking at the breeze in the darkness, knowing that all was all right and that all would be all right tomorrow and in the days to come. The overwhelming peace that was filling Gigot's heart and mind was like the cool, smoky air filling his lungs and his mind with peace, but this time a peace that he had never known before. The atmosphere on the porch was relaxing and expectant at the same time.

"Gigot," Floyd explained, "When you get up in the morning, you're gonna go searching for somethin' that you're gonna find. You gotta know it when you see it and hear it and I don't want chu to run… whatever you do…don't run. Will you promise me that?"

As Gigot was quickly learning to be obedient in his new found environment, he replied,

"Yes, sir, I will, but can I ask you something?"

"Sure," Floyd responded, rocking slowly expecting the obvious question.

"You all seem to know what I'm searching for and you all seem to know what that something is. Will you tell me what it is so I'll know it when I see it?"

Alfred chuckled and smiled, "Gigot, you've already seen it and heard it. You just gotta not run when you see it and hear it again. Is that understood? Will you agree to that?"

Gigot twisted his mouth as though he were deciding with his mouth on whether he would go through with their challenge, or not, and blurted out,

"Does it have anything to do with that mirror in your bathroom?"

As Gigot was rocking in his chair in-between Alfred and Floyd,

Alfred and Floyd leaned over to look at one another and huffed a smile.

"They don't make 'em none too bright down in Florida, do they Floyd?" Alfred said and Floyd responded,

"No, they don't Uncle Al, no they don't."

And with that, Alfred slapped Gigot on the thigh and said,

"Let's go git your van. You can bed down here for the night and we'll git you up at dawn. You gotta big day ahead of you and I don't want you to miss a moment of it hanging out around here."

Gigot felt for his van keys in his pocket and with an agreeing nod, they all got up and jumped into Alfred's truck to go and get Gigot's van. Along the way, Floyd pointed out the roads he would take in the morning that would lead him to where he needed to go in order to get out on his hike, his hunt and his journey. Gigot felt like he was riding along with two Dad's showing him the ropes before he went out on his first hunt. They were so experienced in their knowledge of the land and the great expansiveness of the region got tremendously smaller and more manageable with the time he spent with them on the ride back into town.

By the time he got into his van to follow them back to the ranch, he felt like he knew the place…the town and its surroundings. He knew the turns he would have to make along the country miles he would go in the morning. All was making sense even though it didn't really make any sense.

He wondered to himself,

"I guess this is what moving in faith is all about." He had been given knowledge and with that he had been given courage. He had been given a little insight and with that he had been strengthened. He had been fed very, very well and with that, he couldn't wait to eat that packed lunch tomorrow of beef brisket and home-made bread. He had all that he needed and with that, he was extremely thankful.

A late night now and soon the sun would rise for a brand new day, a day of great expectation into a world that only a few had had the opportunity to see.

## Chapter 15

## Who is Gigot?

Even though the sun does rise early on a morning of expectation, Alfred and Pete had risen far earlier than that. Breakfast biscuits had been made, along with a slab of thick bacon and eggs made just right. The coffee, though, was almost as thick as the bacon and even though Gigot was used to his name brand, he had not drank anything like this since his days in Louisiana with Gill Brantley and his concoctions of dark roasted beans cut with chickory served in a tiny demitasse cup for the afternoon visit.

This morning coffee competed well with the Louisiana blend for it must have included some residue of coffee grounds leftover from a trail ride many moons ago. Gigot choked at first taste of the morning brew and asked for some creamer.

Pete replied, "Gigot, real men don't drink creamer in their coffee, besides, we don't own any of that chemical stuff, you want some milk?"

Gigot choked again and said, "Yes, ma'am," and he filled the half-filled cup of coffee with the rest of it being milk and all of a sudden, it didn't taste so bad after all.

As Gigot was making his way out to the van to finish packing up, Alfred took a look at the box that the 410 was packaged in and said,

"What's that?"

"It's a 410 shotgun…" Gigot called it that because he didn't know any better than to call it what he thought it was.

Alfred laughed, "I reckon you never shot it, huh?"

"No, I haven't, I guess that's plain to see."

"Well, if you've never shot that thang before, you might better go someplace off somewhere and shoot a spell to get the hang of it. 'Sides, guys don't use shotguns to go huntin' out chere, they use rifles with scopes for long range. You do know that animals can smell you from afar off, don't chu?"

"I've heard that, but I'm not too experienced at huntin' and I may end up using the gun more for my protection than for killin'."

"Suit yoself, but where you're goin', there's more hiking than anything. Still, ya need to get a few practice shots off so ya know wut chure doin'. That way, you don't hurt yoself or nobody else, for that matter…I'm jus' sayin'. You got enough shot to practice with?"

"Yep!" Gigot had already grown a little embarrassed from the conversation and his own personal ignorance of shooting a gun. He had not shot a gun since the days of his brothers before they went off to the Vietnam War. Just thinking about a shotgun reminded him of his much older brother who didn't make it back from Pleiku alive. Alfred could tell that Gigot had already moved on somewhere in his mind and he wasn't willing to inquire about it at the moment.

Alfred spoke apologetically to Gigot,

"Ya know, Gigot, I can tell you've had some hard times and whatever it was that you've gone through or whatever it is that you're going through right now, it comes out in your demeanor, in how you talk. And you must be going through some stuff even now. I jus' want chu to know you don't have to do it alone. Try to relax out there, otherwise, if you don't learn to relax out there, you might not make it back in one piece. There's a lake out there I want you to find. You'll know the one I'm talkin' 'bout when you come to it cause there's lots of lakes out there, but there is this one special place that will help you to relax. When you get there, engage it, don't run, remember what we told chu last night, whatever you do, don't run from it. Keep moving forward. You understand?" He said firmly.

"Alfred, I got it, I understand and I thank you for all you guys have done for me. It's almost like you knew I was coming up here and were waiting for me and you've really been gracious and hospitable."

"You don't know the half of it, Gigot, now get up on out of here, cause you're…" and they both yelled at the same time, "…burning daylight!" as they both went back to John Wayne in their minds and his remarks to the young boys that were in his keep.

With the directions in hand and a few meals packed from Pete, Gigot was off on his journey to find the whatever in the wherever it was he was supposed to find it. He was to drive an hour and a half down south past all of the park land to a little known piece of land of about 1,000 acres square. The land was privately owned and little to no one ever ventured out on it anymore, as Floyd and Alfred suspected anyway. This would be the land that he would find what he was looking for, again, according to Floyd and Alfred. It was extremely funny to Gigot that Floyd and Alfred knew more about what Gigot needed than Gigot did and he had not even spent 24 hours with them.

In no time, he had arrived at the markers that were on the map that Floyd had drawn up for him. There it was, the old broken down for sale sign that had been there for almost thirty or forty years. There was hardly any paint left on it, except for a few of the numbers of the telephone number that had been painted on what used to be a nice realty sign that had not weathered the passage of time. The painted wooden sign had broken legs and was lying in the brush. Floyd said that the owner still had it for sale, but no one ever looked at it and that the sign was placed directly in the front middle of the property. He had also told him something else he didn't know and that was that 1,000 acres square was 10 miles square…five on the right of the sign and five to the left; and that the lake they wanted him to see was exactly in the middle of the property. According to his rather intellectual calculations, that would put the lake five miles into the middle of the property and Gigot laughed to himself of what could be so special about this lake…it must be something extraordinary.

Alfred had also told him to go onto to the property before he started shooting the gun because he absolutely was not to get caught firing a weapon on government park property.

Gigot opened the trunk of the van got out his backpack and placed the lunch inside the outside cover. Then, he took the 410 out of all of its packaging and about four boxes of shells and proceeded with his backpack and shotgun out into the brush towards the lower hills.

He traveled for about a half mile and created a practice range at an open area that had some good size rocks that he could place on a mound. After carefully placing the rocks on the top of the mound, he walked back about twenty yards and loaded the shotgun. He was pretty sure that he had put the gun together properly, but had wished that he'd asked Alfred to make sure. At times, Gigot would second guess himself so much, he bordered on inactivity, but this time, he had to trust himself in putting the gun together right and that he was not about to blow himself up with it.

Shot after shot, he fired towards the rocks making crumbles of the rocks hitting the targets, not missing one time. He had remembered his 12 gauge shotgun days with his brothers and it brought back some fond memories of a long time ago. Confident, he attached the shotgun to a strap and placed it on his shoulder and started walking forward over the rocks and the deserted areas towards the forest. He kept climbing and climbing, attempting to get to an overlook to see what he could see. Stone and rock leading to mountains in the distance and foliage unlike he'd ever seen before made the place beautiful for everything around him was absolutely gorgeous in its own rustic, western type of way.

He walked up towards a cliff area that had a steep ledge that looked terribly dangerous and, being a bit afraid of heights, he felt he had gone far enough up and began to make his way back down the sloping rock, sliding a little and then sliding a lot more. As he was kicking up dust sliding down the rocky slope, he caught the site of a deer out of the corner of his eye. He stumbled to his feet and yanked the shotgun off of his shoulder and placed an aim at the deer that was standing just to his left about two hundred feet away on the top of another mount of rock. It was quite majestic as it stood perched there atop the rock as if he owned that rock and was looking over his entire territory.

Gigot took careful aim of the loaded gun when this overwhelming sense of violence took over his mind. He could see the deer getting shot and collapsing in pain. He could sense the violent gush of blood coming from the animal at the point of impact and then as if something simply clicked in his brain instead of his finger, he released the pressure from the trigger and relaxed. He wasn't going to kill a deer. What was he thinking? What was he going to do with it anyway? Tie it to the front of his van for all to see? Hang the horns from a wall? What was he doing out there thinking of killing a defenseless animal?

He let go of his tenseness of the aim and allowed his arms to simply hang with the shotgun resting on his thigh. Breathing a sigh of relief, he allowed himself to see the deer for all of its beauty and worth as it stood perched atop the rock viewing its territory. And, just about the time he had fully gained his own senses of what he'd almost done, the deer turned his way and stared.

Gigot remained still, frozen in movement, thinking rather silly thoughts like, "Is this thing going to turn and run at me?" Motionless, he stood there, being ever so careful to breathe as the deer stood in its perch staring at him and yet staring through him all the same.

The deer did not blink, but tilted its head a bit in wonder and then scratched the rock with his front right hoof and huffed. Gigot straightened his back and didn't move further. The deer huffed again in the cool air, bowing his head as he huffed, as though he was saying something, but Gigot had no clue. Scratching again, the deer hoofed his front right hoof over the rock and huffed louder this time, bowing in release and then standing erect.

Gigot stood in amazement for he had never been out in the wild before and didn't know exactly what was happening on the ridge. All of a sudden, Gigot relaxed as the deer continued to stare and then Gigot nodded his head as though he were acknowledging the deer's presence and saying 'hello'.

The deer stood motionless as it stared for another moment as Gigot made his greeting and then the deer took off down the other side of the ridge out of sight, but certainly not out of Gigot's mind. Gigot stood there for a few more moments believing he had just made a friend, or at the very least, acknowledged the life in another being other than his own. Then, his eyes opened to see the mountain ridge, from a different perspective. No longer was he focusing on the deer, he was able to see the sky and all of his surroundings as it all took on a new meaning of life. He was surrounded by glory and beauty and the fantastic vision of God was playing out before his eyes.

In these moments, he realized he was not out there to hunt or to kill. He was out there to meet his maker and the living maker of all these living things. Within an instant, he was breathing again, relaxed, breathing deeper this time and happy, oh, how he was happy, he was overwhelmed with joy.

He quickly placed the gun strap on his shoulder and was taken over by an urge to move to the forest. He started to sing like he used to sing years and years ago…songs that he had not sung since being in church, seemingly a lifetime ago.

As he picked up the pace in his walking towards the thick forest, his thoughts traveled back in time to a time when he felt like he had a life worth living and a purpose under heaven. And, even though he had begun to sing now, the singing quickly faded into silence as he felt the sense of someone having walked this trail before many years before. His spirit went dark as he approached the edge of the tall and darkening forest. He could see the forest and the trees and his level of awareness as he proceeded forward began to tighten his chest with stress the further he walked into the depths of the wood.

"Wait," he thought to himself. "What are you doing? You've never been here before, what are you doing?" He sat on a tree stump that was wider than he was and, as he sat there, he continued to question himself as to what he was doing there and pondered the validity of listening to the four people last night and all the mumbo jumbo of his destiny.

"How could they possibly have any idea what he was searching for? Who told them I was searching for anything, anyway?" he thought to himself in a rather confused sort of state.

He sat there pondering his life and some of his failures began to erupt again.

"You know, so many people would be better off if I was not around." He thought and thought as he sat there on the stump getting deeper and deeper into his own selfish concentration. When he realized what he was doing, he started laughing, trying to remember the old limerick, "the skunk sat on a stump, the skunk thunk as he sat on the stump and the stump thunk the skunk stunk…"

This made him laugh and for a moment he forgot the seriousness and the uselessness of his debilitating thoughts.

"Useless! Utterly useless," he thought to himself as his mind wandered back to his perceived lack of purpose. He shook his head back and forth as if to jog the thoughts and memories away.

A different thought began to occur to him, though,

"Perhaps if you didn't dwell so much on your negative moments, you would be free to see the good in thee," and with that, he thought,

"Where did that come from?"

"Where do you think?" a thought pondered.

"Well, where do you think?" he pondered back to himself.

The thought came back, "When are you going to stop?"

"Stop what?" he said aloud, this time seeing if the thoughts he thought would start speaking out loud and just that time, he started laughing out loud. He laughed so hard he fell off the stump and onto the ground cover below. He lay there relaxing in the brush feeling like there was someone there talking to him, but it was in his mind. So, he didn't know if he was going crazy or was already crazy and the opportunity had just presented itself making his crazy self known.

As he lay there, he missed Bessy and Daniel and James; he began to miss them alot. They were his own flesh and blood and he could not live without them. They were his life and he followed his mind in remembering some times of great memories of the past as they used to play together in the basement with that silly basketball game and have fun…they all loved to have fun together.

"Life goes on living, doesn't it?" he spoke aloud. "Yes, it does, doesn't it? I know you're right. Life does go on living. It doesn't take itself out or just leave, life keeps on living no matter what happens."

"So, what life are you going to live?" the thought pondered a thought.

As Gigot lay there in the brush, tears came to his eyes and he said,

"I can only live today. I can't take back yesterday and I can't take back the wrong things I've done. I can't undo all the ugly things I did and I can't take back the words I've said. I only have today."

"So today it is then, is it?" the thought pondered again.

Sighing, he took a deep breath and gained the strength to raise himself upright. As he sat there, he repeated the thought, "Today…today is the day to live today. I can't live yesterday again and I can't live out tomorrow. My future is in Your hands I know, Lord."

And with that, he remembered the lunch that Pete had packed for him, the brisket and the homemade bread, some cold beans and, oh, the homemade berry cobbler, what a treat!

# Chapter 16

## The Water is Waiting

As Gigot continued to eat his lunch, he sat there wondering again why it seemed he would make so many blunders in his life because he knew he was smarter than his decisions had made him out to be. He had heard of people making it big, with just one decision, or about how some rich folk had 'lost it all' even a couple times over, and then hit it big again. He had also read about how some very notable people had a very rewarding life and then ended it all senselessly through suicide. He didn't seem to quite get the rationale of why some people were successful business-wise, but they didn't have a lick of common sense and then there were others who constantly failed miserably even though they had been born with a silver spoon in their mouths.

Gigot pondered as to why Hemingway committed suicide at the age of 61. It seemed he had the richest of life, although he did go through four wives. And why was it that one of his favorite writers, Oswald Chambers…why was it that he died in his forties of complications from an emergency appendectomy while doing ministry in World War I? And, how is it that the rich get richer and the poor get poorer? He had seen that one to be a pure fact as he watched both rich and poor go through life and seemingly live on a track that had been created just for them.

"Surely it can't be that we're just going through the motions down here, with some to live free and others to be enslaved all their lives," he thought.

No, even though that may occur, he continued to think, he had seen where many people had come up from where they were and made stars out of themselves, or someone else had made a star out of them.

What was it about life and who decides who succeeds and who fails and is it all left up to the individual, their peers, or chance? Or did God arrange everything by some great design and we're all simply going through the motions?

Does the individual make his own breaks or are the breaks made for him? Is it his responses to his circumstances or is his circumstances created with the known response already known? Why is it that corrupt men get into leadership in politics, religion and business and succeed as though they are God's gift to mankind, but are really the blind leading the blind into hell?

"Why is that?" he asked out loud.

He had seen it when power corrupted men with fame, money, women or addictions. He had found himself to be no different with just a little bit of glory. Perhaps that was why he refused to sing anymore…maybe he wasn't so free from pride as he used to think he was.

"And wisdom! Who has any Godly wisdom?" he shouted in thoughts to himself. "Is there any wise in the earth now?" shaking his head back and forth, no one came to mind.

He remembered the times in his youth and young adult age, that he would have dreams and visions of things that would actually come to pass, just like he dreamed it. The pictures and visions were so real they were frightening. There would be nights that he would not sleep so as not to go where his mind took him in the night. Vivid nightmares of horror and the visions remaining with him even to that day.

"What about the snake and the tiger?" he asked in his mind. The dream was so real, yet symbolizing his fate that day and his fate up to that point. "Fate, I don't believe in fate!" he rebuked his thinking. "That was not my fate!" shaking his head again.

But what had happened to the tiger had happened to him for he had been crushed by such a venomous force, it left him dazed and weak for months on end. The dream was like his life. It wasn't the episode so much as it was the entire time he had spent in the jungle. He thought he was the protector of that area of the jungle, but the snake was far more devilish than he could comprehend and he underestimated the swiftness of the beast. He had been shut down and shut out, so to speak, but not dead, no, he was not dead. He was alive, but he wasn't.

What had happened? Did he die and become reborn?

He deeply wanted to know of all that had transpired in his life and of all of the events that had taken place in his life, was it God's design, people's goodwill or meanness, or was it his own personal mistakes and the chance good decisions that led him to the path where he now found himself?

When Gigot came to himself, he realized he had wandered away from the stump and he did not know where he was. He had been drifting in the brush; the greenery lush to the knees was brushing him along, yet making sure his pathway took its turn where it decided.

"Did I eat?" he asked himself. He honestly did not know where he was and he spinned a slow spin around himself and continued to turn until he saw something he recognized, but everything looked the same. Tall trees and brush up to the knees were in every direction and he did not know how he got to where he was.

He had his backpack on, his gun strapped to his shoulder and his hands were free in front of him. He lifted his hands to his face and felt his face to make sure it was him that he was standing in.

"Where am I?" he thought again to himself. He had walked himself alone in thought and alone he was, but wasn't.

"Oh, God, where have You gone?" he said aloud.

There was no answer, not even in his mind. A cool breeze brushed by him and sent a chill down his spine.

"That was cold!" he said aloud as he watched the brush sway from the breeze away from him. He reached down with his hand to touch the top of the leaves of the brush and walked forward toward the ending breeze as though he were being guided to go a particular way.

It was late in the afternoon and the sunlight was waning through the trees to his back. It was fascinating how the sun's rays glistened through the tree branches and his shadow was in front of him. At least now he had someone to walk with that wasn't condemning or judgmental. He didn't mind following his own shadow, he sort of respected himself that way, but not many other folk.

That's what was so amazing about Floyd and Alfred, he respected them immediately and he never questioned their ways, their advice or their demeanor. They were firm, kind, thoughtful and wise.

"Ummph! I guess I do know somebody who's wise, don't I?" he said aloud as he thought to himself about Floyd and Alfred. They weren't rich, didn't need to be. They had all they needed in their homes with their wives, their trucks and their lives that they lived on the ranch as simple old cowboys. He kept walking in a jaunting fashion now, being relieved by the pressure of continuous thought. He'd known ole preacher Chambers to say that if someone continually thought within themselves as an obsession, that it would drive a them insane or something like that. He was beginning to understand that sentiment.

As he continued to walk further into the forest, the breeze had picked up and gotten cooler. He could tell the sun was going down and although he had packed for a night's stay, he hadn't really wanted to stay out in the wild by himself in the middle of nowhere…all by himself…alone...in the middle of the forest...alone.

As he approached a rise in the mound, he climbed up and over the sloping ridge and there it was, the lake that Floyd and Alfred were talking about. He disfigured his face a bit with a few twitches because he did not want to be at the wrong lake, especially since they had said that he would know the lake when he saw it and that he was not supposed to run from it. Laughing to himself as he looked down at the lake, he said,

"Why would anyone run from a lake? What could be so special about this lake that Floyd and Alfred would intimate that this was what I was searching for…a lake?"

With that sentiment spoken aloud, the lake rippled from the middle and the ripple affect came in his direction.

"The lake must have burped. Hmm." he thought. And then it did it again.

Turning his head in bewilderment, this must have been what they were talking about when they said he would know when he saw it. Just then, a soft breeze whirled around the edge of the sizable lake. It reminded him of being at the football stadium when the people would 'do the wave'. The breeze continued to 'wave' the leaves of the brush in a circular motion around the lake and he could hear the trees above him as their branches moved and swayed in the wind as well.

"Maybe this is something that happens every night when the sun goes down," he thought, figuring that what he had just witnessed was the usual and customary of the evening lake breezes.

"Must have something to do with the air and water temperature," he continued, "but it sure is fascinating to watch." He felt like he was in an arena and the trees and underbrush were the audience cheering what was in the lake.

"What was in the lake?" he imagined as he thought his thoughts. "Oh, crap! What is in this lake?" All of a sudden it came to him that something was in this lake and terror gripped him like he was watching an anaconda movie.

"Oh, my goodness, what is in this lake?" he questioned again, this time referring his question to the absent Floyd and Alfred.

He slipped down the slope, sliding a bit and stumbling as he approached the edge of the lake. He had gotten quicker down the slope than he had intended to and found himself standing just at the edge and looking over the lake.

"What is in this lake?" he pondered as he observed that the lake was crystal clear, pristine and even with the sun going down over the ridge there was still enough daylight for him to see the crystal clear clarity of pure water as it nestle itself with calm ripples from the center.

"If I die here, I'll have seen something I've never seen before," he said aloud to himself. "Wow! What a sight! I wonder what this lake looks like in direct sunlight? This is amazing!"

He stood there overwhelmed by the beauty of clarity and purity and there it went again. There was a burp in the middle of the lake and soft ripples of water moved towards the edges on que. He could see the soft current straight down as he could see the bottom of the lake, but couldn't really tell how deep it was. Looking straight over the water, it looked deep, but how could it be that deep and still be so clear with no fish, no algae or lake-bottom foliage.

"How could that be? There's absolutely nothing in this lake, but crystal clear water!"

He stepped back a little and let his gun strap off his shoulder as well as his backpack. Intrigued, he wanted to touch the water, so he knelt down and as he was kneeling, a rush of joy came over him. He brushed his chin and scratched his face, excited by the connection that was in him. He felt drawn to the water and suddenly another breeze came flowing down from over the ridge, sending a chill up and down his spine. The rush of the wind rustled the brush and trees. There was a clap of branches moving and swaying with one another up above him and the leaves of the underbrush whistled with delight.

He was about to fall forward into the water, but caught himself falling to his knees right at the edge of the water. His opened palms fell flat into the water splashing water up his arms and into his face and a shrill came out of his mouth.

An electrical-type current was rushing from the water up through his arms through his shoulders and back again. He was alive shrilling and watching these currents of light pulsate up his arms from the surface of the water and tears of fright and delight began falling from his eyes and face.

As the tears hit the water, his mind was taken to his past, all his past, with nothing left out, his life was flashing before his mind and he could see all that he had seen and all that he had forgotten along the way to nowhere. Memories flashed like lightning, zing, zing, zing, they flashed of all the things he had done both great and small, good and bad, nothing was left out to chance or to be forgotten. All his life was before his eyes and he could see who he was and what he had been and the water told him all that he was.

Choking and pulling, crying in fright, he tried to pull himself from the water, but the water would not let go.

"Why are you doing this to me?" he screamed. He could see his past, his sin now, the woman, the faces, it finally hit him what he had done and the water would not let him go.

Crying out for mercy, he cried,

"Father, forgive me. Forgive me, Lord!" and he fell face forward into the water shaking and convulsing in the water with all of the lighted current around him as he cried drowning and gurgling in the water. He was shown the moment in time, as when most men have that moment, when he chose his own path instead of following the spirit. He had been told to do something specific by the spirit and he chose not to do it, consequently and simultaneously he chose what his soul and his flesh wanted to do. In that moment in time, the spirit gave him over to do as he pleased, even to the further most. These moments come to all men and he was shown that the spirit will let you have your way if you choose the lesser road.

Here, he sensed God's mercy on his lesser road and saw the prodigal son as himself. In his humiliation he was ashamed.

He garnished enough strength to lift his face from out of the water as drips of lightning fell from his head.

He fell back away from the water crying in grief, falling and drifting away from his past and the sight of who he really was and all that he had been. With eyes clinched shut and yet an openness no more to fight, he drifted into a deep sleep, so deep that night fell and dispelled the breeze with stillness as only silence and stillness can be.

Peace was over the water as the trees and the brush rested from their sway. All had to come to rest in the land of the water that speaks as the water rested, comforted and waited for the sun to rise to a new dawn in this time out of time where there is no need or want and all is at the disposal of the one who takes what was and makes all things new.

## Chapter 17

## The Morning After

As daylight approached, Gigot awoke to the screams and screeches of every animal surounding the lake. Vicious growling was coming from the far side of the lake and the sounds of fear and survival were coming from a victim. He didn't know what was going on.  Gathering his composure from a rough night sleeping on the ground, his body was stiff from the cold and the rigidness in his muscles made it extremely difficult to jump to his feet. He basically rolled over and forward pushing himself up with his knees and lower legs with enough effort to see across the lake where the screams and the fight was coming from.

A lone wolf was attacking a deer by the water's edge and the other animals within the periphery of the water were screaming their screams of danger, warning and escape all over the forest. The unfortunate deer getting attacked was fighting in moans and honks and the animals in the forest were reacting to the violent attack. Gigot didn't blink twice as he quickly grabbed the 410 and headed straight into the fray. He was moving on impulse and wasn't thinking about his reaction. He was moving as fast as he could towards the salvation of the deer from the raging wolf.

Running to within a safe firing distance and aim, he knelt in a battlefield firing position and as if he had done this all his life, he took aim and fired, not once, but twice, no, three times as the wolf took all three hits of the small shotgun in stride, not knowing what had just hit him. Rattled and flinching, the wolf stumbled away from the deer, crippled fatally from the three shots, one in the rear and two in the abdomen.

Without fear, Gigot ran to the aid of the fallen deer that lie panting from the attack and placed the head of the deer in his lap. He looked at the wolf bleeding profusely from his wounds as the deer was doing the same from his. Blood was everywhere flowing from both animals and the dying breath of the wolf escaped just moments before that of the deer as the deer's pants grew deeper and slower until there was no more breath to breathe.

In what seemed to be a matter of seconds, both animals lie dead with the blood flow slowing to nothing. There were no more pants, no more gush of the blood, no breathing at all from either one. Life was gone from the two and Gigot convulsed in tears having never seen or done anything like this. As Gigot gained his composure, his own panting ceased to a regular beat as he sat there on his legs with the head of the deer in his lap.

"Life," was all he could think to think or say.

"How could this happen? Here?" This place of beauty and wonder, a place of perfect peace and rest and yet he had been awakened to murder in the wild…a sight that he had never seen before.

He immediately began to internalize what he had just seen, intuitively analyzing each and every moment. He marveled at the blood, yes, but what made him most reflective in introspection was the fact that he'd actually killed an animal. How could this be…when just the day before he couldn't bear the thought of killing a deer. But just now, without a moment's notice, he instantly fired three shots into a ravaging wolf!

When Gigot was able to gather himself and realize that two dead animals lie before him, he didn't want to simply leave them there unattended. So, he found a plot of ground for the two beasts and started digging with his hands and a broken tree branch to break up any soil that was too hard. The soil was actually quite soft which made it much easier to dig deep enough to place the animals in a shallow grave and cover them with the exhumed dirt.

The dirt wasn't the only thing that he was exhuming in those moments. He was sensing the internal rationale for the ability to kill a predator and his inability to kill the innocent, yet he was willing to bury them both in respect.

What was it about the predator that brought out of him the desire to protect and defend the defenseless? What was it about the defenseless that brought out of him the need to defend and take matters into his own hands?

Was this person that had just responded who he truly was? Was he the defender of the weak and powerless from the ruthless predators that stalked the earth for prey? He, once again, was brought to his past to remember memories of what he had done years ago to defend the defenseless and the connection grew full circle. There was some purpose he had in all of this and this experience was bringing it to light.

He completed the burial of the two animals and knelt beside their grave in moments of silence. His heart had said enough and he realized his heart's motives. His Creator knew his heart as well.

He looked back at the water from his venue of the other side of the lake. The sun was at his back in the east and as he peered down at the lake, it had this shimmering shine and mirror reflection that he had not noticed the night before. When he had arrived last evening, his marveling took him to the clarity and purity of the lake water…its essence was pure, if not seemingly holy. As the water had spoken to him last evening, its reflection was now beaming loud and clear as a mirror lain flat on the ground.

He stood in amazement as the sun was rising at the mirror he was seeing before his eyes. The mirror of the water portrayed a dazzling image of the trees and sky above. At this angle and purview, he no longer saw straight through to the bottom of the lake in clarity, no, this view gave an incredible mirror reflection he'd never before seen in a pool of water.

The water was wooing him closer and closer in his spirit and as he approached the water, the brighter the shine of the reflection became. Of all of the mirrors he had had in his store, none was as a perfect reflection as this. His breathing ceased momentarily as the stillness of the scene illuminated what was before him.

All was still…all was silent…all was. It was as though the lake had turned to a mirror frozen in time and he was fearful to move so as not to disturb the moment. His thinking went to being "out of time" in the stillness where existence in living breath is a dimension all its own.

He had been brought into a kinship with the water. He could see it for what it was for it was clear and pure, seeing and knowing, revealing and kind, free and flowing and even though he did not see its source, he knew the source all the same.

It had become obvious to him that this water was fed by an underground spring that renewed itself as only pool pump could ever dream of being. The lake had turned itself, for these moments, into another state of being; it seemed, frozen still, reflecting its surroundings.

He moved closer to the edge of the water and fell to his knees marveling at the purity of the reflection. He leaned just a bit over the water and saw himself, ragged and disheveled, dirty from the night and the morning's event. There were no ripples in the water now, just an incredible reflection. As he looked at himself, he found himself not thinking about himself, but of the water's power to reflect. Remembering last night's shocking and revealing experience, he said,

"You know me, don't you? You know who I am and all that I've done and yet you are kind to me. You know that I am no longer that person and you've made me into someone new, haven't you?"

The water remained still and motionless. Gigot was already expressing the truth of his own personal experience with the water. Gigot still was, but he wasn't. Gigot looked the same on the outside, but inside his life had changed forever. As the water spoke in his spirit, Gigot no longer found himself confounded at anything, but was relaxed and at peace with the water. It was as though it was waiting on him to reach out and touch the water in trust, rather than fear. Gigot's eyes glazed in amazement over the water and his breathing began to increase as he could feel his heart relax in peace.

"You know me," he whispered to the water.

Gigot's heart pounded with excruciating joy at what he was experiencing realizing that all of his self-doubt and self-pity had no part of him anymore. Breathing with courage, he gently placed the palm of his hand on top of the water expecting a surge of electricity as he had experienced the night before. As he placed his hand on the water, he turned his head away in expectation of a shock, but this time, the water received his hand and brought comfort to his spirit.

Gently, his hand lie flat on the water and as the ripples of water moved away from his hand, the mirrored reflection rippled into striations of beauty. He turned his hand under the water, cupping the water and bringing it to his face. His face shined in his hand as drops of mirror fell gracefully back into the water. The substance of the water was like mercury, but it wasn't mercury, it was water. It was like mercury, but it was water. It was a solid and a liquid at the same time. It was a mirror substance, but it was as clear, pure and clean just from looking at it from a different angle.

This water had life and was brimming with life and its very essence was life.

Gigot's mind was baffled and restful at the same time. He knelt there by the water and cup by cup, he turned the water over and over with his hands intrigued as he watched the mirrored substance drop from his hands. This kinship that he was having with the water was a kind of getting to know it type of experience that Gigot found to be all too inviting. As he watched the water flow through his hands in mirrored substance, he relaxed back momentarily on his legs with his hands pulling back from the water.

Drops of the water fell on the ground by the water's edge and strikingly did not become absorbed into the earth, but remained on top of the earth as tiny pellets of mirror. The character of the water remained intact as it gently hit the earth. Curiosity now had Gigot's mind, so he carefully cupped more water into his hands and gently placed the water onto the ground.

There it was again! The water's substance remained as mirrored glass on the ground and so he picked up a piece of the water, which had become mirror and tossed it back into the water. Strangely, there was no 'plop' as one might hear when you throw a hardened object into a pool of water, no, the water re-absorbed itself with no sound at all.

Marveling at this new found experience, Gigot said aloud,

"Hello?" for he was wondering if he had lost his ability to hear. No, he could hear himself just fine, but when he placed the mirrored water back into itself, it made no sound.

Gathering more water, he continued to probe what else the water could do. He got cupful after cupful of water with his hands and placed it on the soil by the lake and eventually surrounded himself with mirror. Out of the water, the mirror remained intact, but once placed back into the lake, the mirror became the water.

When he placed two pieces of the mirror together, they became one, joining together automatically.

"Fascinating," he thought to himself, "extraordinarily fascinating!"

He placed together over twenty-five pieces of the mirror on the ground and stood there looking at himself and marveled at what had just occurred.

"Amazing!" he said aloud, "utterly amazing!"

As he spoke his mind aloud, an even stranger transition occurred. Transfixed on the mirrored image of himself on the ground, the mirror reflected back his image, but spoke these words to his mind,

"What  do you see?"

Pondering the question, he realized that although he thought he'd been staring at himself, he discovered that he was actually looking at the water that spoke, the water that wooed, the water that wasn't water. He was looking at what could see within for it knew all and could see all and all of a sudden, he fell to his knees in tears at his discovery that he was not looking at himself, but that the water was looking at him.

# Chapter 18

## The Idea or the Directive

Gigot spent the rest of the morning cleaning up with the use of all the pure water at hand. He had more than enough to drink and more than enough to wash thoroughly in the refreshing cool, clean water. Had it not been for the summer camps where he had spent his life as a youth counselor, he wouldn't have known that cold water was bearable to bath in. Those summer camp environments provided the coldest water from the bottom of a forest well and was always the only water of choice. The temperature of this water brought back memories of extreme summer days and the God given way to cool off.

After washing his face and arms, he asked the water if it was ok to jump into and the water glistened. Unreservedly, he took off all his clothes and jumped feet first into the chill. When he came up for air, he shot up as fast as he could power himself up and as he rushed straight up out of the water, he screamed, "Hallelujah! I'm free!"

He had this awesome sense of presence about him as he dove deeper into the water. He knew that what he had found here was what he had needed all along. He needed to be free and this freedom had not cost him a dime. The deeper he swam, the more free he was freed from himself.

As he swam, he realized that not only was he free from his past, he was free from any worries, free from any pain; he was free even in the midst of chilling water, he was free. He swam and the faster he swam, the more tired he became, yet his spirit was more energized than ever before.

He had let go and he was being able to tell the difference between his spirit listening and speaking with the spirit of the water and engaging his mind and emotions, but not allowing his feelings to get in the way. He had heard and obeyed this spirit long ago yet over time, his own self had gotten in the way. It occurred to him that just about everywhere he had been in his life, his thoughts and his feelings had become a distraction from the voice of the spirit. The water had its own language that it spoke and he was clearly receiving all that it said.

The smile on his face rang clear because it was coming from deep within him and he sighed and breathed big sighs of relief and joy. This new found freedom within was all around him and he was swimming in it. In the time he had spent at the lake, he discovered that he had become a new person…no more fear, no more worry, no more past, no more of the desire for more for all that he needed was here around him and within him. He had drunk the water of freedom and was basking in its reflection and drawn by its source.

As the middle of the lake gurgled and its power pulled him within, he dove downward and swam deeper into its depths towards the gurgling source. Swimming downward, he saw a lasso coming towards him as though to retreive him from the depths. As the lasso approached his neck, it dissapeared and he was shaken by the vision. The water spoke and said,

"Gigot, you have confessed and repented and confessed and relented. What I have forgiven, I have forgiven. Listen to me."

At that moment, he reached the bottom and realized he had no more breath to make it back to the surface. Immediately, a surge of powerful and relentless water bolted him upward towards the surface of the lake with such a surge of power no man or no thing could have resisted. At the surface of the water, Gigot choked and coughed, gasping and sucking in air, as his mind and flesh were overwhelemed by the flight and his thoughts of dying. The water surged again and pushed him upward above the surface as though raising his brow and said,

"Relax, Gigot, you're not drowning."

Immediately Gigot breathed a breath and relaxed floating atop the water. As he did, the water spoke again to his spirit,

"You know Gigot, at times you have been one of the most obedient sons and at other times when you decided not to engage in thinking through thoughts that did not come from me, you allowed yourself to be played the fool and didn't even realize it. You do now, but have you truly learned faith from foolishness and foolishness from stupidity?"

"Faith is not blind, neither is it foolish. If you continue to dwell with me and listen to my voice, you will hear me in your spirit and know my sound. If another sound comes into your mind...would it be me?"

"I speak to your spirit and in your impertinence, you have listened to another in your mind or your feelings and have become confused. You are to listen to me in your spirit, using your mind for I gave it to you to fully engage you so that you can decide to listen, obey and follow. Passive minds permit promiscuity, yes?"

"I gave you the gift to analyze and, at times, you have taken the gift to the extremes and caused paralyses to my desires. At other times, you created a vacuum without thinking, listening to another voice and passively following it to the doorstep of doom. Use your gift Gigot. Listen, think and move."

"How do you know what manner of spirit is speaking to you if you do not employ your mind? Am I your feelings? A dark spiritual thought? How will you know the difference? Will you recognize my voice in the future or will you listen to yet another and another not knowing the difference? You are not confused for I speak plainly to you and you see that, don't you?"

Gigot was humbly and fully engaged in spirit and mind listening intently to the water's wooing absorbing not only what the water had to say, but to the voice in his spirit logging into his memory the sound of the water as it gently spoke within.

He was exhausted from the swim, so he made his way to the shoreline. As he walked up out of the water, the water, once again, fell like water, but landed like pieces of mirror. He dried himself off quickly from the chill of the air and as he sat there in his shorts with his towel over his back, he looked out over the lake from where he had just been and he saw the lasso in his mind.

"What was the lasso?" he spoke openly to the water. Softly the water rippled to his spirit and said,

"The lasso is desire. It is the desire of men to not allow the repentant to let go of their past. You have had brothers who do not understand forgiveness and refuse to allow you to let go of who you have been, so they hold you back and keep you from me. It's their desire to keep you bound to them. These unforgiving brothers treat most men this way as their way to make the repentant beholden to them for their forgiveness in this life. You have been shown what all men need to see."

"What is that?" Gigot asked.

"There is no rope."

Gigot breathed quietly by the shore of the lake reflecting on where he had been and what had just been revealed. As he sat there by the shore, he looked down at the pieces of mirror that had dropped from him as water and fell as mirror to the ground. Alfred's mirror came to his mind.

"You remember, don't you?" the water spoke quietly to his spirit.

"It was you, wasn't it?" he replied with excitement figuring out what all of this was and where it might be going.

"So Floyd and Alfred know, don't they?"

The water glistened in response and all of a sudden, Gigot jumped to his feet and shouted, "I got it, I got it, I got it!" The water gurgled from the middle and rippled a ripple to the edges.

"I see now, I understand!"

Gigot fell backward trying to pull up his pants, laughing, as he pulled and pulled his pants over his shorts. He got a clean pair of socks from his bag, along with a clean shirt, got himself dressed as fast as he could and gathered his belongings as quickly as he was able and in his exuberance said, "I need to take you to Lewis, don't I?"

The water offered only a response of glistening in the sunlight reflecting the sun's rays from above. In that moment of reflection, Gigot saw what he needed to do.

He took the containers of leftover food that he had had the day before, eating what was left and discarding anything in the covered containers that was unnecessary. This gave him three containers to fill up with the water that he could take it back to Lewis in order to see if Lewis could make something out of it. He knew if he and Lewis could put their heads together on this idea, then he would never lack for another mirror…and the mirror would be shared with all it came in contact with.

He was excited beyond belief and then it dawned on him that this wasn't his lake or his land. He couldn't just come up here anytime he wanted and get what he wanted out of the lake because he didn't own the land, besides the fact that he lived in Florida and this is Wyoming.

"Who owns the land?" he thought to himself. "Who would know who owns this land?"

"Alfred!" he shouted aloud as the water gurgled another pump from below and upward rose the ripples towards the edge of the lake.

Gathering his three containers of water together, he thanked the water excitedly and told it that he would be back as soon as he could with the deed to the property.

He ran the five miles through the forest, through the brush and out towards the van that had been parked by the roadside.

"The sign, the owner is on the sign," remembering that the property had been for sale and that the sign was the marker that Floyd had told him about. Scrounging through the roadside brush, he pulled back the old, broken limbs and brush that covered the sign from the years of age and forest growth.

He scraped the debris away as much as he could and blew and blew with his breath to get as much dust off of it as was possible. There it was, the telephone number that had stood the test of time. The crusty and worn sign, with flaking old paint was still legible enough to read. The telephone number must be the number of a local realtor, he thought, but the sign was so old, he wondered if the realtor was still alive.

Running back to his van to get a pen and paper, he went ahead and threw everything into the trunk of the van, except for the three containers of lake water, he placed those on the floorboard in the middle of the van.

With pen and paper in hand, he figured out the telephone number. Confusion arose in his mind and on his face, however, because the area code for the number was his area code where he lived.

"How could that be?" he thought to himself. "The owner lives in

Florida?"

He jumped into the van and was on the road again, heading back to Alfred's to show him what he'd found. He kept a careful eye on the containers to make sure that there was no chance of turning over and spilling. He had failed to comprehend, though, that even if the water were to fall out of the containers, it would become the mirror and congeal together as one. But, that was not what he wanted.

What he wanted was the purity of the essence of the water in its liquid form to show Lewis the changing properties of the water and to see if the water would speak to Lewis as it had spoken to him and changed his life. His thinking was maybe that's why Alfred and Floyd were as they were; they had been changed by the water.

When he arrived at Alfred's property to take the long drive onto Alfred's ranch, he noticed something entirely different about the property. It was overgrown and brush was rolling across the plains as a desert. He stopped momentarily in the long driveway and felt the wind blowing through the car as he proceeded slowly towards the ranch house. Creaking along in the van, he was dumbfounded to see that the house was abandoned, rusted and breaking apart. He stopped about a hundred yards away from the house and came to himself and thought,

"I must have taken a wrong turn too soon. I'm pretty certain that this was the right driveway."

But his eyes did not deceive him, the ranch house before him that he believed he had spent the night in just two days ago, was falling apart and abandoned. Slowly, he drove closer and closer to the house and with a great amount of hesitation he put his foot on the brake and stopped the van.

"I know this is their house. What's going on? Certainly this is no joke."

Getting out of the van, he walked slowly towards the house. Everything on the outside was as he had left it the day before. But now, it was old, creaking and empty. The windows were broken and the front door was swinging open in the gusts of wind.

"What's going on here?" he said aloud, expecting no response for no one was around. No one was there and there were no sounds but the racing wind across the land.

Swallowing hard, he braced himself as he walked through the threshold. The floors creaked with age and dust was flying everywhere. There it was…the huge fireplace and mantle to the left with the sofas and chairs that they all had sat in together just two nights ago. Missing was the life and the fragrance of grilled brisket over an open flame in the fireplace. Gigot's left arm began to shake a little from nervous tension and fear began to well up inside of him.

"No!" he said to the fear, "there's no such thing as a twilight zone." But what he was feeling now as he went from room to room was doubt and the possibility that what he was seeing was what he was seeing.

"This is, or was, your house, Alfred, what's going on?" he spoke to Alfred, who was not there.

"The mirror…" he thought to himself, as he turned and went the other way towards the hallway bath. He marched inside the bath expecting to see the beautiful mirror that had spoken to him the other night, but it was gone. The mirror that had been on the wall had left its mark on the wall, but the mirror was not there. Everything was still in the house, just as it was the other night, except for Alfred, Pete, Floyd and Ruth and that mirror. Yet, the house looked like no one had lived in it for twenty years, or more.

"Ok, I have the wrong house, ok, I accept that," he said to himself, "I've taken a wrong turn and it must be the next house down the road."

He raced out of the house and jumped into the van, quickly opening the covers to the containers that contained the lake water. Everything was just as he had left it there. The water was still the reflective water, clear and pure. But outside, that was a different story.

Backing up the van as quickly as he could, he proceeded out of the drive and back onto the road heading back towards town knowing that the next drive on the left would be Alfred's…but there was no other driveway to the left…or to the right. In about ten minutes time, he found himself back in the town of Bodie.

Gigot bit the inside of his mouth a bit in tension wavering with the idea that he would just go back twenty minutes, or so, on the drive and then he would find Alfred's house, but rather than waste his time looking for something that was unsure, he decided to go into the general store and ask them where Alfred and Pete lived.

Pulling up to the store front, everything was he had seen it two days before, or "…was it two days?" He began to question himself as to how long it really had been. The bench on the front porch was worn, but it was still there and so he walked on inside the store to find no one minding the store.

"Hello…hello, anybody here?" he shouted with a broken voice, disturbed by the possibility that this, too, was empty. But, here, music was playing, the lights were on and there was the smell of leather and old produce, kinda mixed together by the blowing of the ceiling fans up above.

"Howdy, sir, sorry, was out back rustlin' up some food for the dog, how can I help ye?" the store owner quipped as his thick eyebrows moved like a catapillar on his brow.

"Hey," Gigot responded and extended his hand in greeting to the shop owner, "You doing alright?"

"Sure 'nough, fine and dandy, can I git sometin' for ye?" he asked again.

Gigot hesitated and got up enough gumption to ask the question, "Do you know of an Alfred and Pete and a Floyd and Ruth? I met them the other night and had a dinner with them and I went back by their house and took a wrong turn. I was wondering if you knew exactly where they lived so that I could drop by their house and say thank you for their hospitality."

The store owner had an inquisitive look on his face, turned all the way around as if someone was watching from a corner and said, "You one of those fellers who does that candied camera?"

Baffled at the response, Gigot's eyebrows twitched, rose up and down, and then he asked the same question again a little differently, "Well, maybe you misunderstood what I said, I said, do you know…"

The store owner got testy with Gigot, interrupting him and said,

"I know wut you said, or asked, I jus' thought you wus playing a joke, but you don't look like the joking type, now, do ye?"

Gigot stepped back a step from the man still wondering if he needed to re-phrase his question or just go down the street and ask someone else. Silence became the order of the moment and they both stood there and stared at one another.

The store owner paused for a few minutes, then shuffled his feet and walked behind the counter.

"Let me git this straight. You said you jus' et with Alfred and Pete and Floyd and Ruth the other night and you wanted to know where they live? Is that right?"

"Yes, that's right."

"Well, if you et wit dem, how come you don't know how to git back to their place, maybe you didn't et wit dem," the owner scratching his cheek as he reasoned this thing out in his mind.

Obviously frustrated with the man's demeanor, Gigot replied,

"Look, I just came from what I thought was their ranch, about ten miles up Falls Pass Road. Alfred and Floyd took me there two nights ago, but it was getting dark and I actually don't know if I have the right house, or not. Now, can you help me out, or do I need to go down the street and find someone who can?"

By this time, the store owner had sat down on his revolving counter chair and was rotating back and forth, scratching flecks of skin from his dry scalp and placing the dried specks of scalp skin on the counter. Gigot didn't know whether to ignore him with what he was doing or be repulsed and leave, so he just stood there with a defiant look on his face.

"Hi there, my name is Arthur Dyess, what's yours?" as he stretched out his hand to shake Gigot's.

Gigot was thinking they had already done this, but he did remember that no names had been mentioned, so he said, "I'm Gigot."

And before he could breathe another syllable, the store owner interrupted again and said, "What the hell kinda name is Gigot?" shiftting amd tilting his head in curiosity.

Gigot didn't want to go there with this gentleman, so he asked again with disdain, "Do you know where Alfred lives?"

Arthur could see Gigot's flustered face and puffed up his lower lip and said, "Well, I tell ye wut! I can tell ye where Alfred is, but I cain't tell ye where he lives!"

Gigot cocked his head in bewilderment and said, "What does that mean?"

"It means wut it means, jus' like I said, Alfred and Pete and Floyd and Ruth are in heaven! Now that's where dey are, but I cain't tell ye where dey live!"

Arthur thought that Gigot was some dumb fool investigator from the government or a develeoper out to get Alfred and Pete's ranch and he was not going to play along. Gigot thought Arthur was a tyrannical knob who didn't really care whether Gigot discovered where Alfred lived, so, again they just stood there at a stalemate and stared at each other.

Then, an idea dawned with Gigot and Gigot explained, "You see, Arthur, I'm sure you can tell I'm from out of town. But the other day, I came into this store, late, right at closing time and used your rest room right over there. I stopped at this town because I thought that there was something in this town that would help me to get through this awful life of mine. Alfred and Floyd were sitting out on your front porch bench chewing and spitting tobacco and when I went back outside, we sat and talked and watched the sunset. Then, they invited me out to their place and fed me and told me everything I needed to know in order to find the thing that I needed to get through this miserable life of mine. So, I went exactly to the place where they told me to go and I found it, I found the one thing that has saved me from a miserable life and so I'm not miserable anymore, you see, I'm not miserable at all, now, dam'it, tell me where Alfred lives!!"

Arthur sat back against his chair and started to pant a little. Then a tear came to his eye. He pulled out his handkerchief and before he could raise the handkerchief to his face, he started bawling in tears. He choked up and his face fell forward into his arms placed on the counter.

Just then, a huge gust of wind, rushed through the front of the store throwing open the front door slamming it against the wall and you could hear the creak of a pickup truck coming to a stop just outside the door. As the wind was gusting and howling outside, Alfred and

Floyd rushed inside with their coats pulled over their heads shielding themselves from the wind and the sand.

Startled, Gigot thought he was seeing two ghosts before him and Alfred and Floyd looked and smiled at Gigot and looked and frowned at Arthur and then Alfred said, "Hey there, what's going on here?"

Arthur had regained a bit of his composure and said, "This government feller wus asking too many questions about you two, making up some cockamainey story about eatin' dinner wit you two jus' so he could fine out from me where ya'll lived."

Gigot, dumbfounded, was speechless and didn't know what to say except, "I, I, I was only askin' where you…" and Arthur interrupted him again saying, "Ya'll know how I's git upset wen too much pressure is put on me." Arthur wiped his face and blew his nose from how upset he had gotten.

Alfred and Floyd surmised the situation quickly and laughed. "Now you two need to shake and make up, ya here," Floyd quipped with a grin.

Gigot and Arthur looked at each other with the exact same eyebrow twitch and Gigot thought silently to himself, "I hope I never have eyebrows on my face that look like a crawling catapillar."

Arthur wagged his head at Gigot and said, "I feel the same!"

Gigot's neck flipped back and then Alfred lunged at Gigot, "Great to see you, young man, great to see you, did you find what you were looking for?"

"Yes, as a matter of fact, I did, Alfred."

Floyd responded, "Yea, but do you act like it?"

Gigot stood frozen in his breath because he knew exactly what he had just done. He had gotten frustrated and undone with Arthur's behavior and shouted and cursed at Arthur when Arthur was only protecting the living whereabouts of his friends. Gigot stood there guilty as charged and yet no one exactly had charged him with anything.

Alfred said, "You know, you're gonna have to work on that don't you?"

Gigot knew what he said and he knew what he meant. Gigot had to work on this spiritual man of his, the old self wasn't going to all go away overnight and he felt like he had just failed his first test. He had just learned that even though he was changed from within, it was his responsibility to work on his without.

"Alfred, I just went out to you and Pete's ranch and I know that I was in the right place and it was abandoned. The ranch house was the same, but it was falling apart, everything was falling apart and you and Pete and Floyd and Ruth were not there and neither was the mirror. Then, Arthur tells me that all ya'll went to heaven and wouldn't tell me where ya'll lived."

Floyd and Alfred looked at each other; looked at Arthur, looked at each other and then both of them started laughing. Arthur was the worst, his laughter brought out the mucus that was in his sinuses from his crying earlier.

"Gigot, you went to Floyd's abandoned property!" Alfred chuckled.

"What abandoned propery? No, I didn't. I took the turn to the left and..." Gigot stopped there, realizing that this was no Twilight Zone movie. "Well, what did I do wrong, then?"

"You shoulda turned to the property on the right, Gigot, the drive's right across the road directly in front of it," Alfred grinned as he realized Gigot's mistake.

"Oh…" and at that moment, Gigot came to his senses realizing that he was so focused on the left side of the road that it didn't occur to him to look to the right, let alone something as simple as looking across the street. Breathing a sigh of relief that Alfred and Floyd had not been taken to heaven as Arthur had said, he stood there embarassed at how he had totally confused himself by his wrong direction belief. And at how he had just treated Arthur and upset him as he did. Gigot's demeanor was dropping fast and Floyd, Alfred and Arthur could see it drop faster than a penny down a well.

"You found the water, didn't you?" Floyd asked expectantly.

Gigot's shoulders lifted and he said, "Yes, Floyd, but it looks like it hasn't made much difference." Gigot lowered his head in embarrassment and humiliation at the prospect that he had believed he was a changed man, but he was still acting a tad bit the same as he always had.

"You hungry?" Alfred asked Gigot as Gigot's eyes lifted and brimmed with a smile.

"How 'bout you, Arthur?"

Arthur responded, "Let's lock this thing down for lunch! What we having today, Al?"

Alfred replied, "Brisket, I think, Arthur."

"Gigot, lock the inside of the door bein' since you the last one out and turn that sign around that says, 'Be back after lunch'" Arthur ordered Gigot, slapping him on the back and smiling a Mona Lisa smile as though he knew something that Gigot didn't know.

Alfred and Arthur piled into Alfred's truck with Floyd standing by Gigot's van. After Gigot locked the handle and slammed the door shut, he bounced down the front porch steps as Floyd looked back at him and said,

"Gigot, I'm ridin' with you so you don't get lost in the daylight, ok?"

## Chapter 19

## Corporate Agreement

Gigot had another great meal with Alfred and Pete and Floyd and Ruth and, this time, Arthur, too. The grilled brisket seemed to be everyone's favorite. Floyd explained the reasoning behind their move into Alfred's ranch; it was because of their age and health, but they all got along so well, it just seemed the right thing to do.

As far as Arthur thinking Gigot was a government or banking man, Floyd didn't want anyone knowing about his property, particularly real estate developers…Arthur had just gotten confused about the what's what. And, he also didn't want any land developer knowing the whereabouts of the property that Gigot had just come from. In a sense, they were the protectors of that land and all that was in it.

The main thing was the property that contained the lake. Alfred and Floyd were getting up in age and they didn't feel like they could protect that land anymore from onlookers, hikers, real estate brokers and anyone else that might get their hands wet from that lake. They had been sitting out on that porch waiting for Gigot, or whoever, that was supposed to be the one to buy that property.

Their dads' were friends with Jefferson B. Case who had sold the land to Samuel Whitegold years ago with the promise that he would never sell the property, and, Samuel had kept that promise. However, his grandson, Victor, who had never worked a day in his life, had put the land up for sale years ago. Supposedly no one ever cared enough about looking at it. That was a possible reason or maybe it was because the investigators could never find the "For Sale" sign and had been directed to looking on the wrong road…

"Gigot, are you able to buy that land from Victor Whitegold?"

asked Alfred.

"Uh, I don't know if I have the funds for that, or not, I don't know how much it is. I would think at the market rate, 1,000 acres would cost way more than I can afford, but I did take the number down to call him. It's actually a phone number in my area code back home in Florida," Gigot replied.

"But let me ask you this…why is it that other people don't just go on the land and jump in the water like I did. The water told me all that I was and it humbled me, or I humbled myself to it and I'm changed. I believe it made me a new man. I can see that you all know what I'm talking about."

Ruth spoke up and said, "Gigot, I can see in you where the water wooed you and changed you, but you had to submit to it. All kinds of folk have been up there to that property, good men, bad men, wicked men and so-so men and the stories we've heard is that the water speaks to whoever it comes in contact with, but not everybody is the same in their response because not everybody is the same. Some folk simply don't care and so the water doesn't faze them at all and others are so wicked, all that water does to them is make them so angry, they want to destroy something. Not everybody's like you, Gigot, you submitted your self to the water. You have purpose and possibility."

"Well, I'm a little confused to be honest with you, but I do have something to confess," Gigot looked down embarrassed and then looked up again. "I took some of the water and I have it in the van. I was going to take some of the water to one of my friends and see if he could help me make a mirror out of it. Does that sound stupid? I thought that if I could buy the land, then the water would be mine to do as I pleased."

They all sat back down at the table at this point and looked at one another and searched their minds for the right response. Then, Pete spoke, "Well, you all know that Gigot's the one to buy that property and if he wants to go make something out of it, then that would be his choice. That is, if you can buy that property."

"I hear you, Pete," Floyd answered, "but that's what we've been afraid of all this time, somebody buying up that property and making a goldmine out of it because of that lake. Shoot, we all grew up on that lake and we all know what a fantastic find that is and I, for one, do not want some hi-falutin' money guru coming up here, buying that property for the water and then making money off of the lake. Well, that would be jus' downright sac-religious, or something."

Alfred piped in, "Now, Floyd, you and I both know that Gigot's not that kind of person. You and I know the good from the bad by the fruit on the tree and Gigot's not rotten. We know rotten, don't we, Pete?"

"We sure do!" Pete responded.

As slow to speak as Ruth usually was, this time was no different. She would usually wait until everyone had had their say and then she would speak. She figured now was a good a time as any and said,

"Gigot, what do you figure to do with the water?"

"I never got around to telling you all that I own a mirror retail store," Gigot began to say and then Arthur choked on his afternoon chew,

"Whua, wat chu say? A mirror store? Who the hell owns a mirror store? All you sell is mirrors? Don't chu sell anything else?"

Gigot just looked at Alfred and then looked at Arthur and chose not to respond to Arthur's question.

"Like I was saying, I own a mirror store and after all the experiences I've had with the water, I figured that if I could get my friend Lewis to help me, I could make mirrors out of the water and then all kinds of people could see for themselves what the water could do by the mirrors. Can you imagine all the people that the water could change? We could have a completely changed town in no time with these mirrors made from this water! And, don't dare tell me that that's a dumb idea, 'cause you two have already done the same thing."

"But we don't go selling the thangs to the public, Gigot," Floyd retorted. "That's jus', jus' blasphemy! That's what we've been against all along. Can you imagine if the right voo-doo man got ahold of that property and found out what he could do with that lake, well, we'd have another Branson out chere in the middle of nowhere, right down front of the Tetons with lights and a circus and a ferris wheel and everything else, and him selling that water that never runs dry causin' its from an arti, artis, artiz-un…"

Arthur interrupted Floyd, "Ar-ti-si-an, Floyd, ar-ti-si-an well," and then he spit his chew into a cup. "It jus' comes up," and then he accidentally spit on himself with his chaw spittle.

Pete immediately got up and got Arthur a wet towel to wipe himself off and sat down disgusted with him.

Ruth said, "Is that what you plan to do, Gigot, make a spectacle and a profit off of the very thing that's changed your life?"

"Well, I think what I'll do is this: go buy the property and build a building over the lake and sell tickets to have people come in one by one; take a number walking into the building and come out the other side after they swim through the lake and then they can leave an offering if they want to as they leave the property…" Gigot snorted growing tired of the conversation because he hadn't called the owner to see if he could even buy the property or not.

"Now, we all know what that sounds like," Alfred stated as they all looked around the room and agreed with one another.

Gigot said, "If I'm able to buy that property, then, what would you have me do with it? I'm not going to leave that water in that lake by itself. I don't think for a minute that that is what it was for. I believe that water was to be shared with whoever would find it and it would change their life and they would be whole and have a purpose and…"

Arthur interrupted Gigot in mid-stride and said, "I agree with Gigot! You four great protectors have been protecting this land and that lake for as long as I can remember and I knew that water's changing my life afore any of ye! Why can't the whole world be changed? Don't ye git it? It's not jus' for storin' it up and keepin' it safe! So wut if he messes it up, that water gots more sense than any of us, includin' you, Alfred, no offense. And it's high past time that that water is sent to the world 'cause this world is messed up and I'm tired o keepin' secrets! For once, dag-nabbit, trust somebody that the water dun wooed itself up chere and ya'll still wanna control it."

By this time, Arthur's excitement and preaching had caused him to spit his entire chew up from his inner lip and his chew was all over his chin and running down his overalls.

Silence fell over the room and Pete and Ruth helped Arthur clean himself up, throwing that nasty chewing tobacco away in a tin out on the front porch. There were lots of sighs and deep breaths going on now and no one had anything else to say…for a few minutes anyway.

Alfred winced and sighed, looking at Floyd, saying, "Will you trust him to do the right thing with that water? You know Arthur's right. It's time for the real water that can change lives for eternity to get out and change the world the right way, don't you agree?"

Taking a sip of water, Floyd gulped and acknowledged, "Yes, I guess it's time. It's time for the truth to come out about the water. Gigot, we're gonna trust you to make the right decisions about the water 'cause I know the water has helped us in everything we've done and we're safe and secure. The mirror of that water speaking to us has made us know ourselves as we are…or were. I'm thankful that what we've seen and heard through that water keeps us on the straight and narrow. I knowd the water's gonna do the same for you so you can be the spreader of the water that speaks to ye and tells ye all that ye are. I guess the water knows wut its doin', huh?"

Each one said, "I agree…"

"Then, it's settled," Gigot said smiling, "I'll not do anything until I know what to do and whatever it is, there won't be any doubt this time in my life. I know by the experience of making hundreds of mistakes that I don't want to make a mistake with this treasure that changes peoples' lives. I'm sure that the water knows and wll guide. Then if need be and Lewis is up to it, we'll cross that bridge when we come to it. I'll call you all every step of the way, but first, let me use your phone to call that phone number from the sign."

Pete had already dialed the number. She had written it down years ago and it was etched into the inside cupboard of the coffee cups. She had seen that number so many times in her life, she had it memorized. The phone was already ringing when she handed Gigot the receiver.

## Chapter 20


## The Cost


"Hello?" the old man on the other end breathed a gruff. "I said, hello!"

"Uh, hello, hello there!" Gigot smiled at Pete as he was hoping this was the owner of the land on the other end. "Hello, this is Gigot Bengal,"

"Who?" he asked.

"Gigot Bengal," Gigot said again in an energetic voice.

"What kinda name is Gigot Bengal? You wanting money for the circus?" the man laughed to himself on the other end of the line and was quickly growing agitated.

"No, I was calling about a piece of property that I believe that you own in Wyoming."

"Wyoming, I don't own any land in Wyo…wait a minute…you talking about that land near the mountains, I thought that was Idaho; anyway, I had forgotten about that piece of land," he said with a wry expression. "My name's Victor Whitegold, what's yours?"

"Gigot…Gigot Bengal," Gigot had paused and then responded again, pleasantly. "I was calling to see if you were still interested in selling that property. I found the phone number on the sign by the road."

"Yes, yes, the sign by the road. Say, I bet that sign's been out there at least 30 years, or more," Victor continued. "I'm surprised you could still read the numbering on it. Have you taken a look at the property? How's it looking lately?"

"Well, it looks great," Gigot didn't want to come off too excited because he knew the more interest and excitement he showed, the more it would probably cost him. "Have you been out to the property lately yourself?"

"No, I've never seen it. I'm always too busy."

Victor was busy going through his files while he was talking, trying to find the information on the property as he spoke with Gigot. It just so happened that Victor had received his final demand from the county, state and federal tax authorities expecting a full payment of some taxes that were long overdue. Victor's usual and customary was to sell an asset in order to fulfill any taxes or liens on any of the properties that his family had owned and yet the only things left to pay for was the estate he was living on and that property out west. He didn't care one thing about that property, yet he could remember there was something tied to it, but for the life of him, he couldn't remember what it was.

"There we go, I found it," Victor said joyfully. "I found the paperwork on the property in question. What do you need to know about?"

While he was on the phone, Victor began to read the notes on the property agreement that stated  the conditions of the property...under no circumstances was he to sell that property.

Gigot replied, "Well, sir, I've been out on the property and it looks like something I might be interested in if the price is right. The sign states that it's 1,000 acres and if that's the case, I would need to know your asking price on the whole property."

"Well, you know 1,000 acres is a lot of land, what's your interest in that property, if you don't mind me asking? According to my notes here, this property has some great value to it." Victor was being obviously deceptive for he had no idea why the property would have conditions on it.

"Interest, uh, interest?" Gigot responded looking at Alfred and Floyd in an unwary state at this point because he hadn't thought through what he was going to say if the owner started asking too many questions.

Alfred said, "Tell him the truth!" Alfred knew the man didn't know one thing about the property, but he had an unction that the truth would be all he needed to hear.

"Sir," Gigot continued, "That's a mighty fine piece of property and it's so fine, that I thought it was time to put it in the hands of someone who would admire and take care of the property and not let anything happen to it with someone else who might try to destroy the land and what's on it."

"Uh-huh, go on," Victor's interest was peaked in what Gigot knew that he didn't.

"Well, let me put it this way, I'm out here now with some folk who used to know the original owner and they said that the property had to stay in safe hands and they have put their trust in me to continue to keep it in safe hands so that the property would never be abused, but enjoyed for its original purpose," Gigot seemed to feel like he was meandering with his responses, but he was saying what he knew to be the truth.

"Uh-huh! So, you think it's time that the property needs to be in safer hands than mine, huh? Just who do you think you are, young man?" Victor retorted bluntly.

Gigot was shocked at what Victor was saying and how he had interpreted what he had said. Gigot thought about what he had said and it did sound like that's what he was saying so he quickly apologized and said, "Oh, Mr. Whitegold, oh, no, I didn't mean to say that I'm more worthy of owning the property than you, I'm sorry that came out that way. What I guess I should have said was that I'm so interested in that property that I would really like to take it off of your hands so it would be one less thing for you to be concerned with."

By this time, Gigot was sweating profusely and Floyd was walking over to the fireplace shaking his head back and forth in defeat. He could tell Gigot hadn't really negotiated much along these lines and didn't have a clue on how to talk to Mr. Whitegold.

Victor sounded off agitated by now, "You know, 30 years ago, that property was valued at over $600,000.00. By now, it ought to be valued in the millions, you got that kinda money, 'cause it sure sounds like you don't!"

Completely dejected at this point, Gigot sighed and his entire countenance deflated. "Sir, Mr. Whitegold, sir, I have to say, no sir, I don't have that kinda of money. I've thought about it and all the money I have that I could put into the land is $60,000.00, that's all I have and I'm pretty certain that no bank would lend me money for the difference. I guess I'm not ready for that kind of purchase. It looks like I've wasted your time."

While Gigot was talking to Victor about the state of his personal finances, Victor was looking down at the tax lien that was going to go against his home estate if he didn't get the bills paid that amounted to $58,768.65. Victor had gotten up in age and having never worked a day in his life didn't really know what to do. He knew he could simply obtain an equity line of credit to pay the bills and he had seriously considered doing just that…but, this opportunity to get some quick cash was all too tempting for him. Besides, he would have to go to the bank and deal with the bankers that would be asking all kinds of questions and then they would need to come out and value his estate and, and, and. He knew in his heart that this was no coincidence.

"Tell you what I'll do. I'll think about what you have in your hand 'cause you might just be the one to own that land after all. I'll have to think about it!" And with that, Victor hung up the phone.

After he hung up the phone, Victor sat in his elegant leather chair and intensely stared at the amount of money he had to immediately come up with. He thought about the possibility of creating some type of loan for Gigot so that he could get his $60,000.00 and then maybe Gigot could take up payments on what was owed.

"But how much would he owe?" he thought to himself, that was a huge variable. If he charged him too much money, he'd end up with nothing and he couldn't afford to do that.

Victor went to the drawing room, poured himself a brandy and brought it to his nose in a light whiff. Slowly swirling the expensive liquor, he continued to take small whiffs of the brew, which was his custom anytime he went deep in thought. Somehow, according to his thinking, he could make better decisions when he sniffed and whiffed and sipped his cordials to the point where much of his money was being spent on expensive alcoholic beverages that only the richest of folk could afford.

"What's a man like me to do, to do?" he politely asked Selby, the glass he was drinking from. On one hand, he already knew what he was going to do…take the money. He had always been impulsive that way. Yet he was running out of funds way too quickly with the boorish behavior of impulsivity but he simply couldn't help himself.

On the other hand, though, if he took some time and thought this thing through, he could end up with the cash and a nice monthly payment to boot. Victor took a look back at the phone and verified there was a return number on the dial and there was. Hitting the return dial, he waited, sipping on his brandy ready to see if a deal was on its way.

"Hello," Pete answered her phone.

"Yes, yes, this is Mr. Whitegold, I believe a Mr. Bengal just called me from this phone, is that correct?" Victor asked.

"Yes!" Pete replied, "Here he is."

Gigot received the ear set from Pete as she shoved it to his ear. "Ouch," Gigot smarted from her pushing the ear set too hard to his ear, "Hello, this is Gigot, is this Mr. Whitegold?"

"Yes it is, I was wondering if I might ask you a few questions if I may?" Victor was trying to sound persuasive in order to get as much information out of Gigot as he could. He suspected Gigot might be a novice at this type of deal, so he continued, "I'm interested in your offer to purchase and I realize you told me that you have $60,000.00 at your disposal. That actually sounds interesting and so I'm wondering if you would have the finances to complete the payment of one million dollars on a monthly note?"

Gigot raised his entire forehead with that idea and dropped his jaw. "You said one million dollars?"

"Yes, I believe that's a fair price to ask for such a prestigious plot of land. Why 1,000 acres where I currently live would cost $10 million, or more, maybe even $100 million." Victor felt if he played it up big enough, then one million wouldn't seem too great a price to pay.

Everyone sitting at the table could hear what Victor was saying because Pete had turned up the volume on the receiver and as Victor made his proposal to Gigot, they were all shaking their heads back and forth silently saying no to his proposition.

"Sir," Gigot pleaded, "I don't have that kind of money. I'm actually financially strapped and do not have any extra money to pay you."

This made Victor a little perturbed, squinching his eyes, he shot back, "Young man, why are you wasting my time. That land was purchased by my father and it meant everything to him. That land is so valuable, it's priceless! And now, you want me to sell it to you for $60,000.00. You must think me an idiot!" Victor slammed the phone down and hung up on Gigot again. He took the entire swig of brandy down and started to reach for the bottle when his chest went, "Boom!" and he was shot through with pain.

Victor fell to his knees from his chair as his favorite brandy glass of fifty years fell to the floor shattering to pieces.

"Oh, no, Selby..." He had called his crystal brandy goblet, Selby, as was his custom to call his most used items a name. There was no one in the house and hadn't been there much for years because he couldn't afford to pay any hired help except a cleaning lady once a month and his chef that would come in once a week and prepare his meals. He found himself staring at the floor as sweat beaded down his forehead and dripped to the walnut flooring.

"Breathe, just breathe," he coached himself to relax as he maintained his position on all fours.

He was thinking he might have a heart attack, because he was at the age that his Dad had died years ago from a severe attack and he supposed his fate would be the same. But this time, there wasn't a hoard of people around like his Dad had. Victor was alone and that just made his situation far worse, so he began to well up from within gasping,

"What have I done? What am I going to do?"

And, as the wind blows swiftly, so did the thoughts fire right through to his heart,

"Sell the land!" the thought said, "Sell that land and take the $60,000.00 now!"

# Chapter 21

## The Acquisition

Pete had already put on a pot of hot tea, the green kind that's supposed to help you think better.

"What are you going to do, Gigot?" Ruth asked baiting him to express his presumed lack of faith in the deal.

"I don't know, right now, Ruth," Gigot said calmly. "The man just hung the phone up again, so, what I think I'll do is to get on the road and go and meet with him personally to see if a face to face meeting will touch him in some way."

"That sounds like the way to go," Floyd chimed in as they all had sensed in their spirit that this was the direction to take. As the rest of the three elders nodded in agreement, a true calm came over the room.

Alfred got up from the table and walked over to Gigot and hugged him tightly, approving him as only a father can do. He then took Gigot by the shoulders and looked him square in the face and said,

"This is going to work out for you Gigot, just don't give up, even if that man slams the door in your face, don't ever give up!"

Gigot smiled back at Alfred and as was Gigot's way, he wouldn't verbally make any promises, but he smiled a smile that they all knew that he understood. He agreed with them that this would work out and the land would be his one day and the water that woos would be for the world to receive.

Pete and Ruth packed Gigot enough food for more than a couple of meals and all the snacks in-between. With the van packed and ready for the trip back home, Gigot gave each one a long hug. He didn't know when he would see them again and somehow when he looked at Floyd, his breathing got really deep and his eyes teared up some really big tears.

Floyd coughed, waved his hand back at Gigot and said,

"Now you stop that young man! It's time you started getting down the road. Git on otta here before I have to take a switch to ya!"

Gigot smiled again and jumped into the van and took off looking in the rearview mirror of the friendliest faces he had ever met. They waved until he was out of sight and once he was out of sight, it seemed like no time had past until he found himself in a motel room back in Nebraska.

All along his journey back to Lewis' house, he continued to pray and think through what he might do with the water that woos and whether Lewis would be able to work his engineering magic in the production of mirrors if he were able to get the land and the access to the endless supply of water from the lake. He had a sense of overwhelming calm and peace as he traveled the same roads that he had traveled not too many days hence with all of his worrying and crying and stressing himself out. Now, that seemed like a lifetime ago for he was indeed a new man and learning in his moments what being a new man was all about and giving up his self to a far greater power than his own.

That evening he called Pauline and the kids were up ready to talk. They were all so excited to hear from their dad and each one had a story to tell, except for James, he just answered questions with not much else to say. That gave Bessie and Daniel more time to fight over the phone and eventually it was bedtime so all of the "I love you's" and "good-byes" were said over and over and over and over until Gigot could hear them screaming, leaving the room yelling, "I love you, Daddy, I love you, Daddy…"

Later that night, after Pauline had put the children to bed, Gigot called back and told her all about his experiences, that is, as much as he could remember in detail for his stories seemed to get longer and more detailed the older he was getting. However, by the time he got to the part where he wanted to buy the land for $60,000, Pauline had already fallen asleep on the phone.

Gigot was hemming and hawing, hesitating telling her everything yet little did he know that she hadn't heard much of anything he said because she would breathe heavy into the phone as she napped while he talked. Gigot asked her a few questions and by the time he realized that she wasn't listening, he just said, "I love you dearly" and waited on her response which was like talking to someone in their sleep and them mumbling back what you just said.

The next day, Gigot pondered what Lewis and Diane's response to the water might be and he caught himself thinking too much about it to the point that he realized that whatever their response to the water was, it would be their response and he would love them just the same. As he meditated on that upcoming event, he pondered the idea of not even telling Lewis and Diane about it to sharing it with them face to face. He knew that the water would speak to them and he prayed for them in his spirit.

Somehow, though, that very thought led him to see that all that they were or are was none of his business for this was so extremely personal, he didn't want to invade their space or try to manipulate them into thinking something about it all that were his thoughts and not theirs at all. He wanted to share the water with them, but how was he going to do it? He didn't want to demand anything of them nor did he want to manipulate or cajole anything out of them. He loved them as friends and he wanted to keep it that way…but, the water and its importance was far more important than personal friendship, so what was he going to do? He thought and thought for hours as he drove because it seemed to him that whatever it was that he did with Lewis and Diane was probably what he was going to with the water from now on. He knew that whatever powerful properties were emanating from the water, it had changed his life, but the water was what had the power to change people and not him. He had seen it for years where people constantly try to manipulate or deceive other people with power and he wasn't going to be like that or let this thing end up in the hands of people that would trade the truth of the water for a lie by covering it with their own form of perspective.

As time drew closer to Lewis' home, Gigot came to the conclusion that he would simply present the water to Lewis and let the water do the talking. The water knew better what to do than he did and he had all the confidence in the water that the water knew best in what the water was going to say to Lewis, Diane or whoever came into contact with the water.

In a sense, that's what Alfred and Floyd had done for him. They pointed him in the right direction of the water and they let the water speak for itself. This relieved Gigot of any pressure to make some grandiose presentation and it was also making the way clearer on how Gigot might present this water to the public in his store.

The simplicity of Alfred's mirror was just that…simplistic. It needed to go in a homemade frame like Alfred's or much like the mirrored frame that he saw at the Kitty Hawk Grill.

"Haha," he laughed to himself, "the Kitty Hawk Grill. Imagine this wooing mirrored water in a Kitty Hawk frame…imagine that, indeed!"

**Chapter 22**


**Getting Out of the Way**


As Gigot drove into Lewis and Diane's, he had the sense that it was like some adventure movie where he was entering the lair of some kind of government hideout where the most secret of conjurings were being conjured up. If anybody could help fix problems of the engineering or nuclear kind, it was Lewis.

Diane's expertise was of the social persuasion. She was the perfect example of southern hospitality and it seemed that the mold of southern charm had been created from her style.

With all of the welcomes out of the way, Lewis got back to his office in his basement and Diane started working on a very late dinner. Gigot didn't unpack everything for he was only staying over one night again, so he decided to take a container of water to Lewis to see what he thought of it. Gigot knocked on Lewis' door to his cramped, tiny office that led to an even more elaborate laboratory of sorts that every purebred scientist would envy. Gigot respected Lewis' demeanor and his intelligence so he didn't feel the need to present the water to him with fanfare and then tell him all about the water, he thought it best to let the water do its own work and talking for itself. Lewis did note something different about Gigot as Gigot stood at the corner of the desk looking outside the window towards the Mississippi River.

"Aren't you ever afraid of flooding from the river, Lewis?" Gigot asked respectfully.

Lewis merely looked up at Gigot with a slight smile and said,

"Well, it has flooded here in times past, I have all of the studies here of the levels and years that it did that, but I'm not concerned about it.

If it floods, it floods and if it's too severe, we'll move back to the coast where I was planning to build in the first place. You know I built this house to float, don't you? The company paid to have this built here for its proximity to…" and then Lewis just trailed off back into his work as though he had completely finished the thought.

"Lewis, I found something that I want you to take a look at and then tell me what you think. Maybe you can look at it before you come up for supper and then we can talk about it over a glass of your favorite Chardonnay."

Both eyebrows on Lewis' forehead lifted gleefully as he anticipated that thought and he immediately moved his chair as if to go and get a bottle that moment, but came to himself and said,

"I'm almost willing to do that now, but I have about ten more minutes on this project that I need to complete before the night ends so that it can be sent up in the morning. I'll take a look at what you have before I come up, ok?"

"Sounds good, thanks, Lewis, I know how busy they keep you, so I'll get out of here and let you work," Gigot walked out of the room and up the stair well to the first floor having left one of the water containers with Lewis to see in private.

Gigot went into the kitchen and chit-chatted with Diane about his travels and how excited he was to get back home to see Pauline and the kids. Time always passed too quickly there as steaming pots of pasta in one and crawfish over to the side to steam at the last moment. In another pot there was some type of creole sauce that Diane had concocted from an old recipe of hers from Louisiana. They had lived in a few places and had traveled all over the world as a result of Lewis' company…or was it the government…Diane didn't really know for sure.

Gigot kept looking at the clock for the first ten minutes, waiting for Lewis to finish his work and then open that container, but time past quickly and the next thing he knew, supper was ready and over thirty minutes had past. Just as Gigot looked at the clock one more time and Diane was beginning to get a little agitated that Lewis had not come up from his office, Lewis yelled loudly from the basement area,

"Diane, come down here, there's something here I want you to see…"

Diane looked at Gigot, exasperated from having prepared the meal that was now going to get cold, shrugged her shoulders and yelled back at Lewis, "Lewis, I don't know what you've got going on down there, but the dinner's going to get cold if I come down there."

"Hey, Diane," Lewis exclaimed, yelling again from the basement office, "You've got to see this thing that Gigot found!"

Diane twirled her facial expressions before Gigot knowing that if Gigot had brought something to Lewis that was at all of the scientific kind, Lewis would not let it go until she went down there to see what he was talking about. She loosened the back of her apron and threw it down on the counter pointing her finger at Gigot saying,

"Now if this dinner gets cold, it's your fault." Wincing her eyes and smiling at Gigot, they both knew she meant no malice in the comment. Gigot volunteered to work his kitchen magic to keep the pasta, crawfish and creole sauce warm while she trudged down the stairs to involuntarily see what it was that was so important as to make all of the work with dinner second place.

When she walked into Lewis' office, Lewis was beaming from ear to ear and wiping tears from his eyes.

Diane looked intently at Lewis and remarked, "What have you and Gigot gotten into?"

"Take a look at this Diane, I'll be right back!" Lewis said as he darted out of the room to the bathroom to get himself cleaned up for dinner. He remained in the bathroom long enough for Diane to open the container and see what she was going to see for what she was going to see was for her and only for her. When Lewis went back into his office, he found Diane sitting in his chair with her head propped in her arms resting on his desk.

He stood there at the door, breathing deeply waiting for her to arise, but not saying a word. He walked over to her gently touching her shoulders as only a real man could touched his wife. He pulled back her hair and said, "I love you, Diane, I always have."

Diane, having already placed the top back onto the container, lifted her head and swiveled the chair around and with a beam of sunlight on her face, jumped up into his arms and squeezed Lewis with a hug that would last for eternity.

After some time, Diane screamed to Gigot upstairs, "Gigot, I knew you were up to something and I knew if anybody could find what you found it would be you!"

Gigot was still standing at the doorway of the kitchen area where it headed to the top of the stairs and gleamed for he knew the water had said what it needed to say and Lewis and Diane had gladly received what it said.

Lewis and Diane rushed up the stairs to celebrate. Once in the kitchen, they all hugged and with huge tears rolling down Diane's face, she grabbed her glass of chardonnay and proclaimed as they all raised their glasses,

"Cheers to you, Gigot! But cheers to the water and cheers to life, Cheers!"

Laughing, they all took a sip from their glasses and took a sip once more, "Boy, this tastes good!" Lewis said to Gigot and Gigot replied,

"You always serve the best, Lewis! Now, let's eat that crawfish, I'm starving…"

And with that, Diane threw together the feast of feasts with warm pasta and crawfish that would knock any chef silly. They ate and feasted and drank and cheered all the while talking of yesterday's memories and of all their children's achievements. One by one each child was brought up and bragged on and they all thanked God for their children and the love they had shared in their lives. How wonderful the time was and how wonderful the peace was that had overtaken them all…oh, how wonderful it was indeed.

After cleaning up the dishes from the scrumptious meal, Lewis and Gigot meandered over to the family room and vegetated in front of the new components that Lewis had just created for testing purposes. It was the latest gadgets known to technology and as they sat there with their Panor glasses on, Lewis asked Gigot,

"What are you planning to do with that water?"

Gigot breathed a deep breath and responded,

"I was hoping you could help me with that, Lewis. Were you able to tell how it becomes a mirror?"

"No, I didn't see that, all I saw was what it showed me, I didn't know it could do that."

"I have two other containers out in the car, I can go and get them and maybe we can spread the water out on a surface and I can show you what it does," Gigot said, hesitating to get up as a result of their interest in this Panor movie. Lewis had just put in a new vision projector that could display images that had the look of looking out a window on a clear day.

"I've never seen anything like this, outside of real life, that is, Lewis, what do you call this contraption, it's certainly beyond any blu-ray I've ever seen?"

"It's called the New Vision Optic, I'm testing it to see what it does to the eye and the mind as it is viewed from this particular projector. What do you think so far?" Lewis inquired.

"Like I said, it's like nothing I've ever seen so far, who makes it?"

"I did," Lewis said smiling his Mona Lisa smile. "You're the only one that's seen what it can do. It can turn a blu-ray disc into a lifelike image. I built it with that in mind."

"It's like we're in the room with them on the screen, how did you do that?" Gigot continued reaching his hands out to touch the images portrayed in front of him for they seemed to be in the same room with the actors' images in panoramic view. It was as though they were in the motion picture themselves. This was beyond 3D and rendered 4D unecessary.

Lewis simply chuckled and as Diane was standing at the back of the room, Diane inquisitively said, "Well, I don't see a thing. You two are just sitting there with those new-fangled glasses that Lewis just created and I don't see a thing from where I'm standing."

Lewis joked with Diane and said,

"Diane, you have to try these glasses on first, you won't see anything without these glasses. From your perspective, nothing is there because you have to have the right lens on. You could stand there all night and not see what we see because the instruments only work together in tandem and if you don't use the glasses, you don't see the image that's being projected from the screen."

Diane calmly walked over to Lewis and Lewis gently handed her a pair of the Panor glasses that he had developed in his basement laboratory. She sat down beside him and placed the glasses on her face and gulped. She immediately took the glasses off her nose and then raised them back up to sight and did the same thing thrice more not believing what she was seeing. There was indeed a panoramic image shown in the room from the projector that Lewis had built, but it could only be seen with the glasses on. With the glasses in place, she could see the panoramic images as though she were in real life as the movie was projected back off the screen into the room. If she removed the glasses from her sight, she didn't see a thing.

After a few minutes of this going back and forth in curiosity, doubt and disbelief, she finally relaxed and sat back on the sofa beside Lewis and watched the movie…if that was what you'd call it.

She breathed deep sighs of relief as she watched the movie through the new fangled lense and then to her husband as they both sat there mesmerized by Lewis' own invention. She leaned over to Lewis and gave him a hug and a tug on his arm realizing that she was probably looking at history being made here because she was looking at something the naked eye could not see, but with the help of the glasses that Lewis had made, real life was made out into the room and she found herself enthralled by the images. She had been taken to a place where only a visionary could envision the future to be and the only way to see it was through a new lense.

## Chapter 23

## If the Truth Be Told

Early the next morning, Gigot found himself on the road again heading back home through the northern end of Mississippi where he had met Apostle Hananiah's spirit and he knew he didn't want anything to do with that. He continued to travel southward through the hills of Alabama and desperately needed another stop. It was about the time of church time this sunny Sunday morning and even though Gigot simply had no need of going into a building to hear from God, he decided to give it a go at a traditional looking church in a town called Alabaster, just south of Birmingham.

Gigot was so joyfully happy inside that he was beaming. He was in communion and nothing was ever going to drive him away again from his dwelling with this water and the possibiltiy of sharing the water with anyone that would care to listen. He thought,

"Maybe this is the place to start…a place where people at least want to hear from God." So, he jumped out of the van excited about the prospect of being able to talk with someone about this water of life.

As Gigot approached the front doors, he realized that they had started right on time and the deacons were standing at the back to walk down to receive the day's offering. He waited at the front doors of the sanctuary with the deacons, mostly because they wouldn't let him in as he might disturb the hymn that was playing and so that they could walk down on the last stanza.

They told him to wait at the door and when they got back after the offering was collected, they would then walk him to his seat. For the life of him, he couldn't understand why they wouldn't just let him sit down on the last pew where there were plenty of seats, but he obliged them with cooperation and a tremendous smile.

He overheard one deacon ask another,

"What is he smiling at?"

The other deacon responded,

"I dunno, but keep an eye on him, he seems to be up to something."

In Gigot's hearing of these rather unseemly comments, Gigot choked with laughter on the inside for he did not take them personal, but thought the gentlemen to be quite predictable in their demeanor and tasks. It was easy to see that they had practiced their religion this way for years and they didn't care for interruptions.

As soon as they returned to the back of the sanctuary with the offering plates, one of the deacons said to Gigot,

"Follow me to the front."

Gigot had no idea that their custom was to have guests and visitors sit on the front pew so that the pastor and everyone else in the church would easily know who they were in order to greet them right after the service was over with. As the two men were walking towards the front, a young man got up and spoke from behind the pulpit with a warm Alabama drawl,

"Today's Bible reading comes from a place we all know too well, it's Matthew 26, verses 6 through 13. Today is our annual sermon message on "The Woman with the Alabaster Box" and our Pastor will be preaching his sixth message on this passage to celebrate as many years as he has been here. Let's all stand for the reading of the Word,"

After pausing for a few moments for everyone to stand, he read,

"And when Jesus was in Bethany at the house of Simon the leper, a woman came to Him having an alabaster flask of very costly fragrant oil, and she poured it on his head as He sat at the table. But when his disciples saw it, they were indignant, saying, 'Why this waste? For this fragrant oil might have been sold for much and given to the poor.' But when Jesus was aware of it, He said to them, 'Why do you trouble this woman? For she has done a good work for me. For you have the poor with you always, but Me you do not have always. For in pouring this fragrant oil on my body, she did it for my burial. Assuredly, I say to you, wherever this gospel is preached in the whole world, what this woman has done will also be told as a memorial to her." This reading is from the New King James Version of the Holy Bible, may God bless His Holy Word and all God's people said…"

"Amen!" the entire congregation replied in timely unison and sat down.

Gigot had found his place alone on the front pew and as the Pastor stood up to walk to the pulpit, he acknowledged Gigot sitting there and gave him a smile. Gigot smiled back at the Pastor and looked around the sanctuary a bit and saw that everyone was looking at him. He just Mona Lisa-ed a smile back at the crowd and began to feel uncomfortable like something was about to happen. His eyebrows began to twitch involuntarily like they would when he would find himself unwarily stressed out for some unknown reason. The Pastor nodded at him and smiled again, but Gigot discovered that the man wasn't smiling at Gigot, but at the woman sitting directly behind Gigot on the second row.

"I love this passage of scripture…about the wonderful woman with the alabaster box," the Pastor commented as he raised his hand and waved it in the air as though there was some fragrance already in the air.

"Can you smell the fragrance, my people? Can you smell the fragrance of God in the room?" he continued on and there seemed to be quite a bit of abrupt movement going on behind Gigot as it flowed across the sanctuary.

The rustling of the people was becoming quite obvious and even the woman behind Gigot was clearing her throat and coughing as though she were trying to get the attention of the oblivious pastor that was so into his sermon, he was not paying attention to the restlessness of the crowd.

Suddenly a jolt went up the back of Gigot's head as it felt like someone had just cut him with a knife straight up the back of his neck through the back of his head. Gigot lunged forward in pain and immediately turned his head backward as the woman behind him had abruptly jumped to her feet and sliced the back of Gigot's head with her huge diamond ring. Gigot quickly began rubbing the back of his head to see if he was bleeding, but realized that she had not broken the skin. She unwittingly ripped up through the back of his head with her wedding ring as she jumped from her seat in the pew.

"What the hell at you doing?" she yelled at the pastor, "this is what you preached last year on this passage and the year before that and the year before that!"

The woman had been sitting alone and Gigot immediately surmised by the tone of the woman and the look of the pastor, that she had to be the man's wife who evidently had tired of her husband's repetitive message.

"Sit down, woman, you're out of order!" the pastor retorted and as he did so, the other women in the church began moving and shuffling in shock as to what was transpiring in their beloved church on this sunny Sunday morning. The men had not said a word as the women were coughing and clearing their throats as a sign to the pastor that all of this was completely uncalled for.

The pastor continued, "I told you this morning, you witch, that I'm not putting up with your shenanigans anymore, you don't tell me what to do…"

And about that time, the woman behind Gigot had gotten her purse in her hand and threw it at him, yelling,

"You are not my husband, you son of a…well, it's not your mother's fault you're such a selfish pig! But maybe it is…"

"What's gotten into you this morning?" the pastor interrupted, "You just can't stand it when we all get together to talk about the Lord and His goodness. It's His beautiful fragrance that you're jealous of, isn't it, you tiresome hag, and I'm not going to stand for you any longer, ya hear? I'm the man of God, I tell you, not you, you wicked wench!"

"Wicked wench, you godless man of the devil, you're a devil in sheep's clothing," the wife fell forward as she tried to get out from behind the pew where she had been sitting.

Gigot's head fell forward because he did not want to be involved in a husband and wife argument, let alone in a sanctuary where the 'fragrance of the Lord' was supposed to be exuded. Gigot was embarrassed for the two of them, but he was also embarrassed for the church as they sat there dumbfounded by the way their beloved pastor and his wife addressed one another.

As they berated one another with one name after another, the young man who had read the scripture quietly stepped down from the pulpit chairs. All of this was no joke and it certainly wasn't a bad play gone bad; this was all for real and evidently how they must talk to each other when they're alone.

Other women had already stood up to help the unhappy wife as their husbands had moved forward towards the pulpit to intercept the pastor before he could say another word.

"What's happening here?" one of the men questioned the pastor as he approached the front. "What has gotten into the both of you? Is this how you really are when you're at home? Is it, pastor?"

The wife had already collapsed on the floor in front of the pulpit and the pastor stood in a daze as though he had just come out of a trance. Huge tears started flowing from his eyes and as he looked around the room, the people both standing and sitting were struck with shock as to what had just transpired in their hearing.

The room fell silent with the exception of grave tears and weeping from the majority of the women in the room as the men mostly stood with their heads drooped in shame. It was as though they all had just been found out a most heinous crime and the chief sinner was the pastor, but none of them were exempt. The whole room of folk began weeping as the pastor stood there alone, not understanding what had just transpired.

"What is happening?" the pastor asked amiss with no one desiring to answer him due to their own self-incrimination.

Gigot looked up, turned and glanced over the room of people and every single one of them were crying and weeping from the place of seeing themselves in their pastor's heart. It was as though they had all just been found out through the mouths of their pastor and his wife. Tears were flowing down Gigot's cheeks from the embarrassment and shame that was filling the room.

The pastor, now on his knees, crawled to his wife on the floor as she lay there struggling to breathe from the exhausting play that had just been played out in a very public forum. Gigot watched as the pastor crawled over to his wife and covered her with his person, apologizing profusely in the torment of his shame. He had been found out, humiliated and in the sadness of his weeping he looked in Gigot's direction and said,

"Who are you? Who are you that you would visit us today in our hour of torment?"

The entire room had taken on an air of humiliation and the people shuttered at his words for they knew that something far different than anything they had ever experienced had just occurred. They all looked at Gigot in wonder and with swollen eyes spiritually seeing that Gigot was no longer sitting alone in the pew, for there was another sitting there beside him that seemingly held their hearts in his hand.

They all moaned as they wept in their humiliation and then the air that filled the room was filled with the fragrance of spikenard.

Each man who had a wife there wept with their wives and covered them in flowing hugs of repentance and tears. Eventually the cries subsided to whimpers and signs of relaxed peace. Gigot took a few moments to touch the heads of every man there even though no one looked up. He prayed as he walked out of the room that the spirit of the water would be well with these people and that forgiveness would rule their hearts in holy love.

## Chapter 24


## Another Fragrance


As Gigot made his way through the penitent believers and out the door of the church building, he couldn't help notice the air outside was filled with the smell of fresh fried chicken. The local fried chicken joint was across the street and the waffling aroma sent his taste buds to jumping. He left his car parked in the church parking lot since his senses had been overwhelmed with the smells of fried chicken and potatoes and by the time he had gotten inside the restaurant, he could tell that this was one of those home-cooking places that fried just about everything, except for the greens.

The hostess smiled her smile of welcome and exhibited a warm, hospitable style that made all of the patrons want to come back to restaurant just to see her. Friendly was an understatement for this gal named Gail for she had a smile that was larger than life. She knew exactly what to say to each person that walked through the door. She walked Gigot to his table and placed the menu on the table as he was sitting down.

"I see you've just come from the church across the street, how was church today? Did you leave early? I didn't see anyone else come out with you?"

She was about to ask another question when the waitress walked up and interrupted her,

"Now Gail, don't bother this poor man, I'm certain he's just been through hell and back and needs a good meal to get over what he's just been through…"

Gail looked at Delores, the waitress, and scrunched her eyes as if to tell Delores to shut her mouth with just a look. Delores must have gotten the message because the next words out of her mouth were, "I'm sorry, sir, that was an ugly thing to say about those people over there. My name's Delores, but you can call me Dee."

Gigot looked up with a raised brow and said, "Those people?"

"Yes, sir, I mean, those people over there that go to that church." Dee caught herself with her criticism and quickly changed the subject as she was feeling Gail's wrath back at the entrance area. Dee leaned over and whispered to Gigot,

"That's my sister, and me and her don't go to that church no more. They don't like me and I don't like them. I like the smell of fried chicken better than the smell they put off when they walk out of that high-fallutin' place. My mama and daddy go there, but they don't have much to do with me and my son, so I don't have nuttin' to do wit them and neither does Gail…most of the time."

Then she straightened her back and pleasantly smiled saying,

"Now what can I do you for today?"

About that time, some more people began pouring into the restaurant and Gigot recognized the majority of them, they were from the church. They had come in extremely pleasant and smiling and as Dee turned to see what was going on, she dropped her pen and pad and said,

"What the…"

A woman had broken through the rush of people and as Gigot recalled, it was the pastor's wife. By her demeanor, he didn't know why she was coming over to say, but 'Hello' wasn't one of them. He quickly surmised a surprise.

"Oh, Dee, I'm so sorry for the way I've been to you all these years, I'm so sorry…" and she fell at Dee's feet, weeping. Gigot could see out of the corner of Dee's eyes that her eyes were welling up with tears and all she could say was,

"Uh, Mama, uh, uh, what's happened Mama? Mama, are you all right?"

The pastor's wife shuttered again at the feet of her daughter, weeping, and as Dee stood there in amazement, other church members were gradually making their way into the restaurant, going from table to table, hugging and confessing their past gievances and faults to the people sitting at the tables. It seemed like they were all long-lost friends that they hadn't seen or communicated with in years and yet Gigot sensed that this town wasn't that big for that to have occurred.

Gigot sat there in amazement as each table experienced shock and surprise and apologies and confessions. Joy and gladness came to the people sitting at the tables and more and more people from the church were filling up the restaurant with tears, joy and eventual laughter.

As Gigot perused the room and he looked back at Dee and her mom. Dee had fallen to her knees to see in her mother's eyes the love that she had not seen since she had been a young child. They were sniffling and crying and apologizing and blowing and sniffling and crying. The whole room seemed to be in some kind of tizzy with all of the apologizing, confessing, hugging and renewing old aquaintances and friendships.

No one in the place was making any orders, so the kitchen cooks came out from behind the counter to see what was going on. They stood there bewildered because no one was working and no one was eating. They were all talking and celebrating their renewed friendships in love. Not knowing what to do, the cooks stopped cooking their fries and chicken and sat at the counter waiting for the waitresses to come back with some more orders of what to prepare for all of the people in the restaurant. Little by little, the fragrance of the room began to change. There were more and more people there from the little church and as they continued to express themselves, the aroma of the room did as well.

Since the fry cooks weren't in the back of the kitchen frying stuff, they could smell a different fragrance that had overcome the room. The restaurant had been changed from one aroma to quite another and smiles were all over the faces of the cooks as they watched the transformation of the town take place in one moment. It was the fragrance of the oil, but not the frying kind. This was the fragrance of the oil of change, of well-doing and the fruits of repentance. It was the fragrant oil of new life and fresh air. The air of the room was now spikenard and it was a pleasant air indeed.

As Gail watched all of this unfold from the entrance, the last man to open the door was the Pastor, her Dad. Gail took a deep breath not understanding all that was taking place and looked up at her Dad's swollen eyes for he looked like someone had just pummeled him with their fists.

They stood there, father and daughter, and as if through some transcendent reflection Gail could sense his remorse and repentance all at once. He had been a good Dad to her, but a horrible role-model in the home. She and Dee had left their mom and dad behind with their troubles because neither one of the girls could handle the hatred that had been spewed in the home and the hypocrisy that followed them everywhere they went.

The fragrance in the room had filled the air, but now with her Daddy there, a smile broke on her face as she saw the tears roll down his cheeks and she exclaimed, "Oh, Daddy, I love you." She threw her arms around his neck and shouted, "I love you, Daddy, I love you, I love you, I love you!"

## Chapter 25


## Anonymity


It took quite a while for everyone in the restaurant to be served that sunny Sunday afternoon in Alabaster. The kitchen ran out of chicken and just about everything else that day. The banana pudding was the first to go, but the patrons didn't seem to mind at all. Hours past and the joy and good times were expressed at every table. Gigot didn't know anyone there and no one knew his name or even asked. Different people from all over town had the filled the small restaurant with old acquaintance and renewing friendship. It was as though the fragrance in the air had moved from the church building to the restaurant and out into the township just by their willingness to set themselves aside and remember no more all the grievances of the past.

The air was filled with repentance, confession, love, forgiveness, fried chicken and potatoes. Everyone was enjoying the work of the water and hardly no one seemed to pay Gigot any mind.

Gigot enjoyed his meal, this feast of fried chicken, fried okra and squash, the best greens he'd ever had in his life and a super big bowl of banana pudding that someone dropped off at his table. He ate all he could and then some. Someone there picked up his tab, but he didn't know who. It was like being an invited guest at a wedding reception where everyone knew everybody else, except for him; he didn't know anyone. He was simply an invited guest to a homecoming reunion enjoying the flavors of the day.

He continued to peruse the room and saw laughter and good times in the making. Dee and Gail were no longer serving anyone, they had taken a place with their mom and dad and even Dee's son, Jacob, had come in from the back to sit down with his grandparents that he had not seen in years. Pastor Joe had gotten Jacob and was hugging him like there was no tomorrow. He seemed to be saying with all of his loving might, "I'll never let you go again."

Abigail, his wife, had both of her daughters on each side of her with them resting under her arms as she rested with them just like they used to do when they were little girls. The sentiment bore the same with Abigail for the fragrance of the water had touched her and made her into a brand new woman. Her eyes gazed across the table at her husband that she no longer saw neither as a Pastor or a son of the devil, but the incredible God-given man that she had loved so many years ago.

Their eyes met in those moments, with all of the cheering, joy and laughter surrounding them, and the subtle solemnity of peace overcame them both as they had another chance at mercy with with each other, their daughters, their grandson and their future.

Gigot spied the room, politely got up and quietly left the room knowing that his bill had been paid and the waitresses well taken care of. He left the restaurant, gently closing the door with the ringing bell behind him and walked across the dusty gravel parking lot listening to the crunching gravel beneath his feet. The sound of the gravel was awfully loud as there were no other sounds to be heard. There was no traffic on the street since the probability that every known soul in the town of Alabaster was either in the restaurant or had already left to go home for their afternoon nap.

As was Gigot's custom to evaluate and reflect on what he would say or go through, he walked across the street realizing that he had not said a word about the water. In fact, he'd not said much of anything at all. No one had asked him his name or asked him to do anything for them.

He got back into his van trying to remember anything that he had said and he remembered talking to Dee, the waitress, but couldn't remember anything else that he might have said or done in the hours that were spent on that sunny Sunday day in Alabaster, Alabama. All he knew was that the air had changed around him and somehow people saw and heard something that they gladly received and then history was made in the town.

He turned the key in the ignition to start the car and then it struck him that he had not personally shared anything with these people.

He thought, "Maybe I should go and get someone's name just to have a contact for the future in order to see how everything plays out with the future of the town."

Yet, something far gentler moved his spirit to peace that their business was in the hands of someone far greater than he.

"But nobody knows who I am," he said in his mind. And as he spoke that in his mind, he sensed the silence in the car, for no one was there to answer the mood of his pride.

"So no one is supposed to know who I am. Is that it?" he spoke aloud in the car. The silence was deafening to him. He rolled his window down to hear some sound, even if came from the birds singing in the trees. The silence in the car seemed to be telling him something.

As he listened to the birds all around him, he glanced over to the front door of the church building and saw where both front doors had been left wide open. The parking lot was full and yet everyone he had seen earlier at the church service was now at the restaurant.

The loudest noise was coming from the restaurant's open front door where he saw Gail standing there, waving at him. She wasn't trying to get his attention to come back, but was waving good-bye with that totally infectious smile that everyone in the town dearly loved.

He stared at Gail, smiled and waved his right hand. Gail continued to wave, but waved in such a way that it gave Gigot some sort of loving peaceful good-bye in the spirit that said,

"It's time to go now. Put your foot on the pedal and go home."

Her shoulders shrugged a bit from a deep breath and she turned and walked back into the restaurant where cheers suddenly erupted from inside the door.

Gigot sat there, awestruck by the event of the day, realizing that absolutely nothing about this sunny Sunday in Alabaster was about him and his spirit smiled within him.

With that acknowledgement, he put his foot on the gas pedal and spun out of the gravel parking lot back onto the interstate heading south towards home. He was full in every way breathing in deep the warm air that flowed off the highway into the van and out again. He looked down at the containers of water that were safely in the seat beside him and as he breathed, he took in the idea of the air, that no longer was the water contained to a container, but had gotten into him and was being expelled into the world.

The rumble of the interstate and the warmth of the southern air were at his disposal. All was coming to pass as it was intended, it seemed, and the realization of the purpose of the water and his own purpose was coming to a divine union, of sorts, in a way that he didn't understand, but willingly accepted in his heart.

As he made his way towards home, his thoughts fled back to Pastor Joe and the look on his face when Abigail told him off in public and the ensuing fight that led to a breaking point that none of them saw coming. He laughed to himself at the spirit of the day and how he had finally realized that all he had to do was what he was supposed to do and go where he was supposed to go and say what needed to be said and the water would do the talking, the revealing, the mending and the loving. He smiled to himself as he drove and smiled once more knowing that his life had taken on new meaning and it didn't have anything to do with him for nobody knew his name.

## Chapter 26

## The Unexpected

As Gigot continued to head south into Florida, he called Victor Whitegold to set up an appointment to go and see him about the land. Victor was still playing coy, but accepted the invitation for a meeting and invited Gigot to meet him at his palatial estate east of Tampa. Gigot was overwhelmed at the prospect of meeting Victor and prayed the whole day through that the meeting would definitely be in the power of the water and that all would go well with what was desired of him.

Gigot figured life couldn't get any better than it was that day and as the day grew into night he kept driving to get home to see Pauline and the kids. Every so often he would look down at the water containers knowing that he was doing the right thing, but how it was all going to work out, he did not know. The end of the road couldn't come soon enough as he pressed forward pushing the van as fast as he could safely go. He arrived at midnight, tired from the drive, but excited about being home.

"Home…where life could begin again," he thought.

There was a dim light left on in the front living area as he arrived at the door. He quietly tip-toed through the house hoping not to awaken the kids, but also hoping that Pauline might still have some life in her from her day off with the kids. And, just as he was hoping, Pauline was awake and greeted him in the kitchen. She was smiling, brimming with joy that he had made it home safely and asked him if he needed something to eat.

After a good, long hug, they both sat down at the breakfast table to eat a bowl of cereal together and talk about the events of the kids and a little that had transpired around the house and the neighborhood while he was gone. Because work was still coming in the morning, Gigot didn't get into much about his journey, but promised Pauline that he would when they all got together for dinner the next night.

Of all the praying, thinking, analyzing and hoping that he had done about the purchase of the land and the water, he was still a little leery of talking with Pauline about what that meant and the depth of it. Pauline had mixed emotions about Gigot for she had truly missed him and could tell that there was something about him that was entirely different. But…there was also something that he seemed to be hiding and that made her shut down from anything positive that he might have said that night.

They both got cleaned up for bed for it was getting quite late and the morning with the kids getting to school on time was going to be an exhausting task with their expected excitement of seeing their Dad for the first time in more than 10 days.

Some folk would have simply taken the time off to reconnect, but not this family. They were stuck in the grind of doing the obligatory with the ought's and the should's and doing what was right and proper. Somehow, any excitement that they had both had in anticipation of Gigot's arrival back home had fizzled to nothingness and they both went to bed ambivalent; which was the case so many nights in their long, but not so long marriage.

Within a few minutes of touching the pillow, Pauline was asleep and Gigot lay there completely awake from the excitement, adrenaline, expectation and caffeine induced alertness.

"What just happened?" Gigot thought to himself.

Certainly, he could have planned this better, either by arriving earlier in the day or having made plans for everyone to take the day off on Monday…but neither he nor Pauline thought that far in advance.

"Why?" he thought to himself. "Why didn't I plan for everyone to take tomorrow off, including myself?"

Gigot sighed silently to himself knowing that he was the one responsible for not planning or communicating. He found himself being himself and he couldn't blame this major disappointment on Pauline or anyone else. It was his fault and now he was feeling really down and disappointed in himself for not planning properly.

"How in the world could I go from being truly free to coming home and being captured by my own lack of ingenuity? I'm so stupid!" he thought to himself.

He prayed aloud, "Father, please help me to get out of myself and to stay where You are!"

Pauline was not entirely asleep and heard what he'd just said to the Lord and wondered to herself that she needed to learn that lesson as well. She reached her hand over to Gigot and grabbed his hand and squeezed gently, then pushed her body over to his. They held each other as a husband and wife really should, then Gigot said,

"I love you, Pauline."

Pauline responded, "I love you, too, Gigot."

A peaceful rest came over the two of them as they held each other to sleep. Rest, real rest was in their home that night where there was absolutely no expectation but relaxation and for those few moments of sleep, nothing in the world mattered at all.

Neither one of them knew that that night Bessie had planned with Daniel and James to awaken a little early the next morning to surprise their Dad by jumping into their bed. The next morning, the kids crept crept up to the foot of their bed and shouted,

"Daddy, you're home, we love you, Daddy!" Then, they jumped into the bed with their mom and dad and loved on them, pouncing and jumping and loving all at the same time.

Each child gave memorable hugs to their mom and dad and told him how much they missed him the last 10 days.

Bessie said, "I can't wait to get back home from school today, will you be here for us, will you Daddy?"

"Yes, I will Bessie, I'll close the shop early today just for you all I can't wait to hug you all when you get off the bus. I'll be there for you when you arrive!"

Daniel and James hugged Gigot all the more and then Daniel asked his mom, "Will you be here, mommy, will you be here and put some film in the camera so we can take some pictures of you and daddy and and me and Bessie and James?"

Pauline replied, "Yes, Daniel, I'll be here, we'll all be here today when you get home from school and we'll take pictures and have a great time eating a great, big feast to celebrate your Dad being home."

And with that, they all hugged and hugged and hugged and told each other how much they loved each other over and over again. It was a great morning and Gigot was seeing where all things come in their season so was learning to enjoy the moments rather than dwell on regrets. He caught a glimpse of how expectation could cause frustration, but being in the moment, the each and every moment was, perhaps, the way to learn to be.

They all smiled their smiles of wonder and got ready for school and work. After they ate their breakfast together they went to work and to school with the expectation of an even more enjoyable time that afternoon. They were all looking forward to the kind of time well spent with the family that is the memorable kind...the kind that you want to remember and never forget.

## Chapter 27

## Due Diligence

That morning, Gigot went back into the store to get himself acclimated to the scheme of things of having to go to work and attempting to sell mirrors to the public while his interests had moved sharply towards investigating the purchase of the land and obtaining the rights to the lake water. He fidgeted while customer after customer came in the store, some buying, but most merely browsing, not knowing what they were looking for. He had an inside philosophy that he had learned from other boutique retailers that if a person came in merely browsing with no intent or purpose, they were the easiest ones to sell. He remembered one shop owner that owned a pretty large women's clothing boutique at the Outer Banks that boasted,

"If you're a customer without a purpose in mind, you're moving on dangerous waters, cause you'll buy just about anything that fancies you if you don't have a purpose in shopping."

He accomplished the reasoning of not taking advantage of people with selling them something that they didn't need for two reasons. He was too honest and he was a terrible salesman. He figured if someone needed a mirror, then they were in the right place, but he wasn't pushy or intimidating to folk who simply wanted to come into his store because they like being in there or they liked being around him. He spent so much time alone in the store that when anyone came in the store, he wanted to make a friend, rather than a customer. That philosophy doesn't bode well with an outstanding bottom line for sales productivity, but somehow they had had their provisions made and he considered that to be good and well and believed that he would always be provided for, as he and his family always had.

He decided to wait to call Victor until after he had a real heart to heart talk with Pauline and so he warmed up his lunch in the tiny microwave behind the counter and had just pulled the leftovers out that Pauline had provided from Sunday's lunch when the phone rang.

"Hello, thanks for calling the Looking Glass, this is Gigot…" Gigot said, but was preoccupied and ready to eat his lunch because it was hot yet now he had to talk to somebody.

"Gigot! This is Victor, Victor Whitegold," Victor stated rather curtly, "What are you doing?"

"Why, hello, Victor, how are you? I'm here at my store ready to eat some lunch," Gigot said respectfully.

"Why don't you come down here to my place and let's talk. Our place is Whitegold Estates in Sarasota, have you ever heard of Lake Stephen?" Victor inquired.

"I don't think so, we live in Tampa, just an hour north of you, it's a small world, isn't it" Gigot replied.

"What is that supposed to mean?" Victor sounded cold in his response. He really wasn't very good at talking to people and he didn't trust anyone. Gigot could tell that Victor was getting nervous again and his voice was shaking and quivering, but Gigot didn't know why, he thought that maybe he's just old and weak.

"Sir, I didn't mean anything by the comment, I was just remarking about how close we live to each other, it's relevancy to how great our nation is and yet we only live an hour from each other." Gigot was rather apologetic in his reply because he didn't want to mess this thing up like he'd done other things in his life.

"Well, are you coming down here or not?" Victor imposed sharply.

"Yes, sir, yes, I am, but I need to talk with my wife about all of this first to make certain she's ok with it all…" Gigot was the one becoming nervous now because he knew he had had his chances to talk this thing through with Pauline, but was afraid she would say 'no', then what was he going to do? Gigot sighed deeply and said firmly,

"Mr. Whitegold, I'm going to your house in Whitegold Estates and buy that land from you because it's what I'm supposed to do.

But first, I have to thoroughly discuss this with my wife, ok?"

Silence, of course, was on the phone, yet Gigot could hear Victor breathing heavily, taking deep breaths and sniffling. Victor had never been married and not since his father and mother had passed had he ever had the obligation to answer to someone. He did not understand why a man would have to answer to a woman for anything, especially if it had to do with money and land. That was a man's obligation and prerogative always and forever.

"How about this Friday, Gigot, at ten o'clock in the morning?" Victor was insistent on getting his way, but something inside of him wanted to give a little time to Gigot so that Gigot could get his affairs in order. This way, Victor wouldn't necessarily have to agree with Gigot's current philosophy on how to handle a woman.

"Do you have a pen and paper to write the address down?"

"Certainly, Mr. Whitegold, I do, but like I said…" Gigot couldn't finish his sentence from being interrupted by Victor.

"Son, let me tell you something that I want you to hear. The appointment is set for this Friday at ten o'clock in the morning. My address is 10,000 Whitegold Boulevard, Sarasota, got that!"

Gigot responded, "Yes, sir, but…"

Victor interrupted again, "Bring the $60,000 with you, you'll need it to show me you know what you're doing and you believe in what you're doing, do you understand me? I'll have the papers here along with my attorney, he'll be the witness."

Gigot felt like he was being railroaded into something devious all of a sudden because it sounded to him that as long as he produced that $60,000, that the land would be his, but what did that mean? That was all the money that he and Pauline had to their name and that was the net proceeds that would be coming out of his retirement account.

Then, he would be penniless, with nothing to show for his life but the house they lived in with a mortgage and a store full of mirrors that he didn't know if he would ever sell.

All of a sudden, a dreadful reality hit him square in the face and in the heart that said,

"What are you doing?" he thought to himself, "Are you crazy?"

As he was thinking this to himself, he had dropped the phone from his ear and he could hear Victor on the other end saying,

"Gigot, Gigot, are you still there? Gigot, do you hear me?"

"Yesss, yes, Mr. Whitegold, I'm still here, I'll be there Friday with the money. Is a cashier's check ok with you?" Gigot pleaded because there was no way he was driving to Sarasota with $60,000 in cash.

"Of course, young man, of course, it is. Now you go talk to that wife of yours and I'll see you here this Friday to take care of business. Understood?" Victor politely demanded.

"Understood, Mr. Whitegold, understood," and with that Gigot could hear the click on the phone and the microwave still beeping that his food was still ready to be eaten. His head was aching a bit, but he had lost his appetite. He pulled the leftovers out of the microwave and gobbled it down quickly knowing he needed to eat whether he felt like it or not.

No one came in the store that afternoon, so it gave him a little time to come up with a plan for dinner that night. He closed down the store early so that he could get to the bus stop on time to pick up his kids, but on his way home, he decided to go by the grocery store and purchase a couple of racks of baby back ribs.

"This will do nicely with all that we have to talk about tonight," he said to himself. "Everyone will love this and we'll picnic outside with some baked beans and slaw." He encouraged himself with those edible sentiments and raced to the bus stop right on time to get the kids.

"Just breathe Gigot, just breathe," he told himself all the way home or was it him telling himself that?

The evening was the best it had ever been at home with his family. With the smoked bar-b-q ribs, the love of his children and all of Pauline's attention directed right at Gigot, he couldn't see life getting any better than this. There was absolutely nothing that he would rather do or anyone that he would rather be with than his family and having fun. There was no homework that night, nothing but food, fun and cheer. It all happened too quickly and then it was bedtime and the kids went to sleep with hugs and kisses and 'I love you's' galore.

Pauline was back in the kitchen tidying up and as Gigot walked in the door, Pauline inquired,

"So, Gigot, tell me about this land that you're wanting to buy. It must be something for you to want to buy land out in Wyoming, cause I've never thought about moving out there. It's not something we've ever discussed and all of our family is close by…I just don't think that I'd be happy out in Wyoming, why would you ever want to live out in Wyoming?"

Gigot had learned, or was learning to keep his mouth shut and allow Pauline to talk and ask all the questions she needed to, but she was going down a road that he had not even considered.

She continued, "What is it about this land that you feel like you have go out and be gone for 10 days and all you want to do is to buy a piece of property that I certainly do not want to move to? What does that land have that no land around here has?"

She waited for a moment for him to respond and just as he had taken a breath to respond, she started up again, "Tell me, ok, tell me, what did you do out there that would make you want to make us sell our home and move to only God knows where, that, well, I'm not moving, nope, I'm not moving again, not right now and certainly not to Montana or Idaho…or, Wyoming, that's it, I'm not moving to Wyoming!"

"Are you finished?" Gigot had grown tired of her speech, if that is what you'd call it and said,

"Pauline, I do want to buy some land out in Wyoming, but I never, not once said that I wanted to move out there. The land isn't about moving our family our to Wyoming, it's about a lake full of water that I can't explain, but if you'd listen for just a bit, you might be able to make some sense of it."

Pauline's chin schrunched and puckered as though she was listening and giving Gigot the benefit of the doubt, but with a great deal of animosity.

Then she asked, "Why do you have to do this? You get a free ride to take some days off and then you have to take more. Now you want to buy land. You've sunk our money into that mirror store and now you want to spend our last dime on a lake out in Wyoming! What's wrong with you, are you insane?"

By this time, Pauline was yelling and Gigot began to yell himself,

"I told you I didn't want to move out there, you got that! All I want to do is to buy the land for the lake water that's on the land, that's all!

"It's to protect the water there, that's all. It's so that the water will be able to fulfill its purpose, you see, the water has purpose, just like I have purpose!"

Pauline had had enough and retorted, "A lake has purpose? Water from a lake out in Wyoming has purpose? Water? Water? Gigot, what is wrong with you, you are insane, I knew it, you are INSANE!"

Pauline threw up her hands in exasperation as Gigot had gone out of the room to go get something. Pauline thought he was just being rude and walked off from her in mid-speech and now, she was really angry.

"Where did you go, Gigot, come back here, I'm not through with you…Gigot! Gigot? Where are you?"

Gigot's heart was depressed as he was walking through the hallway corridor and back into the light of the kitchen. It had already gotten to be late and here they were again having an important discussion about something that Gigot felt deeply about and they were both tired and getting very angry with each other. They just couldn't seem to get it right. They were always on some other page with each other and of all the things to be wrong about in life, Gigot knew that this wasn't wrong.  He just thought that if the water had changed his life and all the lives it had come into contact with, why in the world hadn't Pauline changed?

When he walked back into the kitchen, Pauline was exhausted from the day and the hour. She was so very tired of arguing with Gigot. It seemed that was all they ever did, no matter how good a time they might have earlier in the day…it was as though their lives were doomed to hypocrisy and toxicity and so she was sitting at the table with her head resting in her folded arms on the table. It was late and she needed to go to sleep. He had gone to get a container of the water.

 Gigot didn't say a word, but sat the container of water down in front of Pauline's head. He opened the container and the water itself looked a little different, but still just as clear as clear could be. Pauline didn't move, but just sat there.

Gigot was too tired to face another battle over water. Besides, this was the water that changes lives into something far greater than they could ever imagine and they were arguing over it.

"Imagine that!" he thought to himself in a rather confounded sort of way.

"Imagine that!" something said back to him.

"What?" he thought.

"What did you say?" he didn't know if he was talking to the water, a spirit or to himself. He stood there over Pauline as she had actually fallen asleep with her head in her hands and came to the conclusion that nothing had changed.

He hadn't really changed, he was still Gigot. The room here in his own house had not changed. Yes, the kids were overwhelmingly happy for the last two days, but Pauline hadn't changed, she was still Pauline… argumentative, uncooperative, undeniably the obstinate rock that he knew as Pauline. And the worst part of it…he was stuck with her.

As he stood there, the water spoke and said, "Well, she's stuck with you, too, and everything you just said about her goes for you, too, you unchangeable boulder!"

Needing to breathe, he sat down to listen rather than speak and he sensed the water wooing and speaking once again to him clearly, "I am the change and without me you cannot."

Gigot sat in silence as he was being reprimanded and rebuked for being himself. He could hear himself breathe so loudly, he annoyed himself.

"That's how I feel when you pick yourself back up, Gigot…annoyed, grieved is more like it. It's up to you, Gigot, you can be you or you can be what I have chosen you to be and remade you to be. You have to let your self go. Understand? You are your problem, not Pauline, not your kids, not your business or your lack of money…you are your problem."

The water continued, "To your mind, it seems that I am sitting here in between the two of you, but that is not accurate. You are standing in the way betwen her and me and it's because you are more devoted to your principles and your way than you are to me. This is not how I work. There have been and will be times when I come between people, but it will be because the one person has submitted completely and has allowed me to woo another yet unresponsively. The time is coming when others will attack you personally because of my wooing, but that is not what is happening here. I am not here to divide you from Pauline, but one thing I do is divide your spirit from your soul so that you can know the difference between my voice and your own."

And with that, there was silence.

Gigot thought within himself that whatever came or whatever change there needed to be made, it was up to him, first and foremost, always and forever. He couldn't drink the power of the life-changing water and remain who he had always been. He had to accept the gift of life that the water gave and not return the water to a container when he wanted to pick himself back up again. He realized that he was keeping the water in a container, but that was not the purpose of the water. The water needed to be free…free to free not just him or Pauline, but to free everyone it came in contact with.

Accepting this as fact in faith, he sighed himself away once again. He slid the small open container towards the top of Pauline's head. He placed his hand in the water and with it dripping slightly from his fingers he touched the top of Pauline's head. Nothing happened and Pauline did not move. She sat there asleep.

Gigot had to continue to learn that it was the work of the water that did the work of the water and not him. He had to allow the work of the water to work its work in him and only him and the fruit of that work would be that it worked its work and the evidence would be exhibited in his life and not some act of piety or religious hocus pocus. He realized what he had just done and that was to think he could use the water to touch someone and some miracle would occur. That was not how the water did its work. He failed to remember that the water was the one to show the person all that they are.

He got up and placed his hands onto Pauline's shoulders and leaned down and slid his arms around Pauline whispering,

"I love you, Pauline, I always have."

Pauline breathed a breath of alertness, stretched her arms about, straightened her back and turned her chair around. She stood and gave Gigot a resounding and loving hug.

"I love you, too, Gigot."

"What's this? Is this the water from the lake?" she glanced at it sitting still on the table.

"That's special water, you know, Gigot. You know it has to be protected for as long as we live."

Gigot raised his left eyebrow, tilted his head and was astonished at the words that had just come from Pauline's mouth.

"Gigot, what you've done is good. This is good."

Gigot stood there amazed and looked at the water and its transparency. He took Pauline by the hand, turned out the lights in the kitchen and they both walked together arm in arm up the stairs; something they had never done before.

## Chapter 28

## It's Not What It Seems

The moments passed too quickly in the following days and soon it was Friday morning and time for Gigot to make his way to Sarasota to visit with Victor regarding the land purchase. Gigot and Pauline had come to a consensus about the land and the rights to the water. They agreed that it was purposed for them to buy the land even if it meant giving up everything they had in order to obtain it. It wasn't about the money, it was about the water and the treasure they believed that it possessed. There was something peculiar in their time together that week. Everything seemed to work according to plan and even Gigot had not had any problems obtaining the proceeds from their retirement account. The total amounted to $61,450 and that was sufficient to meet the $60,000 proposal set forth to Victor Whitegold as long as he kept his end of the deal.

There was only an hour's travel from where Gigot lived to get to the Whitegold Estates in Sarasota. Gigot mapped his course and took off believing that this was what he was supposed to be doing. He called Alfred and Floyd along the journey and talked with them all. Their support and encouragement was overwhelming to Gigot and so the ladies said they would give Pauline a call to encourage her as well. They were all praying in one accord that the Lord's purposes would be fulfilled. That was their custom as Gigot and Pauline were quickly learning.

For Alfred and Pete and Floyd and Ruth, life and prayer to them was not about the things they desired, but what the water had purposed to do through them. The water would provide the manner in which all things would be accomplished.

That was how they lived their lives, at least for now. It had not always been that way, but once touched by the water, the desire of the water became their aim and their purpose.

Gigot was learning the course of following as well…learning to lay down what he thought he needed for the purpose in which he was created. It had come time for him to live and breathe with the water's wooing and leading.

As he traveled along the highway to Victor's, he began to kick himself in his mind because he should have packed a container of the water to go along with him. He could remember that one container was in the kitchen and one container was in their bedroom, but he simply could not recall where the third container of water was. It might be in the family room or it could be in one of the kids' bedrooms, he just could not put his finger on where the third container was.

The closer he got to Sarasota, the more anxiety he began to feel. The homes and mansions began to get bigger and bigger and there didn't seem to be any poor areas where he was going. Here, everyone seemed to be rich, or at the very least, far richer than he could ever think of becoming.

Everything was about the aesthetic, beautiful and pristine and when he drove up to the gates of Whitegold Estates he was entering where some of the richest lived and breathed. Victor had given him a code to enter the gated estates where every home looked oddly similar. It wasn't that the homes were similar; it was the expansive landscaping that was perfectly identical. Gigot had done a little investigating himself into the Whitegold Estates and discovered that the land mass had been created and developed by Stephen Bentley, Victor's father. Each palatial estate was developed from ten square acres each on perfectly flat land and each mansion was required to have a minimum of 10,000 square feet in the erecting of their homes. Each home was required to be placed directly in the middle of the property so as to give the impression that each home was the same distance away from the boulevard.

As Gigot drove down Whitegold Boulevard, there was an in-road to the right with a glorified median separating the in and the out road.

Each estate had rich rod iron through the front of their property. All had tremendous iron gates and all of the mail box stantions were made of heavy river stone that set to the right side of each gated entrance. All of the front yards had perfectly sown and mown grass and it seemed that they all had been mowed by the same mower on the same day with the light and dark shadows glistening in the sunlight and the residing morning dew.

Gigot had never seen anything quite like this, not even on television or in one of those architectural magazines. He had never seen anything quite so immaculate and perfectly coordinated in a neighborhood. He was thinking that this must be the real life of the rich and famous, but he didn't know they lived in Sarasota, Florida. The only difference in all of the properties was that Victor Whitegold's estate was at the end of the boulevard and the street ended there with his twenty acres of land instead of the mere ten.

Driving slowly to the end of the boulevard, Gigot approached his destination and was finding it difficult to comprehend and describe in his mind what he was seeing. The vastness of these properties was breathtaking and yet there was something a bit strange about it all. Once entering the Estates gate, he had not seen one human.

He had seen open land gated by rod iron, all the same and all the same kept. Everything was perfect and pristinely procured and managed. And, all led to the originator and developer of the plan, the Whitegold home, located at 10,000 Whitegold Boulevard at the end of Whitegold Estates.

Gigot slowly and quietly pulled up to the huge iron gates, rolled his window down in the van and pressed the buzzer type doorbell to the left of the outside gate. There was a speaker there for communicating and Gigot sat there and waited patiently for a response. After waiting for a few minutes with no response, Gigot decided to press the buzzer again and again he sat there for another couple of minutes with no response. He checked his map and made sure that he was at the right place and laughed to himself in his doubt that he couldn't be in the wrong place…not with entering the right code into the front entrance. Still, in the silence, he doubted.

At least five minutes passed and as he was about to press the buzzer one more time, the tall, heavy iron gates opened with a loud and voracious squeaky squeal as they were moved by motors that sounded like they weren't quite up to the task of opening one more time. He proceeded forward with reserve because he still had not seen or heard anyone since entering the estates. He marveled as he drove down the wide drive as each blade of grass tended to guide him to the place of pristine perfection.

A colorful, flowering garden awaited him in the middle of the circular drive that sported a fountain of water that seemed to spray at least twenty feet upward. The home exuded power and magnificence yet was built in a style that he had never seen. This was the aristocrat's home of the 1930's and 40's and it was so utterly extraordinary that no other home in the estates could possibly be like this one.

There were things on the property that he had seen before, but not of the size and magnitude of this estate. The cemented growling lions parked at the front door were intimidating and yet Gigot could only catch a glimpse of their powerful glory because they were so tall and huge.

"Who could have made something so large?" he thought to himself and "Why? What was it about that era, the 1920's and 30's that caused people to create things that were so far larger than life?"

In his investigation of the Whitegold Estate and name, he had also discovered how the Whitegold's had obtained and accumulated property back in the day at the expense of those who had to sell what they had in order to survive. He found it entirely extraordinary that Mr. Samuel Whitegold had basically taken from the rich as much of their wealth as he could store because they needed to buy the essentials in life during the depression. He had prospered where the majority had failed. He had paid pennies, nickels and dimes on the dollar for prized possessions, artifacts and antiques that the wealthy class had collected in their estates over generations and over a few short years had taken in a haul that was unprecedented in his day.

The front door entrance was just the beginning of going back in time to an era between the late 1800's. The huge wooden doors were so thick it wouldn't have done any good to knock on them. There was no doorbell, but there was a brass door-knocker in the middle of the right door that was heavy enough to make quite a pound when you lifted and released it to make the owner aware of your visitation. Gigot lifted it twice and allowed the resound of the solid brass clacker announce his arrival. He stepped back a few paces as was his custom upon visiting strangers.

Much like the wait at the gate, he waited and then stepped back up to the door-knocker and knocked twice more. Just then, the door began to creak and he could hear a deep, sullen voice in the crack of the door saying,

"You're so impatient, has no one taught you any manners or any level of etiquette?"

As the door opened, Gigot got a whiff of dust blowing out the door and the taste of old air exhumed as the door opened wider. Gigot could taste the air coming from inside and tried to smile, but his wits got the best of him and then he sneezed in Victor's direction as he opened the door completely.

"My good man, do you have any manners at all?" Victor said disparagingly.

"Oh, I'm so sorry, sir, please forgive me, I'm Gigot Bengal…" Gigot replied.

"Yes, I know who you are and I'm Victor Whitegold, please come in! The sun is too bright today, it hurts my eyes," Victor said, trying to be polite and hospitable, but it obviously wasn't his nature.

"What is that you're driving?" Victor asked.

"It's a minivan, sir…" Gigot responded.

"A minivan, what's a minivan? Seems odd to me, please come in." Victor insisted and as Gigot stepped inside, he was astounded as he was seemingly walking into a museum of historical proportions.

Gigot took a breath and dropped his lower jaw in awe of the greeting room presentation. It was as though he was on a movie set for some time back in history, but could not place the era. His knowledge of period furnishings was lacking, although he had had some very familiar mirror frames much like what he was seeing as he followed

Victor slowly away from the door.

The flooring was pure marble, still shiny, like new, but very dusty. There were oriental rugs placed strategically on the floors and European tapestries on the walls with precious artifacts of days and eras long time passed. Not only was the entrance area flooring made of pristine white marble, but every table in the room was marble of different textures, shapes and designs. A remarkable porcelain monkey was sitting on the table to the right that had large spirited eyes that led Gigot to believe that he would be watched while in the home. Much further into the entrance way and directly ahead, the marble stairwell swirled with curled rod iron, upwards to rooms that he would not see.

To the left, was the drawing room where it was impossible not to notice the height of the ceiling on the lower level. The ceilings must have been 20 feet high with rich textures and dark colors. The drawing room floor had a rug that dominated the room with a smattering of pieces of dark wood furniture and thick leather covered sofas and chairs. Gargantuan paintings were on the wall, family portraits they were, as Victor described to him. There were the portraits of his grandfather Samuel Whitegold, the patriarch, his beloved wife, Elizabeth and his father and mother, Stephen and Sarah Bentley. Gigot was already lost in the place and had it not been for Victor's voice leading him forward and around, he would tripped over the head of the bear rug that lie waiting at the fireplace at the floor of the main side wall. Victor had not even asked Gigot for a tour of what seemed to be a museum, but that was not how Victor saw it. Victor was trying to impress Gigot with all that they owned and he had left the hospitable musings out, so Gigot was simply following Victor around not realizing what they were actually doing.

One of the things that Gigot had taken note of was Victor's inability to communicate effectively. Victor was rather abrupt and moved at his own pace walking about the home with the aid of a very strong cane. Victor had lived alone the latter portion of his life and, for the most part, had not inherited the vibrant and lively personalities of his mother or father. Victor was the epitome of inward thinking and introverted communication, which was to move without saying where he was going unless it moved him inwardly to say something specific. Some used to think him extremely arrogant, but arrogance was not his issue in life, it was his uncanny intelligence and presumption that everyone else should know what he already knew and so he didn't tell people what he was doing or where he was going or not much of anything. He expected people to use their minds as he did and he thought that it was beneath him to communicate the common things of life out of boorishness.

What was common to Victor, was severely extraordinary to others. The fact was that he didn't have commonality with anyone that he had met. Fortunately, when he was growing up, his mother and father were the socializing personalities of the region. Unfortunately, though, because they were so talkative, he never learned the need to communicate for himself.

All the while he was leading Gigot along in his tour of the mansion, he was sizing Gigot up regarding his intelligent quotient, his demeanor, but what he was basically after was Gigot's comportment. Victor was taught by his father to measure a man by his comportment and time would reveal in behavior and conduct what mere words often failed to do in truth. Victor was trying to find out who Gigot really was by taking him around his house and not saying much, if anything at all. Victor was almost annoyed at all of Gigot's gawking at the crystal, the chandeliers, the French porcelain and the authentic oil paintings of the French aristocracy of the $18^{th}$ and $19^{th}$ centuries. Gigot was about to touch the harpsichord, but didn't, to Victor's delight. After a short while, Victor found Gigot not saying a word either, but walking alongside him to help him with his weak legs.

As they were entering the library with its tall walls of mahogany and books used and collected from two centuries, Gigot asked Victor if he might intrude on his thoughts with a question. Victor did not respond immediately, but was quintessentially amused by the way Gigot phrased his query. And, as they proceeded to take their seated positions at the main desk in the library, Victor stated,

"This desk used to belong to the brother of Napolean Bonaparte. Treat it with respect."

And with that, they both sat down.

Victor, tired and breathing heavily, inquired,

"What is it that you have to ask of me?"

"Sir," Gigot said softly, "I saw where the patriarch of your family, Samuel Whitegold and his lovely wife, Elizabeth are your grandparents and I also saw that Stephen and Sarah Bentley are your parents. I do hope that you think me not presumptuous to inquire as to the nature of your last name for you call yourself Mr. Victor Whitegold. I would be led to believe as a result of seeing your father's portrait, that your last name should be Bentley."

Victor sat quietly in his favorite leather chair and did not move. Gigot could hear him breathe and could hear himself breathe as well. The silence in the hallowed hall was only moved by the dust particles in the stale air.

Then, Gigot straightened his back, realizing a thought, "Whitegold is your surname. It is the chosen name of your family and household!" Gigot tilted his head attempting to completely understand the spoken thought and the thoughts of the unsaid.

Little did Gigot know that he was playing chess with a champion and had just made a pleasant move of offense without being offensive.

Victor responded by tilting his head and said, "Well played, young man. Well played."

## Chapter 29

## It's Hardly Ever What It Seems

As Gigot sat there with Victor, he quickly thought back over portions of his life and brought his memories up to the present in order to really see where he was sitting. His thoughts were moving quicker than ever and his reflections on his thoughts went to pure analyzation. The construct of the house and of Victor was unlike anything he'd ever been a part of. Mind you, his thoughts weren't about the things in the home that made it a museum, it was about what everything in the home represented, including Victor.

Gigot watched Victor go through a wooden cigar box sitting on top of his desk and then Victor started mumbling something to himself that Gigot couldn't quite make out. Gigot sat still while Victor fumbled around his desk as he was looking for something particular. Gigot would have no idea what it was, let alone, where it was.

It dawned on Gigot that if Victor was initially playing some sort of game to be "well-played", then he could be in the middle of a thinking man's chess match, and if he is, then he must still be in the game and it's Victor's move…according to the way Victor was acting. Victor seemed out of place, yet he was only out of mind. Could it be that Victor's form of playfulness was illusion and distraction? With that in mind, Gigot asked,

"Victor, is there something I can help you find?"

Victor did not respond, but continued searching for whatever it was he was searching for.

"Ah, yes, I remember, it's broken…" Victor subsequently confessed. "I was looking for a glass, but I just recalled I had broken it a few days ago."

Gigot didn't know what was going on, other than he was in a room with the man that had Gigot's destiny in his hands, so he viewed this time as a time to remain silent and wait…seemingly wise, even though he didn't have a clue on what to do or what to say next.

After Victor's fumbling around and lighting his cigar, he sat back in his very comfortable leather chair and said,

"I need a drink!"

Shocked, because it was just a few minutes before eleven o'clock in the morning, Gigot responded with a deep breath and as he prepared to say what he was going to say, he opened his mouth and…nothing came out. Gigot was speechless for he actually had opened his mouth and could not say a word. Something was keeping him from talking. So, he just sat back as Victor had and relaxed. Gigot's mind immediately went into overdrive and the memories of his times of speaking irreverently or out of turn or just plain been stupid came to the forefront and he found himself wincing and being thankful that he was learning to keep his mouth shut...especially when he did not know what to say.

Victor proclaimed, "I said…I need a drink!"

"Can I help you in any way?" Gigot replied.

"Not unless you can bring Selby back…" and Victor's mind just trailed off to someplace that Gigot did not know, nor did he know who Selby was.

"Would you like to get some fresh air, Mr. Whitegold?" Gigot asked, trying to change the subject from drinking.

"Fresh air? Who said anything about fresh air? No, I would really like something to drink, if that's ok with you, would that be alright with you, Gigot? What kind of name is that anyway, Gigot? Where did you get a name like that?" Victor looked sheepishly inquisitive as though he already knew the answer, but how could he, Gigot had never told him, had he?

"Victor, is it alright if I call you Victor instead of Mr. Whitegold?" Gigot inquired.

"Certainly," Victor replied.

"The way I see it is this. This is your house and we're here to talk about your land. If you desire to have a drink, then who am I to stand in your way of having a drink?" Gigot said playfully.

Victor twirled around in his chair and gleefully said, "Now that's what I want to hear, straight talk from a straight man, you want one?" Victor jumped to his feet and immediately withdrew to the drawing room where he kept his brandy in the crystal decanters on the glass shelves. There was so much to see in the drawing room the first time Gigot hadn't noticed the small bar located in between some book shelves.

Victor asked Gigot, "Gigot, have you ever had anything that you loved and admired and then it just vanished?"

Gigot thought for a few moments and then answered, "Victor, the only thing I can think of at the moment is time."

Victor raised his brow and said, "Time, what does that mean?"

Gigot replied, "You see, Victor, I have a wife, Pauline and three adorable children and the one thing that I tend to have and yet it vanishes all too quickly is the time that I have to spend with my family."

Victor had already poured himself a brandy from a familiar glass and was about to take a sip when he managed to manipulate some weird facial expressions and sat the glass down.

"I don't think I've ever heard anyone say that before, Gigot. I've never had a family of my own and my own father and mother were always working or socializing, but you know, they always took me everywhere they went. By joe, I went everywhere with them, even to go and buy some of these old antiques. Do you think my father and mother thought that way?"

"Well, you did say that they took you everywhere they went. I know of parents who, if they have the chance, get a babysitter and leave their children alone as much as possible, but I don't think that way and it sounds like your parents didn't either if they took you everywhere they went." Gigot said pleasantly.

"I sure do miss them, my parents, I mean. After mother died, no one came around anymore. I was always with them so I didn't create a life of my own, I guess. Does that make sense to you, Gigot?" Victor asked.

"I guess so," Gigot continued, "But I don't think that was what they intended do you, Victor? I see it that if they took you everywhere they went and your dad taught you some things on the side, like business, then they were your life and your family and that's ok."

Victor had already sat back down again, scratched his head and said, "We're here to buy land today, aren't we? You know that land is worth 10 million dollars, don't you? Have a seat, Gigot."

Gigot sat down and all of a sudden, Gigot could feel the despondency settling in on him. He knew that all of this idea was too good to be true and reality was finally coming home to roost. He had been royally played by someone or something and now he was going to walk out of the room with nothing.

"Do you have that check for $60,000. Yes, I see by your facial expression that you do...the way I see it, Gigot, is that you give me that 60,000 dollar check and I will finance the rest over ever how many years you want it financed." Victor's demeanor had changed for some reason and Gigot was racking his brain to see if it was something that he had just said or if the real problem was that Victor was a liar and had never intended on selling him the land in the first place.

If that was the case, why was he here? Why was it that he was sitting here in this mansion with the possibility of owning the land and the water and the answer sitting just four feet from him?

Gigot figured he didn't have anything to lose, so he said,

"Victor, now I need a drink!"

Victor tilted his head and smiled a tiny smile like he wanted to chuckle, but that wasn't his style when he was seriously negotiating. One of the things he didn't realize though was the fact that Gigot was not going to give in to any terms of further servicing the land by way of a contractual agreement for further monies. He had not taken Gigot seriously in all that Gigot had communicated. Gigot was spent out and there was no other money and no other way of making any type of payments. But Victor had not been listening, he was still playing his game and it seemed to him that Gigot was playing along, albeit Gigot's own naïve style.

Victor said, "Well, Gigot, if we're both drinking on this deal, do you want a cigar to finalize the transaction?"

"Finalize? Uh, no, I'm not thinking that we're ready to do that, just yet. You do remember that I told you that we have no more money to offer for the land and that the 60,000 dollars is all we have to give. And another thing, where is the attorney that you said would be here to be the witness and draw up the papers?" Gigot stated firmly expressing the facts over to Victor again so as not to proceed any further with Victor's shenanigans.

"Umph!" Victor grunted displeased and took the poured brandy back from Gigot's reach. He sat both brandys back on the table and grunted again thinking to himself about what to say next. Then he turned back to Gigot and said, "Son, you're no match for this man and it's an insult to me that you think you can swindle me out of 1,000 acres of land for 60,000 dollars, I bid you good day!"

Without blinking an eye, Victor proceeded to walk out of the library rather briskly with his cane through the drawing room and then towards the front door. His paces got slower and slower the closer he got to the door because the game he was playing was risky, but deliberate. He was betting that Gigot would start telling the truth and give in with a better offer than 60,000 dollars and the closer he got to the door, the more he began to question his own gamesmanship and stopped when he put his hand on the solid brass door handle.

Victor's hand was on the door handle and his back was to Gigot when he said,

"One last chance young man to come clean and tell the truth. I know that no man wants to buy land that's worth 10 million dollars and only give 60,000 dollars for it without being some kind of fool or thinking I'm some kind of fool. You have so insulted me and my intelligence and not just that, but my business savvy and my family name. I know that the only thing I have left is a little bit of time and all of this that you see before your eyes. My father and mother built this development off of the great name of my grandfather. All that you see here and all that you saw there is all that I have left. There is no more money, just solid, hard assets that are worth millions…many millions and you want me to just hand it over to you. You are a worthless business man and I've grown very tired of your company. I would appreciate it if you left right now."

Victor said all of that without turning to look at Gigot because of the insult. He was not going to please the eyes of Gigot one more time. Victor kept his back to Gigot as he turned the doorknob and lifted the handle to open the door. Victor knew within the depth of what he was doing, but he just didn't care. He knew that if that 60,000 dollars walked out of the door, he might have to sell the precious goods within the house that his grandfather and father had procured over the many years of industrious business that they all had enjoyed. As Victor slowly opened the door, he moved slower and slower and Gigot thought to himself that he must be having a difficult time with the mechanics or the weight of the door.

Gigot didn't know what to say or do with the fact that Victor was asking for the truth. It dawned on Gigot that if there was ever a time to tell the truth, it was now. So, he said as Victor stood there with the door wide open,

"Victor, would you oblige me for a few more minutes so that I can further explain…"

Victor interrupted Gigot and stated, *"J'ordonne que tu me laisses tranquille!"* *(I demand that you leave me alone!)*

A tear floated down Gigot's cheek and as Victor was turning, he caught the tear in his periphery. Gigot didn't know exactly what Victor had just said, but he knew all the same. It was time to go. He trudged out to the van and heard Victor closing the door.

As he opened the door to the van and got in, he leaned over to the right passenger seat and tried to pick up some papers that had fallen onto the floorboard of the van. Bessie, Daniel and James had written notes for his journey that all would go well and that God would take care of everything. As he was picking up the notes, he noticed the tip end of a plastic container and immediately pulled it out from under the front of the passenger car seat. There it was…the third container of water. One of the children must have placed it in the car when they gave him the encouraging notes.

"The truth, Victor needs to know the truth!" Gigot said to himself,

"I've been hiding the truth from Victor all along, what have I been thinking? I've been trying to do this all on my own even though I professed to allow the water to have its way, I haven't even allowed the water to have a say today, what is wrong with me? When will I ever learn? When will I ever learn?"

Gigot sat in the van and wept and repented of taking himself back up and trying to do things on his own, especially when the water had proven over and over to know the right thing to do and the right path to take.

Gigot took the container of water and rushed back to the door and knocked with all of his might. He lurched towards the door-knocker and knocked and knocked and knocked. He waited a few moments and started up the knocking again. By now, he was perspiring all over and not only dripping with perspiration from his forehead, he was about to burst with tears over the possible joy of Victor's return to the door or about to burst with tears over his loss of opportunity and the closed door before him. Exhausted from emotion and the prayer the night before, he stumbled to his knees and knelt before the closed door and cried out in prayer, "You know that I need You, I'm sorry for getting in the way again, oh God, please forgive me..."

The large wooden door creaked its creak and slowly the door opened a tad and Victor stood in the open crack of the door and said,

"Gigot, what are you doing? You must know I don't allow beggars here, what are you doing?"

Without saying another word, Gigot slowly shoved the container of water towards Victor having to trust that this was the right thing to do since Victor was the true owner of the land; he was the rightful owner of the water. Gigot had to give it up…all of it, the knowledge of the water and what it meant. He had not trusted Victor with the knowledge because he didn't know what Victor would do with it since Victor had never entertained himself with the value of the property and its contents. Gigot had become so self-absorbed that he was the chosen one to deliver the water to the world that it had not dawned on him that he was not the true and rightful owner of the water…Victor was.

As Gigot carefully shoved the container of water through the slightly

opened door over to Victor's shoes, he said,
"Victor, you said you wanted to know the truth about the land and about me…here it is in this container."

# Chapter 30

## Living Water

Victor looked down at his feet where Gigot had shoved the container of water and said,

"What is this?"

By this time, both Victor and Gigot had tired of each other and they were both very tired from the events and unfulfilled expectations of the morning.

"Gigot, I'm really tired now and I need to eat my noonday meal. I believe that we have completed what we attempted to do."

"Victor, will you take a look at this, this is what the land is all about. I'm surprised you didn't know anything about it." Gigot said respectfully.

"Didn't know about what? While I was waiting on you this week, the only files I found on that land was that the family was not supposed to sell it, but for business sake, I have no idea why. Is this some natural resource found on the land?" Victor said inquisitively.

"Yes, Victor, it is. I'm pretty sure this is the reason why the family was not supposed to sell the land. What is in this container needs to be protected from the public…" Gigot said as he was still kneeling at Victor's feet.

"My God, man, get up, I told you I do not receive beggars here, stand to your feet and tell me what this is!" Victor insisted as he backed away from the door giving room to Gigot and allowing him to re-enter the massive entry way. They stood there together and Gigot said,

"I need to place this on the table over there and if you will open it yourself and take a look at it, I think what is in the container will explain it itself."

"Umph!" Victor chuckled inside and let out his dismay in the form of doubt. He shook his head back and forth in disagreement and said,

"I doubt that whatever is in that little plastic container could surprise me or explain anything to me, besides, why are you just now telling me something about a natural resource on the land? Have you gone and tried to make yourself rich at my expense? You swindler…"

Victor chuckled as he felt like he finally had the upper hand on Gigot. Whatever was in that container was why Gigot wanted that land so badly…badly enough to try and swindle it away from Victor.

Victor was still shaking his head back and forth as he turned towards the marble table that had a glass top that was two inches thick. There were two crystal lamps on each end of the table with silk tassels dangling from the white lampshades. The whole setting in the entry hall was set upon this focal point. It was among Victor's mother's favorite spots in the entire mansion. The setting of white marble, white silk and crystal with brass overlays made the room glow and provided the perfect presentation for what the rest of the home represented. It was the grand classic style of the best of what the preceding historical eras represented. The home was a historical museum and this focal point invited the guest into the realm of pure gilded gladness.

Gigot walked over to the exquisite table and placed the common container of water directly in the middle of the table. As Victor was slowly making his way to the table with his cane, Gigot stepped over to the corner to retrieve an entry chair that looked as though a royal king had sat in it. Gigot leaned over the chair to pick it up and take it over to the table so that Victor could sit down to view the container, but as Gigot bent over to lift the monstrous seat, he realized that it was either too heavy or it was nailed to the floor… and…it wasn't nailed to the marble floor.

"My land, Victor, what is this chair made of? I can't budge it!" Gigot admitted not being able to move the chair, not even a smidgen.

"Umph!" chuckled Victor, "That is a throne chair from 19th century Europe. It takes at least two men to move that seat made for a king. Go and get a sitting chair from the drawing room."

Gigot didn't waste any time, but did exactly as Victor said.

"Here it is. This is heavy…" Gigot struggled to talk as he bore the weight of the drawing room chair. He carefully placed it within seating distance of the glass table top; close enough for Victor to plainly view what was inside the container set before him.

"If it's ok with you, Victor, do you mind if I carry through to the kitchen for a glass of water?"

Victor waved his hand backwards as to move Gigot along to where he needed to go so that he would be able to see what lie inside the container. Victor was very excited and his eyes sparkled with desire at the prospect of a valuable natural resource found on his property. His mind went to money as whatever it was that was inside the container must be extremely valuable. He carefully lifted the top lid from the bottom and as it opened, he closed his eyes in anticipation. He drew in a breath, held it for just a moment and then simultaneously opened his eyes and blew out his breath to see the magic inside the container.

As filled with expectation as he could possibly be, he gave a resounding, "Umph!" once again in disappointment.

"This is…is…water," he thought to himself. He picked up the container and tilted it from side to side and didn't notice anything unusual about it, it was just plain old water. He was tempted to touch the water and taste it, but he didn't know where it had come from or why Gigot would think it to be something of value.

"Perhaps there must be some mineral property to the water," he thought to himself as he continued to tilt the water and watch it roll in the small hand-size container.

Disappointed, he set the water down in front of him and exclaimed loudly,

"Gigot, I think you're a loon, there's nothing to this container but a little bit of water and just when you'd gotten my hopes up, you let me down again."

Gigot was so far into the house into the kitchen area so he didn't hear Victor file his complaint.

Victor sat there, tired and disappointed and then his mind went back to his need and a most pressing need at that…the need for Gigot's

60,000 dollars. As he sat there exasperated from the disappointment and fumbling in his mind how he might cajole that check out of Gigot, he shoved the container forward in disgust and as he did, the water inside shifted backward, then forward and came back onto his hand. At the moment of touch, the water shocked Victor with a memory of his past. The memory was when he was sitting at the dinner table with his father and mother as he would lovingly sit and listen to their stories of finding each other through the power of the water. Suddenly, another memory came to him as his mother was reading to him of history and geography and telling him that one day, they would take him to the land of the water that speaks and show him the way of it. Then, one by one, vivid shocking scenes appeared in his mind from his past that were pleasant and revealing.

He touched his hand to his forehead to deliberately catch his thoughts to stop the onslaught of the past and he found his hand leaving his forehand and stretching out to the water.

His hand was quivering as he placed his fingers into the container and another shock went through his body and he shivered with amazement of the sights he saw in his mind from his past…the things that he had done and seen, some embarrassing, some frightening, and some disturbing, particularly the decisions that he had made by his mother's deathbed. All of the resentment of the loss of his father and mother was forefront in his mind and he felt terror strike him as he was about to shove the water off of the table in anger.

"No time, there was not enough time with them," he thought in deep resentment to God and to himself. "You took them away from me and left me all alone! Why are you so evil?" he spoke aloud.

Tears had welled up within him and he found himself tightening a fist in the water because he knew…he knew as sure as he was sitting there that there was a God who knew all that he had done.

"You took them away from me and all I have is what Papa and Father and Mother left me, why did you take them away from me?" he sobbingly cried aloud again.

His grip was tight on the water in the container and he would not, or it would not let him go. He sat there weeping and grieving and remembering that he had never cried a tear when they died, he had just felt angry. Now, all that was left was his resentment and the water seemed intent on taking that away as well.

"You have to let it go." He sensed in his spirit.

"No, it's all I have left of them, no, "he cried.

"Let it go," the water pleaded, yet pleaded with such authority and a sense of peace, that it was already working its power in Victor's spirit and Victor listened in his mind.

The water spoke to Victor and changed his life in just a few short moments out of time. Victor sighed an overwhelming sigh of relief and joy and he let go of the water as he let go of his past regret, pain, misery, but most of all, he let go of himself. He sat there and wept for the memories he had just been shown of his mother, missing her, but now knowing that she was in a far better place than he seemed to be. He wept there on the glass table as tears formed small puddles beneath his face and as he saw the water of his tears on the glass, he once again remembered the wonderful stories his father had told him as a very young child about the water that wooed. Victor slumped hard when he realized that that was the one trip that they had always planned to take, but never did. Somehow, what they had had not translated to him, but it has taken Gigot bringing the water to him that now has made his life worth living.

He sat up erect and with a spring in his step, threw the cane down to the floor. The rattle of the cane hitting the floor resounded down the hollow hallway and echoed around the corners.

Gigot heard it and thought that Victor had fallen, so he left the peanuts that he was eating on the kitchen counter and ran down the hallway towards the entry way only to find Victor meeting him in the breezeway, giving him this fatherly hug of the face with his hands clasp around Gigot's cheeks. Victor was squeezing Gigot's face and then he pulled him close to him and said in Gigot's ear,

"I'm alive Gigot, I'm alive! You brought the water to me, it's the water that my father had met many years ago, the same water that my grandfather had met…I'm alive, Gigot, I'm alive!"

All at once, Victor stepped back and took both of Gigot's hands and swung him around like some German polka. They were both dancing a gig with tears of joy flowing from Victor's face and tears of laughter from Gigot's. They danced and twirled around and around until Victor started getting dizzy and had to sit down from his palpating heart. He grabbed his chest and had the most awful look on his face as though he were about to croak. He took a deep breath and then let out a laugh that he had not laughed for more than thirty, or forty years.

"I smell peanuts," Victor exclaimed.

Gigot scratched his face and replied, "Yes, and they were great, I almost ate the whole basket while I was waiting on the water!"

"I have some lamb in the fridge, let's boil some potatoes and eat a feast! I'm starving! Do you like roasted lamb, Gigot?" Victor asked Gigot as Gigot smiled this great big smile in return letting Victor know that if was affirmative on the lamb and the potatoes.

"I'm starving, too, Victor, I hope you didn't mind me getting a few peanuts, those were great, I love to eat them right from the shell like that!" Gigot said gleefully.

"Well, son, there's more where that came from," Victor placed his hand on Gigot's shoulder as he imparted sort of a blessing onto Gigot concerning what he had. He was letting Gigot know that whatever he had in his home, Gigot was welcome to it.

"You're welcome to whatever I have in this old place, Gigot! You've brought to me the one thing that I missed with my parents and it was the one thing that they told me they would show me, but never did."

"Well, Victor, maybe they did show it to you. They just didn't take you to the water themselves, but I bet that if they met the water, the water was with them and in them and you couldn't help but meet the water somehow, someway, someday." Gigot said excited knowing full well what he was talking about.

Gigot knew now that the water was like the wind, it would speak to whoever it came in contact with, but it would speak and then leave the response up to the person. Gigot was shaking his head back and forth fussing at himself on the inside, thinking that he should have brought the water to Victor in the first place. But here he was again, thinking he knew a better way than the water and all of a sudden he had this brief moment of embarrassment when the water peered into his heart and asked,

"When are you going to let go and let me?"

Gigot sighed within himself and continued to smile at Victor as Victor was in the fridge pulling out all kinds of food. It seemed as though Victor had enough food to feed a dozen people. Victor was humming to himself as he placed dish after dish on the kitchen counter. What Gigot didn't know was that Victor would have a chef come in once a week and cook enough food for a week and Victor, not being able to decide exactly what would go with the lamb, pulled everything out that was within reach.

"I'm so happy," Victor hummed to himself. "I'm so happy, I could just sing and I don't know how to sing. But…I do know how to dance! Ha,ha, ha, ha!" he laughed to himself and then he started dancing a jig around the huge island in the middle of the kitchen.

"I tell ya what, Gigot," Victor said as he shook a long pointed carving knife at Gigot. "We may be able to work something out after all, yes, indeedy! Yes, indeedy!" And Victor began to sing all over again, "Yes, indeedy, oh, yes, indeedy." He was dancing around the center island again and Gigot could tell that what he was doing was thinking as he was dancing.

"I know just what we'll do, Gigot, if it's ok with you. I have some bills I have to pay with that 60,000 dollars. How about we do this? How's about we trade the 60,000 for the land. We just swap assets. You give me the 60 and I give you the land and call it even, whadusay to that?" Victor raised both eyebrows fully and left his mouth wide open as if he could catch an elephant with it if it happened to fly by.

Gigot, shocked at the immediate change of mood and behavior of Victor, but knowing the reason why, he shouted,

"Hallelujah, yes, Mr. Whitegold, I mean, Victor, of course, yes, sir, I'm up for a trade like that, that sounds awesome!"

Victor had already sliced two lamb chops apart from the rack of lamb from each other and handed Gigot a rib bone full of cold, braised lamb. He poured out his best Cabernet into two glasses and said,

"Now, take a bite of this and wash it down with a gulp of that!"

Gigot did as he was told, rather willingly and cheered to the best lamb he'd ever eaten and he was too enamored with the quality of the wine to ask how much it must have cost.

"This tastes tremendous! I could eat like this every day, Victor!"

Victor leaned towards Gigot and looked over the rims of his glasses, smiled and said, "And you shall Gigot, you shall…"

In their moments of feasting with the lamb, the wine and the bread, it ocurred to Victor that Gigot had not answered an earlier question. Victor knew that there was significance to most everything so Victor asked Gigot once again,

"What kind of name is Gigot, Gigot? What does it mean?"

## Chapter 31

## Watch the Water Woo

Gigot did't know how gifted Victor was in getting things accomplished with an effective plan and the ability to see far into the future on how a proposed plan would be carried out. Even though the only moments Gigot had seen of Victor was him being a crabby, old, self-indulgent hermit...Victor's awakening from the wooing of the water revealed a morphed man of extreme comprehension and vision. Victor's purpose had lay dormant for decades, but now was at the forefront of his brow and nothing was going to prevent that purpose from coming to fruition. What Gigot had seen in a disturbed recluse had now become a vibrant business man ready to take on the world just like his father and his father before him.

That afternoon, Victor devised a plan that would propel Gigot's destiny and the destiny of the water into unity. Gigot had the 60,000 dollar check in his briefcase and Victor had all of the pertinent contracts available in his office. With one quick phone call, Victor's attorney was on his way and there would be no questioning or negotiating with this attorney as Victor used his services for Victor's desires and not the desire or advice of the attorney.

Victor's change inspired him to see what the water saw instead of dreaming of the past and his past relationships. Victor had been given a glimpse of his immediate future, so he drew up a plan just like he proposed in the kitchen over the lamb chops and wine; that was something that had not changed, for a meal and a drink was always the working way of accomplishing a great task or the culminating of a final decision. Victor's demeanor thrust Gigot into a whirlwind of accomplishment in just a few short hours.

A contract was drawn up to trade the land for the 60,000 dollars and call it what you will, the trade, or sale, was final and all rights to the land and water went to Gigot Bengal that afternoon. In the transaction, Victor signed over the check to the attorney to deposit into his account to pay all outstanding taxes and fees due, which happen to include the over-due retainer fees to the lawyer.

With one fell swoop, Victor signed over all of his remaining assets, including the mansion and all of its belongings to the newly formed Whitegold Museum of History to be located nearby. The proceeds from the sale of the mansion would be used to purchase a former hotel on the waterfront to create a museum of history of the gilded age so that all would be able to enjoy the contents of his home that he had enjoyed all of his life. Victor knew that his heart would not be able to keep him alive much longer, so it was imminent that the lawyer file a proposal to the hotel corporation who had failed to obtain any respectable suitors for their historical district plan. The decisions that Victor made that afternoon would eventually affect untold thousands and millions of people in regards to the museum of history and the eventual release of the water to the world through Gigot's retail establishment.

But here lie the obvious question to Victor and Gigot who had pondered the question before:

"How do you give living water to the world without it becoming tarnished and abused by the depravity and manipulation of man?"

Victor had not been a praying man, not since his childhood days with his mother and father. He had always seen things as the answer to most anything, but the spirit of the water wasn't about material things and there was no thing that was going to tell him the answer to their question.

"Was the water to be bought or sold?" they proposed to one another and the answer was a resounding no.

"Was there to be a huge edifice built so that the masses of people could come and inquire and meet the water for themselves?" and the answer again was a resounding no because that was what had occurred with religion and what it had to offer.

What were they going to do with the water? Neither of them had the answer other than what Gigot had already done and that was to share the water with one individual at a time and allow the water to speak to that individual and not to the masses through some man on a pedestal. They had seen in their lifetime when men are allowed to be put on a pedestal, that no matter the message that they professed, the real substance was always about elevating the man and the message always got lost in the pride of the man and the subservient attitude of the listener. Gigot knew what he was and he was no professional at anything. He didn't want people looking at him; he wanted them to get in touch with the water, first and only.

It seemed to both of them that what Gigot had been doing all along was presenting the water to people that he would run across and in the giving of the water…the water always knew the right thing to say to the individual. So, was that it? Was Gigot supposed to simply keep doing what he was doing…talking with one person at a time? How long would that take for the whole world to meet the water that wooed?

They tossed around the idea that Gigot had of making mirrors out of the water and that seemed to be a viable idea worth looking into. Gigot's friend, Lewis, had the engineering expertise to accomplish the analysis of creating the permanent transformation of taking the water from liquid form onto a solid form base. Could it be as simple as pouring the water onto glass and the water remaining as mirror later to be framed, just as Floyd and Alfred had done, but now it would need to be on a much larger scale? If they did that, though, would they be selling the mirrors or would they leave the mirrors in the store for people to meet the water? They simply could not come up with the final solution because if they sold the mirrors, what would happen to the mirrors once they got into the hands of people who might try to use the mirrors for their own advantage somehow, someway?

Again, they were at a loss for what to do. Victor grew tired of the going back and forth as his style of operating as a businessman did not put up with such antics, so his past spoke up in French and said, "*La question ete' debattue' a maintes reprises, Ca suffit!*" *

And with that, he was done, he wasn't going to discuss it any further. He had quickly surmised that Gigot could go on and on with the 'what-ifs' and he simply wasn't going to do it anymore. Victor was not going to put the question out again and again for repeated repetition.

"Gigot, is this how you run your business? Playing 'what if' games?" Victor questioned Gigot as to his business prowess.

"Sometimes, yes, I do, I guess, I haven't really thought about it much being a type of business prowess," Gigot responded sheepishly knowing he was out of his league when it came to making business decisions as a real Whitegold might do it.

"These are business decisions, you know, Gigot. Even though, the water is not about business, you've made it about business by applying it to the presentation of buying and selling, or, at the very least, making a presentation," Victor said in a very kind, but stern voice.

Victor's entire demeanor had changed towards Gigot and he no longer saw him as the ignorant peckerwood out to waste what little time he had left on this earth, but he had been shown himself through the eyes and ears of the water and the virtue of patience was now needing to draw deep from the well of the water within Victor's heart.

"Gigot, we've gotten a lot accomplished today and I truly thank you for being persistent in showing the water to me. The only way for me to really change was through that water and now that I have and will continue to, I see my purpose and your purpose intertwined in one with the water. I treasure this time that I am having with you, but I know that my time is soon running out. I'm ok with that, in fact, I feel great about it. Yesterday, I had a thousand regrets, but today, the only regret is that I didn't come to know the water sooner in my life," Victor sighed and continued,

"I have no regrets, honestly, not now, and I have the water and you to thank for that. And, even though my life has new meaning and a realized purpose, my time on this earth is coming to a rapid close. The water knows what to do and how to do it and here we have been going back and forth with our pitiful plans of how to do something… anything with the water without consulting with the water. You know, I learned from my grandfather decades ago that if you had the answer staring you in the face, it's a more wise thing to stare right back and give the answer the honor its due, rather than searching under rocks for what has already been placed in your hand. Gigot, let's ask the water what it wants and trust that the water knows for sure, how about that?"

Gigot's eyes softened from the remarks and his face was marked with wonder. Raising his upper lip in a quirky type of agreement, Gigot said,

"I agree, Victor, I agree, completely. And, if I've learned anything today, it's to go to the water first, rather than last. I'm still learning. I just wish I didn't have so much to learn."

Gigot walked briskly into the entry room and retrieved the container of water, but noticed that it seemed far lighter than before. He didn't feel any movement in the container and stopped midway down the hallway to carefully open the container. There was no water in the small container and Gigot choked on the idea that it must have spilt onto the floor or the table when it was dealing with Victor. Gigot ran back into the entry room and no spills of water were there and there were no mirror images on the glass table.

"It must have evaporated…no, this water doesn't evaporate!" Gigot thought to himself.

"So, what happened to it?" he continued to ponder. Just then, he heard Victor calling for him down towards the end of the hallway.

"Gigot, come here, there's something I failed to tell you," Victor stood in the middle of the hallway by the entrance to the dining room. "I drank it…I drank the water!"


* Translation from French, "It has been debated over and over again… stop it!"

## Chapter 32


## Acceptance


"You did what?" Gigot laughed out a chuckle as he walked down the long hallway back to Victor.

"I drank the water," Victor said confidently.

"Why did you do that?" Gigot inquired knowing that he himself had drunk the water while he was swimming in the lake.

"It was the right thing to do. I drank the water so that it would always be with me," Victor said emphatically, "Didn't *you*?"

"Yes, I guess I did," Gigot admitted.

"Well, did you or didn't you, there isn't any guessing about it!" demanded Victor who, again, was easily tiring of having to go back and forth with Gigot.

"Yes, I know that I did, I even swam in the water…when I got to know it," stammered Gigot embarrassed, who was getting it this time that his yes needed to be yes and his no needed to be no.

"You know Victor, in the past few weeks since I've come to know the water, I've seen it where the influence of the water was all around me and in me I didn't need to carry around a container. I've also seen it, like here, when I've talked and talked to people, like you or my wife…and had to leave the container of water with them for the water to privately speak to them. What do you think is the difference? If the water is in me and I know that it is, then the water is in me. But, if the water is in me and the internal influence doesn't seem to work, but the external direct container of water does work, what do you think that means exactly?"

Victor pondered Gigot's questions and thoughts for a few minutes and since Victor's only experience with the water was just a few hours old, he didn't feel adequate to respond with the correct answer so he said, "What does the water say?"

"Well, we don't have any water," Gigot responded, "except for what is in us. And I know that I've been changed by the water and I also believe that the water is with me."

"How do you know for sure, Gigot?" Victor questioned him again, "What makes you so sure? For me, I know I'm a different person…I drank the water, I think the water wanted me to drink it and be inside of me so I gave up and did what the water said and so…the water is in me for sure and it's not just plain water, it's real, it's real living, life-changing water."

"So, where is the water?" Gigot asked him again as tears were beginning to well inside of him and a tear dropped from his right cheek.

Victor was startled by Gigot for a moment and then said, *"il est a l'inte'rieur*…it is within!"

The two stood there looking at each other eye to eye in the expansive hallway with just a few feet between them. Coming to grips with the reality of the water being in them and knowing the power of the water within, they realized they could be as much of themselves as they used to be and yet somehow changed and not be themselves at all.

"So, what is the difference?" Gigot asked.

"The difference is…it is…" Victor pondered for a few moments more before completing the thought. "It is…the difference is us, Gigot. We are the difference. We are the changed, but we are also the hindrance. Not only are we a hindrance to ourselves, we are a hindrance to what others perceive about us. If your wife didn't accept you, then she's not going to accept what's inside of you. Just like I didn't have a clue when you were trying to reach me and I never heard the water until I physically opened the container or, at least I don't think I did. Maybe I did hear the water through you or coming from you and that's what kept me listening to you or listening to it. Yes, that's it, I was hearing the water in you, but me and you and the ideas we have or put off get in the way…I think…I suppose. The difference is not in the water, I believe the water is the same, but the situations change with the people; the people are the difference."

Victor had gone somewhere in his mind trying to grasp what was happening to the two of them.

"So, the container is the carrier or vessel, but it can also be the prohibitor," Gigot concluded. "Even though I have the water in me and the power of the water is real and inside of me, there's something about me that is prohibiting the power of the water to move or reveal itself to others."

"Yes, unfortunately, it seems so, Gigot, but maybe that's only the way it seems. Maybe the water is working and speaking and wooing and we just don't realize it."

Victor had placed his hand on his chin as he had turned to walk back into the kitchen. "Maybe if…what if, oh…"

"What, don't stop now, continue, Victor, I need you to think this through with me, what is it that we need to do as humans to not prohibit the power of the water to do its work through us?" Gigot pleaded with Victor as one might plead with a senior professor who had all of the answers to all of life.

"Gigot, don't put that off on me, ask the water yourself," Victor chided Gigot for his impertinence, not towards him, but towards the water. Gigot simply wasn't getting it that he had all these questions and he needed to address them with the water itself and stop asking Victor because Victor was no oracle of the water.

Gigot and Victor trudged back into the kitchen and it was getting late towards dinner time. They sat by the kitchen counter and Gigot fumbled through the cabinets and quickly found the leftover bread and lamb and asked Victor if he wanted any.

"No," nodding his head, "no, I'm needing to work through this one," Victor confessed, "I'm still adequate from the lamb, you know, old fellows like me don't need to eat three full meals a day and I'm still good from that lamb."

Suddenly, like a room of lights had just been turned on, they both looked at each other and with Gigot having just taken a mouthful of both lamb and bread blurted out, "You're still good from the lamb! It's the change, you see, others have to see, not me, but the change, they have to not see me, but see and hear the water and the only way they're going to see the water is to let the water so change me that the only thing they see or hear is the water. I have to continually let go of me, I'm getting in the way. I think I'm beginning to get it."

Victor stood there smiling because he was getting it, but he was also enjoying seeing Gigot get it a millisecond before he did. He could see the lightning in his eyes and he was so overwhelmed that he said,

"Ok, ok, Gigot, I think we're both getting it, now it's time for you to go home to your lovely family so that I can get some rest. I'm really tired now."

Victor held out his arms to Gigot like a proud father and they gave each other a hug that would seem to last a lifetime and then some. Victor walked Gigot back to the door and as Gigot was prepared to exit the door Victor said,

"Don't be too hard on yourself Gigot. You know it could be that when you show up, that other people just aren't ready for the water or they're just not going to get it. You have to know the water and believe that the power of the water is in you and has changed you…keep believing, don't' stop believing that the water has changed you and has the power to change anybody. But, I also believe that if somebody doesn't want to be changed and they don't receive the power of the water, then they don't receive the water or its power, it's that simple. I could have said no and as mean and ornery as I have been the majority of my life, the water didn't owe me anything. My whole life, I could have gone out there and met the water myself, but I didn't and I'm grateful that it didn't hold it against me. No, I think everybody's gonna be different. Everybody's gonna react differently to the water, Gigot, you'll see. You just be the best water carrier that it has changed you to be and don't look back to what you did or what you used to be cause you're not that man anymore, Gigot, you've been changed!"

"And another thing, Gigot, you need to remember that it's the water that does the wooing, not you or me or someone else that is able to come in contact with the water. The water does the wooing and the speaking and will only do it through a vessel that it has chosen to speak through, so your thoughts about it being abused or misused might be purely suppositional," Victor said as he was now on a roll with his thinking and his immediate desire to believe the right things and not his usual and customary of dwelling on material things that were right before his eyes.

He was remembering his childhood days and all that he had absorbed from his grandparents and parents. Their reflections of the water were coming back to him as in a long lost dream that had gotten misplaced with their removal from his life.

Gigot was standing at the door ready to leave, but Victor had now opened another gate of thought that Gigot needed in order to process the grandeur of the water properly.

"Suppositional?   Suppositional..."   Gigot   pondered   Victor's mentoring.

"Yes, Gigot, suppositions are theories or beliefs we create or are taught that may not necessarily be true."

Victor continued, "I just don't see something as powerful and terrific as this water kneeling to a corrupt mind and allowing itself to be abused or misused. The water is real, I know that as a fact and even though facts can be turned upside down, manipulated, used or abused, this water has real power in and of itself. It doesn't need a false vessel to deliver itself. It's more powerful than that. I don't think that this water would have anything to do with an improper vessel. Just like me and you, the vessel gets changed or it doesn't, but I don't see the water dwelling in an unchanged vessel. You see, your supposition is that the water could or would inhabit an unchanged vessel that would use it for its own purposes. That would mean that the vessel was greater than the water. The water doesn't need that...that would be hypocrisy on the water's part. This water is pure cleansing and an unclean vessel could not hold the purity of this water within by remaining unclean. No, I just don't see that happening. Why would you think that anyway?" Victor stated thinking deeply on the purity of the water as a result of his personal experience.

There were major differences in Victor's life and Gigot's life. Gigot had been out in the contemporary world whereas Victor had remained solitary at home. Gigot had seen for himself in religion, for example,

 Terry Lursen

where leaders, who didn't seem to be real at all, would profit off of what they were preaching and what they were preaching was their beliefs and not necessarily the truth.

"Victor, in some ways, you've been blessed by not getting out into the world lately and seeing some of things that I've seen. There's just not a whole lot of truth spreading out there, but a whole lot of profiting off of people's backs particularly when it comes to matters of the heart. When it comes to matters of the heart, it seems people will believe just about anything somebody tells them and then the purveyor wants to be rewarded handsomely for something that they seemingly just made up. But the people don't know it; they don't know that they are being manipulated by their need. It's kinda sick, actually," Gigot's thoughts were getting the best of him and Victor could see it in his disposition that he didn't possess much trust in man at all.

"Son, you're beginning to sound quite pathetic, like I know I've sounded for many, many years. It sounds like you've seen some real hucksters out there and all they know is manipulation and deception; they probably don't know the real thing. I've sold a few things in my lifetime and in the realm I've walked in, I've seen some real hucksters who said they could pay for something and when it came down to it, no huckster ever outdid me with what I needed to sell. I had the power over creatures like that because I owned the property. Either they had to pay up or shut up, no thief walked away with my property. Think how far greater and more powerful this water is than me," Victor said and then paused for a minute.

"Let's do this…let's trust that the water knows best. Always remain in the water for the water remains in you. Let's leave it at that for now, can you do that?" Victor smiled and Gigot returned the smile adding,

"Yes, we can both do that for sure!"

**Chapter 33**


**Purpose**


Gigot had a difficult time leaving Victor alone, but life had to continue and Victor reassured him that Gigot's path and purpose was definitely intertwined with the water. In no time, Gigot had made it home and was celebrating the acquisition of the land, the water and his purpose in life. It was the purposes of the water that excited Gigot and Pauline the most. The life changing properties of the water was drawing them both to bring the water to view so that it could be shared with others.

Gigot got some help with maintaining the store and went out on another trek back to the land visiting Lewis and Diane along the way and staying a few nights with Alfred and Floyd while he was there. Everyone had had ideas on what to do next and they were all eager to share and Gigot was very open to listen.

Alfred and Floyd reiterated what Victor had quickly surmised and that it was imperative for Gigot to listen intuitively to the water in his spirit and cease from the debilitating questioning of his mind. It isn't that one is not supoosed to think, that's not it, it's the fact that the water is about life in the spirit and the spirit is where it communicates. Alfred contended that Gigot would not learn to listen intuitively in the spirit overnight or soon, for that matter, but that it would take time out of time to pay heed to the water's will and way.

Gigot could not get over the joy of his discovery in his friends. They were so happy for him and even quite ecstatic about the possibilities of the water and Gigot and the future that the water beheld.

He talked over the process of making mirrors with Floyd and Alfred since they were the ones who originally figured it out. Using their ideas, Gigot got with Lewis who developed the ideas even further by transferring the water onto a specific kind of glass that was treated in Lewis' laboratory. He showed Gigot how it was to be done so that when he poured the water onto the glass it stayed according to the parameters created. They went ahead and created three full-size mirrors to use in the store with the possibility of selling them only to the right people. Gigot left a barrel of water in Lewis' basement for whenever the need would arise to create more mirrors.

It took about a month for Gigot to complete his travels and get back to work at the store. One by one, different people would come into the store and Gigot would be so excited and one by one they would leave, some with a purchase and others with none. What was really happening, though, was the opportunity to help others with their issues. As the customers came in the store, more were attracted to what Gigot had to offer by the way of advice, observations and prayer. One observation Gigot was able to make about himself was that he could see the water speaking to people and know that it wasn't him, but it was the water at work.

People would be thankful and appreciative, but Gigot found it very difficult to receive any kind of praise for helping people because he wasn't the one doing the helping. He knew that for a fact. There were things that would come out of his mouth when talking to people that only they knew and when he would speak of them, they would be amazed that Gigot could be so profound, yet seemingly unaware of the intuitive knowledge himself taking no credit for whatever help they might receive from his spirit. Somehow Gigot just 'knew' what the solution to their issue was and, if he didn't know, he didn't offer any advice because he didn't want to get himself involved in other's lives and be wrong in the process. He'd seen it when other counselors were supposed to be helping someone in need, but actually giving them bad advice from inaccurate observations and leading the people astray into more trouble than what they had to begin with.

He set up one of the mirrors made of water in the back along the back wall. It was shaped into a full-length rectangular floor mirror with a simple wooden frame. He had gotten an idea from Victor to name the mirrors like Victor used to do with all of the objects that he had in his mansion.

Victor's family had acquired over 10,000 objects and pieces of furniture in his home. Victor was a pretty smart guy and could remember all the objects' names. In any case, Gigot set up the first mirror in the back and called it, "The Looking Glass".

One day, a bright, young man came in the store and introduced himself as Simon Vain. Simon had made it big in men's boutiques and he loved mirrors, the more mirrors the merrier. When he walked in the store, a sensation came over Gigot like never before. Gigot was uncertain of the man; there was just something about him from Gigot'sensing from the water. Simon had come in with a few of his friends that loved to laugh. Gigot said hello to each one of them, one was very friendly and funny, but the other acted like he was hiding from someone because he kept looking out the windows repeatedly in different directions. There was a certain odor to the three of them, an unusual smokiness that Gigot was unaccustomed to smelling.

Simon Vain went slowly through each aisle of mirrors constantly looking at and smiling to himself as one might do with a great sense of pride. He had on a rich silk shirt, with a few buttons opened up top to show off his chest and a long gold chain cross made of glistening gold. He was a very happy lark and as he walked through the aisles of mirrors, it seemed that he and his cohorts had something funny to say at each one. They were acting goofy as though they were in a fairground funhouse full of mirrors, Gigot loudly exclaimed,

"Let me know if I can help in any way."

As Simon continued through the aisles of mirrors, he had already picked out two and had his friends to bring them to the counter where Gigot was waiting. The man was already purchasing more mirrors than most other customers and Gigot asked the friendly friend what his plans were with all of those mirrors. The guy just smiled a huge smile and said,

"He loves mirrors and he wants a mirror in every room of his house. He likes your store 'cause he likes mirrors and you have the best variety. We don't go to any other mirror stores, I don't think."

Gigot's eyebrow raised with all he had just heard and then smiled going about his business of finding the box casings that the sold mirrors had been shipped in. Mr. Vain's two friends were at the counter joking around and laughing, which must have been their usual and customary thing to do. As Gigot walked towards the back storeroom, he spied Mr. Vain going to the last row of mirrors approaching "The Looking Glass".

Gigot went into the back room to retrieve the right boxes for the mirrors and was returning to the front when he stopped at the entrance to the back room with the two boxes held tightly in his hands. He let them rest upright against his chest as he watched him go mirror by mirror until he arrived at the last one. Simon Vain was to Gigot's far right and the two friends were still standing around by the counter waiting for their leader. The man came to a stop directly in front of the Looking Glass and just stood there with a pushed-up chin on his face. One could easily surmise he was deep in thought about something by the expression on his face. His look had gone from smiling at himself in pride to a look of tense pressure. Gigot could see that he was standing there tightening his jaw and chewing on the inside of his mouth. His eyes got tense as well as he began to scrunch his eyebrows together as though he was thinking about something that made him terribly angry.

Gigot knew that the water was speaking to him directly and had his absolute attention. Mr. Vain seemed to be getting more and more angry the longer he stood before the mirror. He clinched his fists and started heaving as though he were getting ready for a boxing match. He was pumping his fists opening and closing them, over and over again and Gigot could not imagine what the mirror was saying to him to make him so angry. All of a sudden, he raised his right fist as if to threaten the mirror to stop as he jutted out his jaw with gritted teeth seething with venom. Gigot could see the spit falling from his open mouth as he seethed and then he wiped the spit from his mouth as a prize fighter might do in the middle of a bout.

"What are you saying to him?" Gigot silently asked the water,

"Why are you making him so angry?"

Abruptly, the man lowered his fist and his shoulders relaxed as though he had either heard all he was going to hear, or he was taking a break somehow.

The water working through the mirror was telling him all that he was, but Gigot didn't have a clue as to what kind of man that was standing before this mirror. The man looked over to his right at Gigot standing in the corner and he looked rather needy like he needed someone to help him out of his situation. Sweat was pouring from his forehead and he looked at Gigot with fear in his eyes like he'd seen a ghost. Then, all of a sudden, the man was thrust against the mirror as though someone in the mirror had grabbed his collar and was choking him by the neck with his face firmly fixed against the glass of the mirror.

His eyes boiled with anger and his teeth seethed with hatred at what was happening to him. The water that woos had grabbed him and was not going to let him go. He took his fist and thrust it at the mirror like he was fighting an invisible foe. The lightning current that Gigot had seen when the water passed through Gigot vibrantly appeared and shocked the man with scenes of who he really was. Gigot watched him in fear as he shuttered and screamed at what he saw through the eyes of the looking glass. His left face was impressed upon the mirror and his right eye was intent on killing whatever it was that had him.

Gigot stood there in shock as the man responded to the wooing of the water with clinched fists and violent bursts of cursing. To Gigot's dismay, it had never occurred to him that anyone would respond to the wooing water with violence and seething anger, but the revelation of what was really inside the man was frighteningly pouring forth. Gigot simply did not know that the man who loved himself was a violent man ready to kill the water for what it knew. He watched as the man shoved his fists at the mirror that would not let him go. He pounded the mirror with all of his might but the mirror held fast and did not break. Blood was pouring from the man's fists and the thought of the saying, "kicking against the pricks" came to Gigot's mind.

When the man dropped his shoulders in exhaustion, the mirror let him go and he dropped flat to the floor.

Somehow and quite strangely, the two friends standing at the counter joking around with one another were completely oblivious to what had just transpired. They were leaning against the counter waiting on their leader laughing and carrying on with one another.

Gigot ran to the back rest room and got some paper towels and wet a few of them to help the man clean himself up from his experience. By the time he got over to Mr. Vain, the man had already gotten up on all fours and was breathing heavily and wiping his bloody knuckles with his handkerchief.

"Where's my cross, Gigot? What did you do with my cross?" the man said angrily, his teeth still clinched together locked in place from the experience.

"Sir, I haven't done anything with your cross. I didn't know it was missing, but now I see that it is. It must have fallen to the floor. I'll look around for it." Gigot said apologetically because he knew that the man had just undergone through an incredible confrontation with the looking glass, but it was only torment to the man from the way he had been living his life and his refusal to change.

"Forget it," he stated as he raised himself up. "Leave me alone," he said as he threw a forearm at Gigot as Gigot approached him with the towels.

He dusted himself off and straightened his clothing and stared straight into Gigot's eyes and said,

"I guess I didn't see that coming, but I bet you did, didn't you?"

Gigot stood there not saying a word respecting the fact that the water had said what it wanted and needed to say and the fact that he was looking at a violent man and violent men seek revenge, so it was expedient at that point for Gigot to remain silent.

"I have these towels if you want them," Gigot stated unreservedly, "are you going to be all right?"

"Ugh," Mr. Vain grunted, "I've never been better, you can keep that damn cross, I don't need it anyway…" he trailed off his tone as though he had just said something revealing and unnecessary.

"You must be running some kind of voo-doo store here. You won't be seeing me around here anymore and you can keep those two ------- mirrors, I don't have any use for what you're sellin'."

He straightened his clothes one more time and kept a clear distance from the looking glass mirror. As he walked by Gigot, he shoved his shoulder into Gigot's shoulder to push him out of the way like a middle school bully. He walked straight towards the front door and said to his cohorts as he passed them,

"Leave those there. We're not buying anything today, not here, not ever!"

As the two friends followed him out the door, the friendly one looked back with the eyes of a child as he ran out the door chasing his leader saying, "Good-bye, Sir!" The other one stood there with a very strange look as though he were taunting Gigot with his dark, sullen eyes and said, "Looks like we won't be seeing you anymore, Mr. Christian man..."

Gigot didn't say a word as he watched them all leave his store. He stood there motionless and looked through the store windows as they got into the man's Mercedes and screeched out of the parking lot. Then, he quietly walked over to the mirror and stood before it. Not knowing what to say or exactly what to do, he started cleaning the surface of the mirror with the wet towels in his hands. He pushed the blood of the man down to the bottom to collect it all on the paper towels. He cleaned up what he could and went back to the rest room to get more wet towels to finish the job.

As he returned and approached the looking glass mirror, he noticed the gold chain dangling from behind the mirror, but didn't see the cross anywhere. He grabbed the chain, but it was stuck on something underneath the mirror. He had to get down on the floor and crawl around the mirror to pull it from the bottom of the mirror. He couldn't imagine what the chain could possibly be attached to.

The Looking Glass mirror was a piece of heavy glass in-between the rustic wooden frame. He tugged on the chain again and the chain released and fell into his hand. He looked behind and all around the mirror for the cross, but didn't see it anywhere.

After looking around on the floor for the cross, he stood back up to regain his balance and as he stood directly in front of the mirror he saw what seemed to be impossible, but saw it nonetheless.

The cross was in the mirror. It wasn't on the mirror and it wasn't on the other side of the mirror. Somehow, in the exchange with Simon Vain, the cross was absorbed by the mirror. If he had looked at the mirror after his experience, he would have easily seen it, but after the bout with the mirror, Simon didn't dare look into again.

The cross hung there, chest high in the mirror. Gigot choked a bit and looked behind himself to see if the cross was hanging behind him, but to his utter shock the cross was truly imbedded or absorbed, ever how one might come to say it or believe it…it was in the mirror to stay.

Gigot was very kind and careful with the mirror in his cleaning with wet paper towels and it cleaned rather easily. He went back to the rest room with the soiled towels, throwing them away and washing himself up in the sink. Afterwards, he went back to the looking glass mirror and stood there in amazement at how the mirror had taken the cross from the man and absorbed it into itself. Gigot stood before the mirror and with deep respect inquired, "Why?"

With deafening silence in the store, Gigot could hear himself breathe and he waited patiently for the mirror to respond. The water spoke to Gigot in that moment and asked, "What is that to you, Gigot? You follow me."

## Chapter 34

## Life

Gigot reflected all night on the day's experience and wondered what he had gotten himself into. He knew the water for real and what he knew of the water was life changing, necessary, wonderful and a whole lot of other accolades that he could think of, but it had not entered his mind that someone would respond to the water like that man did.

He was realizing what Victor had said that not everybody cared about doing what was right and true and not everyone is going to respond to the water as he had. He knew he hadn't lived in the spirit of the right and true all of his life, but he had not stayed there. He had moved on and knew that he had to continue to move forward to remain with the water.

If the water represented anything to him, it was the true and the right, but it was something far greater than just true and right. He could not conceive of any wrong within the water so he meditated on what it was, exactly, that the water had in conflict with Simon Vain. The water was and is real as it became obvious that Vain is not. Just like Victor had said about the strength and power of the water, it was too great to be used or abused; it wasn't going to submit to a lesser mind, so there never would be what some people call spiritual abuse, you'd have to be a spiritual person to do that and that is inconsistent with the reality of the water.

But what was it going to do the next time somebody who was really bad off and refused to change…what was going to happen then…in his store? Did the looking glass water have the power to destroy if it had the power to do what it did yesterday to that man?

Gigot tossed and turned all night in his questioning and doubts about the water. What was he going to do if the water hurt someone in the store? He could get sued or something. Maybe an even more violent person would come in the store and get so angry with the water that they might really do some damage to the place or to Gigot…or worse, to a another customer in the store! The longer the night went, the longer the night was spent in anguish on what he had done with his 60,000 dollar investment into something that could possibly be destructive. By 4:00 am, he was a nervous wreck and ready to go down to the store and remove the looking glass mirrors from the store.

He got up out of bed, got dressed and went downstairs to get the car keys to go and take care of what he had done. When he opened the kitchen drawer to get his car key, he saw a note on his wallet from his children that had all kinds of drawings on it with happy faces and stick figures. They all had written their own notes on a single page of paper and Pauline had folded it nicely and placed it in the wallet so it would not be missed in the morning. He took the note, unfolded it and walked over to the breakfast table with a dimly lit light so as not to blind himself so early in the morning. The children had written these words,

"Dear Daddy, we love you so very much and we are very happy for you that you are getting to do what you had always wanted to do. We see your happy face and that makes us happy, too. (They had each drawn their own happy faces of themselves at that point in the letter) You and mommy are happy too now and we can tell the difference the water has made in your lives. Maybe one day you can show us the water and we can be as happy as you and mommy even tho we are very happy, happy, happy! We love you, Bessie, Daniel and James."

Tears fell down Gigot's cheeks. Wiping away the tears, he read the short letter again and again. Realizing his own fears had gotten the best of him, again, he folded the letter back together and placed it back in his wallet along with the car key back in the drawer. He went back to the table and sat down to pray and talked and prayed and prayed and meditated to truly listen this time.

The morning light came up with a gleam over the trees and as it shown itself through the windows, he was continuing to learn that he didn't know very much at all and he had the rest of his life to learn from the water about what really mattered and the first thing that had to go was the way that he thought about life and other people.

He realized that he had made so many mistakes in his life and it was about time to stop making them…if that was possible. He realized that he was the majority of his problem and the way that he thought about life in general, other people, Pauline and the kids and so on…it had to change…today…right now. He had to quit blaming others for his mistakes and quit thinking bad about the greatest gift that he had been given and that was this gift of real life with the water.

There was nothing to fear about the water for the water was right and good and it was the water that people needed whether he had everything worked out about it or not. The water needed to be available to the world. The world would have to make their choices on how they would respond, but he wasn't going to hide the water or put it away so that no one would ever know…no, he was going to move forward so that somehow, some way, the water was going to get to the world for all the world to know.

As the sun rose further in the sky, he couldn't help but sense and see the glory of God in it. This was a new day and no longer would he allow fear to rule his heart, his purpose, or, as he was learning, the purpose of the water. The purpose of the water was far greater than any purpose he could have for himself. The water was not about him and it wasn't up to him on whether the purposes of the water were to cover the earth. It was for all mankind, not just for him. He did not know how everything was going to work out, but he did know one thing and that was what he been able to learn thus far…one person at a time until the time came for something more, or different.

It had been a toilsome night on his part, but it had turned into a morning of joy and gladness. Pauline had gotten the kids up for school and soon enough everyone had said their hello's, good mornings, their 'I love you's' and their good-byes as they all traveled to work and school.

With no time to spare, Gigot got to the store and opened it up with the cheeriest of mind and spirit that he had ever had. He had an even further appreciation for his morning coffee which was particularly strong that morning and the aroma in the store made it all the more inviting.

Gigot cleaned and cleaned and then cleaned some more. For some reason, everything had gotten really dusty and as he cleaned he figured the reason was that he had not dusted the store good enough in a while, so it was about time. As he cleaned and wiped each mirror down carefully, he kept a close eye on the front door anticipating a gloriously successful and financially prosperous day. By noon, he had cleaned himself tired and he found it odd that no one had come into the store. Even on his slowest of days financially, he would have new customers to come in and browse…but not today.

He warmed up his lunch in the microwave and in the deafening quiet in the store he could hear the puppies next door at the dog groomers as they whined for their mother in the bath.

"Surely, it couldn't be taking that long to give the mama a bath," he thought to himself for the puppies were going crazy with whimpers, cries, little barks and tiffs.

By 2:00 PM, no one had come in the store and he was beginning to wonder if he had turned the open sign on…and he had. He walked back and forth to the front door, checking the door lock to make sure it was open and it was. By 4:00 PM, he was leaning his head on his arms on the store counter, resting from not having any sleep the night before and dosing from the lack of traffic flow. He kept looking up, pausing and then laying his head back down on his arms until he finally fell asleep there on the counter.

He must have been asleep for some time because his snoring became louder and louder and subconsciously he could feel saliva dripping from his mouth as his head lay careened in his arms on the counter.

"Ding, ding," went the doorbell as a customer came in the door. Gigot jumped up, head first and slobber poured from his waking mouth. He quickly composed himself, or, at least he thought he had, and said,

"Heh-woh, weh-cum to duh Wooking Gwassp!"

His eyes were not quite awake and neither was his body. He wiped his mouth again and shoved his fingers up through his face to wake his face up, but the customer was already in the store and walking through the front aisle of mirrors.

It was a female, one that he had never seen before, or had he?

"Yes," he thought to himself, he had seen her before, but not in the store. He heard her giggle at his greeting as he continued to compose himself and straighten himself from being asleep. He looked at the clock and it was already 5:30 PM.

"My goodness," he accidentally said aloud, but caught himself, realizing that he had been asleep for an hour and an half and that he was talking to himself with a live customer in the store.

She peered through two of the mirrors at Gigot just moments after he said what he said and he noticed her noticing him. She had long, dark hair, wavy and a smile that she smiled at him as she peeked through the mirrors to give him a brief gaze with her eyes.

"Boom!" went Gigot's heart…she was beautiful!

Gigot walked over to the edge of the front aisle and so as to not get too close, he stopped before he came into full view and said,

"Hello, welcome to the Looking Glass, let me know if I can help you in any way."

He smiled when he made the greeting and she turned towards his voice as he was talking and said demurely,

"Thank you, I've seen your store for some time, but it wasn't until today that I had a few minutes to see what you have here."

She glanced away, almost as though she was embarrassed, or something, and as Gigot had had a difficult time in his past with beautiful women, he shied away from her smiling, but dropping his head so as not to stare at her beauty.

She was Gigot's height or maybe taller and was wearing black high heels, black hose and a dress that looked like she was going out on the town, or something. She was completely made up with a perfect complexion and perfect everything as far as Gigot could tell. Her skin was youthful and soft. Her hair was long, dropping off her shoulders and glistening dark in the lights.

As she drifted to the second aisle of mirrors, his heart pounded just being in her presence. He couldn't help but think back to Tolstoy and his, Helene', in War and Peace. She was the woman with such tremendous and captivating beauty that a room full of people would part as she walked through a dance to the other side of the room. The way Tolstoy described his character Helene', he must have had someone in mind that had such untold beauty and perfection in structure, no one had ever seen any other woman as beautiful as she. And, according to Gigot's eyes and Tolstoy's imagination, this woman had just walked into his store.

Gigot caught himself, though, recognizing the beauty of the woman and then leaving it at that. His heart pounded at first because his eye's wanted to see her again. He was captivated, yet, no, he wasn't…he didn't give in to the urge to stare or glare at this new customer that was so intriguing. He did notice, however, that she was pausing carefully at each mirror. Her movements were slow and methodical as though she were there to find something particular and so she was taking her time at each mirror touching the frames, moving her hair, turning to her left or to her right, depending on her mood as she approached each mirror.

His view of her went from the immediate loss of breath at her beauty to "what is she doing, I think she may actually buy something today…" type of thinking.

As she proceeded from one aisle of mirrors to the next, both of their smiles went from the very friendly to the kind of smile you give someone just to make them aware that you see them, but don't come any closer. Gigot finally starting looking away from her when she would glance a glance over to him just being nice. He felt her glare at one point, because she actually was about to say something to him, yet he turned away so as not to be found staring at her. He did not know it, but she shook her head back and forth in disappointment because she had the urge to ask him a question, yet he was seemingly unattentive.

Gigot felt the imposition that she felt and immediately turned to her and said, "Do you have any questions?"

She stopped, looked straight him, took a breath of disbelief that he had heard her thoughts and quipped,

"Oh, no, I'm just enjoying what you have here. I've never seen a store like this, I don't think…ever and I'm a model and you know us models, we have to have our mirrors..." She expressed a faint chuckle as though she were embarrassed to admit the fact that models do have to have their mirrors.

Now, he knew where he had seen her! He had seen her face on the magazine covers in the grocery store aisles. You know the ones that are stacked at the beginning of every checkout register so that it will be either an impulse buy or something you can browse through while you wait on other customers in line.

"That's who that is!" Gigot thought to himself. Then he smiled to himself that he had figured to out, but certainly not on his own.

"Do you live around here?" Gigot questioned her.

"Yes, just a few miles from here. I've lived here for about a year because it's close enough to the airport and I wanted to live in a small town where I wouldn't have to put up with the hustle of a city. I get enough of that everywhere I go. I travel the majority of the year, so when I'm home, I like to be alone, it's better that way," She said as she trailed off in her mind in thought about something she had just said.

She turned away disquieted somehow and Gigot was certain that he had not done anything while she was talking, but he wasn't sure. He had to fight his own pretentiousness and fear of saying the wrong thing because he was actually intimidated by her and her beauty and now her revealed success. He thought about what she said and it came to him that she was going to look at every mirror in the store.

"EVERY MIRROR IN THE STORE!" his mind screamed at him when he realized that she was in the store looking at every mirror intently and she was ultimately going to get to the Looking Glass!

He was glaring wide-eyed while he was thinking silently to himself and all of a sudden, he realized she was standing right in front of him and he had not noticed her walking towards him from being so deep in his thoughts.

"Are you ok?" she smiled a gifted smile as she approached the counter, "You must have been in some deep kind of thought. I hope everything is all right"

"Oh, yes, everything is great, actually, I'm sorry, you found me out, I was deep in thought, but now, I'm not thinking at all," Gigot blurted and suddenly realized what he had just said.

She laughed out loud this time and when she laughed, her back stood further erect and her hair flowed around as she used her left hand to pull her hair from her face.

"So, you're not thinking now, ha, ha," she laughed again. "That sounds like something I'd say, or, that would be said about me or the girls when we all get together. My brother had given me a poster one time for my eighteenth birthday, I believe it was and the poster said something like this…it was a raggedy ann doll sitting on a stool and the caption read, 'sometimes I sits and thinks and sometimes I just sits!' I believe that is a quote from Milne and the Pooh."

"He gave that to me as I was going off to my first photo shoot and all of the people that I worked with just loved it because it reminded them of how people look at us models, all beauty and no brains." She laughed at herself and the way she told the story, Gigot could see a tear come to her eyes.

"Are you ok?" Gigot asked her as he shoved a tissue box towards her across the counter.

Her eyes continued to well up with tears and she grabbed a tissue and brought it to her eyes.

"Yes, well, no, but yes, oh, I guess, the poster reminded me of my brother. I love him, he's such a funny and talented guy, but has had some hard times. And…" at that point she grabbed three more tissues and she was in full blown crying when she said, "Our mom just died last week and I haven't cried until today…just now, oh, my God."

She cried and blew and cried some more, then grabbed more tissues. Gigot just stood there with tears in his eyes at the loss of his own mother and how that made him feel back then. In these moments with her, he missed his mom all over again.

"We had all gotten together last week to celebrate her life, well, her passing, but I felt like I had to keep it all together. I'm usually very emotional, but I wasn't then…but, I am now…" and then she grabbed a few more tissues so that she could not be totally undone in front of Gigot as he didn't have a word to say to her.

He bore her tears with her and smiled when he needed to smile and listened and waited on her as a new found friend. His heart was mingling with hers and she knew it. She was comforted by him and the opportunity to let it all out about the loss of her mom had finally arrived

"Well! I bet you didn't expect that today, did you?" she said embarrassed, gushing from her tears and wiping her eyes and nose as gracefully as she could.

Gigot looked at her with eyes of compassion and still not saying a word, politely brushed her hair back away from her face as only a loving father could do for his child.

"I bet you're a good daddy, aren't you?" she laughed still chuckling up tears as she talked.

"Well," she exclaimed as she raised and dropped her shoulders quickly as to make a transition back into reality of her being in a public place and revealing her emotions which was uncharacteristic of her.

"If you don't mind, I'm going to keep looking through this great store of yours, ok?" she politely moved back with a bit of a curtsy and a bow to step away from the counter to regain her composure on her own by going through the last aisle of mirrors at the back of the store.

She had been raised to always be sophisticated no matter what and now she had found herself in a place of her embarrassing undoing. She had not cried like that, not even the week before when her mother passed.

"What has gotten into you?" she silently asked herself in a punishing kind of way as she continued to go from mirror to mirror on the last aisle. As she moved further away from Gigot at the counter, she moved closer to the Looking Glass mirror.

Gigot noticed that with each mirror on the last row, she would do something different in each mirror. The first mirror, she leaned towards it close and with the tissues, carefully wiped her eyes and cleaned up what was left of her make-up.

As she came to the second mirror, she wiped her nose yet again, straightened and then arched her back so as to creatively fit her dress to a tee on her slender body. Then, she leaned closer to that mirror and intently looked into her eyes and continued to remove what was left of her make-up from her face.

At the third mirror, she stood there, fixing her hair and then coming to a private realization, she looked over at Gigot with her hair all a frizz and with absolutely no make-up on, she said, "Well, how do you like me now?"

Her question came in the form of a joke at first as she stared at Gigot with tears in her eyes, but to Gigot, he knew she needed an honest and forthwith answer…one that would not be placating her with flattery. No, she needed deliberate honesty from a mature man that in just a few moments of time had come to deeply respect.

She stood there with tears in her eyes desperately needing the affirmation of a man that wanted nothing from her, but a quiet moment in time to reflect on what he really saw standing before him. In her mind, she had been undressed emotionally and needed to know if any of this was worth going any further in life. She had succeeded at everything and had failed at nothing. In the eyes of the modeling world, she had hit the top and had the ability to stay there for a while, which said a lot about her own unction to keep going no matter what.

But in these moments, she felt like she had been found out and left desolate as to what she really was and that she was not only alone… she was lonely and had no sense of real value in anything she had accomplished.

"Well…don't leave me hanging like this, I'm embarrassed enough as it is," she said erupting in tears as she spoke. She caught a glimpse of herself in the third mirror and turned quickly away from what she saw and started to weep uncontrollably. Gigot ran over to her with the tissue box and pulled a few more tissues out, wiping her face and giving her more in her hands. Even in her turmoil, she was elegant and strived to remain intact from her inner torment, but it was all too much. With many tissues and a little time of gathering both of their composures, she stopped crying when she saw the tears in Gigot's eyes. She had never seen compassion in the eyes of a man, only stares, galks, lust and want.

With all of her make-up gone and her ability to stand before a man completely undone, she was feeling an emotion that she had not felt since she had been a child. She realized that as she stood there with Gigot and looked into the mirror at the two of them together, she suddenly felt like she used to feel when she was with her Dad so many years ago. She felt 'normal', the kind of normal that a little girl feels when she falls and skins her knee and her Dad rushes over to lovingly take care of his wonderful little girl.

Gigot took her by the hand and said, "You wanna see the most beautiful girl in the whole wide world?" and he smiled as he walked her over to the Looking Glass. The two of them stood in front of the Looking Glass and as he stood beside her, he asked,

"What's your name?"

She looked into the mirror at Gigot and said,

"Juliette."

Gigot looked at her in the Looking Glass and said,

"Juliette, my name is Gigot, welcome to the Looking Glass."

And with that, he took her hand that he was holding and stretched it out and placed her open palm on the mirror and stepped away.

She inquisitively watched him move away from her and in the blink of an eye, her eyes leaped back to the mirror that now had her and was sending those lightning strike strokes through her hand and arm to the rest of her body. She immediately fell to her knees, but kept her hand firmly planted to the surface of the mirror. With great tears she started choking up breaths with great heaves, gulping in air and releasing the tension hyperventilating as she knelt before the mirror. Gigot knew that the water was working its work and speaking to her of who she really was.

After the initial shock and regaining her breath, she moved from her knees and sat gracefully with her head bowed and her arm extended with her hand fixed firmly upon the glass. Gigot could tell that it was her choice to leave her hand there and allow the speaking and the revealing to take place. The immediate transformation of who she really was and was to become was imminent.

After a few minutes, she released her hand from the mirror and then turned her hand backward and brushed the mirror with the back of her hand as a form of politely thanking the mirror in appreciation. Gigot had sat back on the floor himself gazing at the transformation before him and being thankful for the grace to be able to see such a sight.

She came about and looked at Gigot as they both sat there on the floor together. With the beauty of the water at work on the inside, she gracefully smiled at Gigot and asked,

"Gigot, how much is this mirror? I know exactly where it could go…"